About

Two questions the author finds difficult to answer — where are you from and what do you do? Unfortunately, these are common questions, and this is my attempt to answer them.

Where are you from? Born in London, moved to Kent, Somerset, Wales before being moved to France at age six, lived between France and England between ages six and nineteen, due to schooling. Portsmouth Polytechnic. Met a girl, married, children (two), 'career' in insurance and pensions, lived in Worcestershire.

Then everything changed. Since the age of thirty-six the following things happened:

Separation, divorce, boyfriend, publican, hotel manager, bankruptcy, gay pride, global consultant, receptionist, amazing life partner, evicted.

What do you do? He describes himself as a flitter. Currently, he is an amateur writer, freelance trainer, life coach, and small-time property developer. He has a high tolerance for change. He recently counted his life; since leaving home he has had twenty addresses, twenty cars and twenty different jobs!

TRAPPED

Apologies

I trawled my memory for names of characters and have used the names of people I know in many instances. I may have used your name and then killed you off, and for that I apologise. I hold no ill feeling towards anyone in my life. I love you all.

A J STUART

TRAPPED

Vanguard Press

A CIP catalogue record for this title is
available from the British Library.

ISBN 978 1 80016 290 7

*Vanguard Press is an imprint of
Pegasus Elliot MacKenzie Publishers Ltd.*
www.pegasuspublishers.com

First Published in 2022

**Vanguard Press
Sheraton House Castle Park
Cambridge England**

Printed & Bound in Great Britain

Acknowledgements

Many thanks to all those who've helped during the writing of this book! In particular I'd like to thank my partner, Ian, for cajoling me every time I found something else to do when I had allocated time to writing this book and my sister Kate for her proofreading and sense checking. Also, to Doc, and others for their reviews and perspectives, you know who you are. I wrote this book during lockdown, and it encompasses many of the things on my mind at the time. I was furloughed, and spent many months at home, so I'd like to say a special thanks to all the key workers, who risked their own health to go to work in hospitals, supermarkets and distribution centres, amongst many others, allowing me to do something I had been putting off for years. Thank you.

Pronouns

By 2024 I have predicted that a new non-binary pronoun will have been adopted, and will be increasingly widely used, I hope no one takes offence. A key character in this book uses the new pronouns. To help you with reading the book, the non-binary pronouns are as follows:

Ne: she, he, they

Ner: her, his, their

Ner: her, him, them

Ners: hers his theirs

Nerself: herself, himself, themselves

2024

The Committee

He walked slowly down the corridor towards the room number printed on the directions he had been sent two weeks before, on beautiful embossed headed paper. He felt the paper between his fingers and wondered to himself how many more trees are needed to produce thick paper, compared to thin paper. Was it recycled? Do these people really understand the degree to which things have to change? Every aspect of our lives, the way we interact, the way we work, the way we live. 2020, what is now widely referred to as Pandemic One, was just a rehearsal. Although not strictly the first time the world had experienced a cross border epidemic, it was clearly the first to touch every country across the word. He remembered the time he thought what the world needed was a common enemy to pull it together, it turns out that if you treat the common enemy in different ways, then it adds to division, disagreement and conflict in every sense of the word.

He remembered the aftermath of The Pandemic and the disagreements, the challenges within the United Nations. The pressure to share vaccines from the haves to the have-nots.

He was one of the first to reclassify countries from low income and high income, to Low Voice and High Voice; building on the phrase, White Privilege, acknowledging what we all knew, that ten percent of the world's population is white and male, and, as people like himself have such loud voices compared to other groups, he decided to use his voice. He began for the first time to start campaigning, the rise of Extinction Rebellion had been impressive and had no doubt accelerated the rate of change, but still White Minority Control was holding back.

When he was at university back in the eighties, many things were predicted for the twenty-first century, not many of them had come true, but a few had come to pass. Working from home was now the norm rather than the exception; flying cars had arrived; shops had become display and touch centres with home delivery being the norm; computers had invaded every part of our lives. they got smaller and smaller. We wear them on our wrists and they tell us everything we need to know about the world and our bodies. Our smart watches had even started communicating to each other whether someone you met or dated was experiencing emotional turmoil. The most expensive ones even share stress levels during sex, with the prospect of making clumsy, bad sex a thing of the past. Electricity had taken over as almost the sole source of power in people's lives.

His forecasts for the twenty-first century that had not come to pass, were almost as many. Religion still formed the major mart of many people's lives, monarchies across the globe still held favour and unelected second political chambers still existed in many so-called democracies. Public transport had still not broken through to be the dominant way for people to travel, in fact, as the blurring of the lines between flying cars and passenger aircraft develops, longer and longer journeys were being made in private vehicles.

The pressures on production continued as High Voice countries listed more and more items in what they considered necessary to live a fulfilling life, and as Low Voice countries had to content themselves with challenges to overcome flooding, famine and forest fires, High Voice countries continued to worry about standard of living and seek market growth and progress. He remembered, it was three years ago now, that he felt there was no hope for humanity, as even when faced with the clearest signals that change was needed, humanity quickly reverted to type. But we did this, there's no one to blame but ourselves. For fifty years climate change, pollution, ozone depletion, inequality, racism, had persisted, and for fifty years political candidates who could change things have been offered to us at general elections to vote for, we collectively across the globe had not taken that leap, instead we had voted for security and maintaining the status quo. For all the campaigning and protesting and movie making that had taken place, every few years we had all had the opportunity to effect change, but for many, many political cycles the opportunity was not taken. Business as usual returned. Like many High Voice countries, the UK was run by a Centrist government dominated by one party. In the UK the Centrist government in question was right leaning, with constituents who were very right leaning indeed.

All that has now changed.

Last year the Green Movement did something truly radical. All green parties across the world aligned themselves to a code, and the UK Green Party led the way. It was proposed that they set up two boards. A Scientific and Economic Board, in charge of policy recommendations and then a second board made up of leading figures in the Green movement as well as philanthropists. Once Greta Thunberg and David Attenborough were announced as board members, meeting virtually and, acting as a second chamber to comment on policy, the Green Movement became mainstream. The success of the Green Party in Germany was replicated across many countries. As national Green Parties adopted the code, popularity and confidence in the economic credentials increased. The Green Party in the UK thus achieved something of a breakthrough. He liked to think it was because it was now the common-sense vote that had prevailed, that people had voted with their hearts and with hope and positive action in their plans, but, he realised, this was far more likely to have been the love we felt for David Attenborough, and although this move hadn't made him a politician as such, it had made him a figurehead people could vote for. It was also helped in no small way by the scandals associated with contracts during Pandemic One, affecting both sides of the House of Commons, which, unlike all other major debating chambers, still had a them and us, government and opposition, left and right, red and blue.

All that had changed

Of the 650 seats in the United Kingdom parliament only 245 now represented the old two main parties: 405 members of parliament representing Scotland, Wales and Northern Ireland all now exclusively single party countries; for England the majority of the MPs were Green Party MPs followed closely by Independents and the Liberal Democrats. For the first time the 'First Past The Post' system had actually produced a parliament that closely matched the views of the general public. Much was made of an algorithm which had changed people's pattern of voting. You were able to tell the app what type of government you wanted, what your priorities were, and it made a recommendation to vote in your constituency. The more the binary parties argued against the app, asking for it to be shut down, the more people downloaded the app, and when the Electoral Commission told voters not to use the app, its success was assured. All polling was made redundant, and the app grew, changing its predictions by the hour, as people loaded their voting intentions onto the app.

It turns out that what people wanted, wasn't policies at all, they had grown to be dismissive of promises, manifestos, none of which seemed to come to pass, what people wanted for their politicians, was for them not to be politicians, not career politicians, instead the new House of Commons was full of environmentalists, doctors, nurses, business people, charity workers, with minorities and women almost approaching their proportion in the population. A seismic shift had happened.

The Green Party now headed a government free of Labour and the Conservatives, promising a radical human agenda, with change and progress for us as a species rather than us as economic cogs in an increasingly destructive economic machine. For many, this was exciting and scary in equal measures, but you get what you ask for. The media were lost without their traditional political allies and can't decide whether we are heading for bankruptcy or salvation. The headline, in the most right-wing newspaper at the time, told the whole story.

The UK votes to give away everything it has to the animals.

The queen had asked Prince Charles to deliver the Queen's Speech on her behalf, claiming ill health, but many suspected she had reservations about how this would leave her legacy.

A select committee had been set up to provide concrete ideas to present to the nation that fit the mood of the nation, reassure the country that it was in safe hands and that the new government could be trusted with the future.

As he continued his walk along the corridor, he was aware of the softness of the carpet, covering no doubt a wooden floor worn down by centuries of footsteps. The occasional creak, revealing that time had taken its toll, this old building representing as it does, consistency and stability of Britain, of the Empire and now the United Kingdom was straining. It seems the building itself was asking, 'What next? What's to become of me?' He arrived at the number of the committee room as indicated on his paper.

Home Office Select Committee

Chaired by the Right Honorable Minister for Sustainable Living

9.30 a.m. Energy — Attendees: Various energy companies

11.30 a.m. Living — Attendees: Andrew Brown MBE Futurologist

He read no further, he looked at his watch 11.25 a.m., he took a seat. At 11.29 a.m. the door opened, and he was ushered into a seat. In front of him was a U-shaped table with at least twelve people around it. He sat down ready to present.

Future Living

The chairperson looked at him in silence as he sat down and removed his jacket, leaving him smart, in a retro roll-neck jumper and jeans. it left him looking anywhere between age forty and sixty depending on genetics, the amount of manual labour carried out and the amount of sun damage experienced. His round-rimmed tortoiseshell glasses gave him an air of interest, and he was used to being watched. Added to the look, was long shoulder-length blond hair, that could have been dyed, but looked very natural; at six feet two inches, he knew he was difficult to ignore. He allowed the silence to lengthen, a power trick he learned a few years ago when dealing with other professional people whose attitude bordered on arrogance, and, for this purpose, he had decided to include politicians in that category. The trick is to enter and wait for the other person to start the conversation, let them know that you are comfortable with silence and self-assured. He had picked up so much information in his life just by letting people talk and metaphorically hang themselves. He waited. He smiled. He looked around all the faces watching him, waiting for him to speak.

The chairperson cleared her throat. 'Mr Brown, I understand you have come here to present something to the committee, we have a tight schedule. Please tell us what you have to say.'

'Thank you, Madame Chair,' he said looking her in the eye. He determined that although she was open to ideas there were several around the table who were sceptical whether radical change was actually needed, or perhaps more likely scared that big decisions brought big consequences. It was difficult to read their expression exactly through the superiority smugness that permeated the room.

The lighting was poor, and also the ventilation, the room could be suffocating, and then he remembered numerous select committees' hearings that he had seen on TV, which were the adult equivalent of being taken to the headteacher's study, if your company wasn't paying enough UK tax, or your greenhouse emissions were too high. Maybe the atmosphere was planned to create discomfort, it had no effect on him, partly because today he was here to deliver solutions and partly because he had played these games in his career and knew how to deal with them. First rule is to make yourself the owner of the space. His glasses case was in his pocket, instead of reaching for it, he stood up, lifted his jacket up so as not to crease it and took it out, deliberately but not slowly, enough to say this is my space and I am in control of it, but not enough to be considered a time waster. The balance is key, and with such a large audience he will have to risk that some will turn against him. He smiled, sat down, cleaned his glasses and got the paperwork out of his satchel and laid his notes in front of him.

He took a deep breath, sure now that he had everyone's undivided attention and began his pitch.

It was radical, it was surprising, as people were going to interject, he raised a finger imperceptibly but just enough to stop them, he smiled and wrote down their name and the word he had used, so that at the end he could ask them what their question was with a prompt word to help them remember. He spoke non-stop without looking at his notes for thirty-five minutes. He did not take a sip of the complimentary House of Commons branded water, nor make any other distracting movements. His eye contact was even amongst the audience and you could have heard a pin drop, as the expression goes, although the thickness of the carpet meant that was possibly unlikely.

He stopped and started back through the people he felt had questions, with the prompt words, they answered obediently. Where their question was struggling to resurface, he took the opportunity to add more information to the subject area in question. The chair was impressed, he could see that she was not used to having someone command the room quite like he did. He knew he was attractive to women but he knew that wasn't the reason for her warmness towards him, he had seen her in action, and she was a force to be reckoned with. It was probably just that his ideas were exactly in line with her objectives, and she was pleased that she had someone who could put them across in a non-partisan way.

'Mr Brown, thank you very much for your presentation and for answering so many questions. For the record, I'd like to summarise your proposal, which effectively is asking us all to completely change the way we live. You are proposing that we undertake a repeat of the new town projects that were completed between the late 1940s and 1960s to solve an increasing housing and homelessness problem. That these new sites would also attract a mix of demographics from high-net-worth individuals to low income and "just-about-managing" income levels. That these sites would be fully self-sufficient, with doctor surgeries that could be upscaled and all amenities that a population might need, so if necessary, each site could be put into lockdown as a unit, thus protecting it and other sites in the event of Pandemic Two, which as you rightly say is a real scenario, given viral mutation patterns of late.

'You are proposing that over time, more and more of the population would, with incentives, move over to live in these sites, meaning that existing housing, which you categorise, as "land heavy" can be rewilded.

'You are proposing that these sites be constructed vertically, despite the fact that culturally the UK has favoured houses rather than apartments, that these sites would be like 'skyscrapers in the woods', close to railway main lines for connectivity but surrounded by nature and multipurpose land use. I would add at this point that this, I believe, is the biggest hurdle your proposal has to counter, and is one of many proposals being put to the committee, and by far the most radical.

'You claim that with correct planning these sites could be "sights" rather than "eye sores", and you urged us to think Gherkin or Shard, rather than traditional apartment blocks.

'In terms of sustainability, you think there is scope to make most elements of the site multi use, so the gym, the swimming pool, the tennis courts, the football pitch would all be used by clubs, schools and general public. You envisage one catering hub for the site, used by hotel and short-term accommodation in the morning, schools at lunchtime and restaurants in the evening, minimising waste and maximising the use out of all the equipment. You believe there are opportunities to live more simply with significantly less consumption but maintaining the same level of quality, and for most, a significant increase in quality of living. You imagine that car ownership will diminish over time and that car shares will be the way forward. People living in each site would pay on a pay-as-you-go basis for a fleet of cars in the car park, always being charged. The site will use the latest glass panels that generate electricity from the sun and holes in the structure to allow ventilation and generate power on windier days.

'Is that a fair summary of your,' she paused and looked down at her notes, 'Vertical Villages proposal?'

Andrew smiled. 'It is an excellent summary.'

'Any further questions from the panel?' She looked around her fellow committee members, there are no questions, he noticed that he seemed to have won over some of the doubters, just a couple left who would need further persuasion.

'Thank you, Mr Brown, for coming in, I understand that you have a document that you will be sharing with us all.'

'I do.' He got his phone out and with one touch he sent the document, each of their phones pinged and vibrated as the document flew to outer space and back.

She hesitated as they all looked at their phones, the speed of his action had made them all panic for a split second, he saw it in her eye, too many *James Bond* films. Initially, he knew they almost all thought, 'Aargh it's a trap we are all going to die!' The moment passes, she regains control.

'Thank you, very impressive.' The link he had sent is a fully interactive virtual tour with children playing and laughing, the rewilding having been completed, wild boar and deer roaming freely, historic trees reintroduced, babbling brooks and the sound of cricket. It touched every possible demographic, but it was the title that will make the difference.

GREAT Britain, showing the way.

The irony was not lost on Andrew, the Industrial Revolution started in this country and was championed in this very house two hundred and fifty years ago, first to burn coal to create power, first to mass produce in factories. In a sense Britain invented globalisation, it's a stretch, but he had heard people say that the United Kingdom invented global warming, maybe it's not ironic, maybe it's perfectly appropriate that the solutions should come from this place too.

Some of the committee members had accidentally clicked play and one of them had the sound on, gentle Elgar music filled the room. It seemed fitting that he should leave to music. Andrew got up, thanked them, put everything away, put on his jacket and left. And so Project Amadeus was born.

2032

Grand Opening

The mayor waited at the train station for the London party to arrive, the day was warm and intermittent sun peeped through the light clouds, the station platform was new and still looked it. The underground travelator was up and running although this morning there were a number of last-minute hitches and words spoken. But now the guests would be able to get off the train follow an escalator to the lower level and travel on the world's fastest travelator, made possible by having five connected travelators, the middle one reaching a top speed of twelve kilometres an hour. The first two gradually speed you up and then the last two slowing you down, so getting off is no different from getting off a normal travellator. They had tested it last week, with staff running to see if it made a difference, but the test was passed and now the mayor was worried they had accidentally invented a new sport. He was pleased with all their efforts; this initial impression is key and he hoped the guests would be impressed with the travelator and being able to get to VV6 in less than five minutes despite it being over a kilometre away.

This sixth Vertical Village was always going to be special, the first five were built across the country and were a lighter version of the vision of the late Sir Andrew Brown, knighted only a few months before cancer took him. They resembled large apartment complexes, with balconies and a traditional look. They looked like accommodation blocks rather than office blocks, it was felt that Sir Andrew's futuristic vision was too much for investors to fully commit to. The success and over subscription of those Villages had shown that the appetite for change was much greater than anyone expected.

VV6 was a sight to behold and special for a number of reasons. It was the closest to London, it was right on the northern edge of the New Forest National Park and it was a recreation of one of the most iconic buildings in the world: Marina Bay Sands in Singapore, three towers connected on the roof with a sky park. Instead of fifty-five floors, this giant of a building has sixty-two floors and had views across the green spaces around it, to the Isle of Wight and the English Channel beyond.

But to the people on the inside, this was not what would make VV6 so critical for the UK and possibly the world. VV6, secretly, had been located here to house workers from, and to support work at Porton Down, the site of the Ministry of Defence's Science and Technology Lab. In the event of another lockdown, the two sites would act as one. Now that war was relegated to third place behind environmental catastrophes and disease, as the major threats to the nation, Porton Down had become one of the most strategically critical sites in the whole British Isles.

The mayor stood waiting and looked at his watch, the train was due in another four minutes, they were all getting updates on their watches and the station display was showing live video feed from the driver's cab, so you could see exactly where they were. You could see the flood defences on either side of the track as the train sped through open country having just left Andover. The new station simply called VV6 was between Andover and Salisbury, a flat part of the country liable to flooding and other 'Acts of God' such as wildfires and very high winds. The mayor mused at the phrase 'Acts of God' the phrase still persisted in legal contracts and he had had many discussions with contractors and infrastructure planners about such clauses. More accurately they were 'Acts of Mother Nature', acts she had been performing for centuries, to remind the human race that they are not all powerful. Her acts more recently showed signs of rage and betrayal. She had in recent years laid waste to large parts of the world, and this low-lying area was within her sights. In fact, this new building had been designed with that in mind, and all of the lower four levels could quickly be converted for boat docking and transportation, the roof garden could be repurposed to farming, to farm those crops still too difficult to farm in laboratories. These were all details left out of the press release and covered by one phrase: 'VV6 has been designed to be future proof'. The mayor knew the emptiness of these words. How could you make something future proof when the future is in a state of flux? He felt confident that whatever the future threw at them, it would probably be the one thing they hadn't planned for. He didn't know how correct he was.

The train pulled into the station at exactly the right moment, the mayor smiled as it was obvious that the train driver had slowed on approach so that the train would halt at exactly the point when the minutes and the seconds on the clock showed zero. He did not know the driver of this train but felt sure that he would like ner. He found himself using the new pronoun for only the second time but, in his role, he knew he had to get it right. For years many non-binary individuals used they or them, in the absence of a pronoun to suit, but that left a side issue which also needed addressing, and that was when you didn't know the gender identity of the person you were referring to. In legal contracts the male pronoun was chosen as the default. In conversation it had been common to use the plural, particularly when asked to use they or them, but male pronouns still dominated. A few months ago the mayor had heard a conversation on local radio:

'So, you went to see your doctor, what did he say?'

'SHE said it's nothing to worry about!' was the response.

All of those had led to the new pronouns: 'Ne', Ner', 'Ners' and 'Nerself'. The mayor had to relearn his grammar to get the hang of it, ne was an alternative to 'he', 'she' or 'they'. Ner instead of 'his, her, their', ners could be used instead of 'his', 'hers' or 'theirs', and ner was increasingly used to replace 'him', 'her' or 'them'. The English language was after all one of the most changing languages in the world. He had to be especially careful today as Sir Andrew's child was doing the grand opening and ne was very vocal about ner gender identity. Sam had even abandoned traditional titles, instead of Mr, Mrs or Ms, Sam liked to be referred to as Cz Sam Brown, short for citizen. There was a time when the mayor would have ignored such complexities, but it looked like this change was here to stay. The new pronouns were now widely used in employment contracts and Sam Smith's global hit a few years before, *Ne loved Ner,* cemented it into modern English.

The doors of the comfort carriage slid open, double doors giving a grand entrance. The mayor held his breath as the edge of the platform rose gently and moved forward to meet the open doors to allow a step free and danger free exit from the train. The mayor breathed out. Sam Brown had not visited the site, ne had said publicly that ne wanted to see it for the first time when complete. It wasn't in fact complete, they were behind on many of the accommodation floors, but the building looked complete, and some residents had moved in and were waiting on the roof for the drinks that would be served later after the naming of the building. Sam approached the mayor with the prime minister beside ner and they all shook hands. Sam was about five feet ten inches tall, mousey blond hair, short and today, was wearing jacket and trousers, with casual, but the mayor guessed, expensive trainers. The mayor knew he had done everything he could to prepare for this day, now smile and be the charming host, a role he was quite good at.

'The warmest of welcome to you both.' He looked over their shoulders as their party was still getting off the train. 'I am so excited that you are both here, and Sam, I had the great pleasure of meeting your father on many occasions. I hope VV6 will meet his expectations and we are all very pleased that you are the person to name the project and that we will all soon find out what you have chosen.' Smiles all round as the mayor noticed a number of large packages being taken off the train, the signage he assumed for the train station and for the plaque to be unveiled later. Normally, the mayor would have been included in the discussions, but this mayor knew that Sir Andrew wanted to offer this honour to his only child, and the mayor, therefore, asked to be kept out of all the communication that mentioned the name. He had heard rumours of course, some of which had more in common with the Boaty McBoat Face public naming of a ship many years before, but the mayor had no such worries, although he had heard that 'Noah's Park' was being circulated by some on anti-social media. But this was Sam's decision and by all accounts Sam was a very sensible young person. What's more, Sam had been offered one of the penthouse apartments in the upper levels, and the number of questions asked would suggest that Sam was seriously considering becoming one of the more high-profile residents.

They safely managed to use the travelator without hiccups, and oblivious to the six-metre wall above them that surrounded the site. Even the road entered the site through a tunnel in a man-made hill that was just a greener way to disguise the wall, nobody wants to live in a prison, after all.

They arrived at the foot of the building, in all its magnificent glory, shining and breathtaking, even more so because this was the first real skyscraper that's not within a skyscape surrounded by other tall buildings, and that, the mayor knew, made it all the more impressive. The downside, they found, was that people somehow felt that the building was more likely to fall over without being surrounded by similar buildings to provide support. In fact, the opposite was true, this building had been declared the safest in the world, specifically because it was so far from flight paths and there were no other buildings that could collapse into it.

They were standing in the welcome square, with a coffee outlet, and a few parking spaces, with electric charging points. A semicircle of staff created a welcoming party and Sam, and the prime minister were directed to either end, they greeted people and spoke briefly to each person. The mayor's team were making sure that the VIPs worked at a similar pace, and sure enough, by the time they reached each other the crowd divided and revealed the plaque, temporarily hidden by curtains and a traditional drawstring, which had already been fixed in place while the handshakes were being done. The mayor could not have been more pleased with the team.

He was now stood with his two guests, his back to the building, the people in front of him represented those who had accompanied his guests from London and the welcoming group. He waited while more people came out of the building behind him, he recognised the Stevenses and the Du Ponts who had moved in recently. They smiled and the mayor smiled back.

A hush grew and the mayor was handed a microphone.

'Welcome everybody, I am glad you could be here, I am talking to you here and simultaneously broadcasting on our internal radio station, operated from within our high school.' The mayor paused as a single firework was released from about halfway up the building and a cheer went up among the assembled group. 'This is an exciting time for all of us, and I'm delighted to be sharing this moment with our prime minister.' A pause for a cheer, albeit muted, he continued. 'And Sir Andrew's only child, Sam Brown.' The cheer interrupted the mayor this time, he took the time to look out, the cameras from a number of news outlets were in front of him, but they were all pointing at Sam now. The mayor looked over, to see if this moment was affecting ner, but it wasn't, ner composure was intact. Ne seemed to be absorbing it. The mayor continued, 'That is my cue to take a step back, and Sam over to you, we are all very excited to find out the name of the place that so many of us already call home.'

A huge cheer went up and Sam walked closer to the still covered sign. The prime minister didn't move out of the way enough and had to be nudged further to one side, to the amusement of many of the crowd. The noise slowly fell, such that, even though there were perhaps two hundred people now assembled, you could hear the birds in the background and, as if planned, a bird swooped across the assembled ground. Sam looked over as if ne had arranged it. Ne shook ner head and smiled. Ne thought, 'No Sam, this is just what living here will be like.'

Sam cleared ner throat. 'It is with huge regret that I am here today.' A murmur in the crowd. 'I should not be here, my father should.' A round of applause. 'Dad, this is amazing.' Sam said looking up at the building, but also at the heavens. 'I am not an engineer or a builder, I am full of admiration for you and what you have managed to achieve.' Sam looked over at the mayor and smiled, the mayor clapped in the direction of Sam and then swept his hands round to applaud all the people present. 'But I am so honoured to have been asked to name this latest triumph of engineering and imagination, I hereby name your home,' ne paused for effect, you could hear one or two old style cameras, but you could feel the weight of the mobile phone recordings and media cameras on alert, 'New

Horizons.' A huge cheer had gone up and Sam turned and pulled a rope which released the plaque which had a drawing of the top four floors of the building with the words 'New Horizons' hovering above, so that the skygarden underlined the words.

The mayor went over, shook the hands of the prime minister and went to shake Sam's hand but instead they embraced. The mayor could feel the shaking, as Sam cried on his shoulder, the mayor patted ner back and whispered, 'Let me know when you want me to release.'

'Thank you,' came quietly back. A few, but very long, minutes later, the two of them separated and smiled at the crowd. The mayor took hold of Sam's hand, and for completeness, the hand of the prime minister, they raised their hands in unison, much to the politician's surprise.

'Shall we get a drink; I know just the place!' he said to Sam and the prime minister. They nodded in unison. The mayor turned to his team and said, 'You guys set off to the roof, my guests and I will join you later.' The mayor started the tour of the building on the sixth floor, a quick drink in one of the bars, two beers, and a glass of wine for the prime minister.

The tour continued from the bars to the restaurants and the admin area with a bank, a post office and the mayor's office suite. They soon found themselves on the school floors, each classroom had all the modern technology that they could find, including height adjustable desks for maximum accessibility and flexibility. The mayor found himself getting carried away with the design of the desks which not only could cater from nursery school children to adult education evening classes, but also, connect seamlessly to create large tables and fold away to almost nothing for storage. The mayor had spent weeks discussing these desks, to make sure they were right, but he noticed his enthusiasm for them wasn't rubbing off on his guests. He moved on through the science labs within the school, which were in part funded by Porton Down, but like the external wall around the site this was not something included in the brochure. The gym, the tranquillity centre, the sensory room for those who needed it and for those who would benefit from it.

They took the lift to the ground floor and had a quick look round the supermarket and deli, the hydroponic plant centre for indoor gardens, the storage units which could be hired by residents and then the underground garage with electric points in every space. The garage covered an enormous area far greater than the space needed for vehicle parking. Flood defences in disguise.

Outside they took a walk around the grounds, into the woods, the playing fields, the outdoor swimming pool, the large fishing pond, the vegetable patches and allotments. They walked for a long time until the mayor could see they were tiring.

'I have arranged a room for you and your guests in the hotel on level twenty, perhaps now would be a good time to leave you to your own devices, the drinks this evening start at six p.m. on the roof, I'll leave you with a communicator each.' He handed over a small device, that reminded Sam of an iPod ne had had when younger, except this device also had the four coloured buttons you usually find on a TV remote control, although Sam had only ever used the red button on TV control. 'The top button will allow you to talk to our reception team, you can ask them anything, on the back is your room number. This device also gains you access to your room, the coloured buttons at the bottom will operate the technology in your room. Just hold the device near something and a light will come on matching one of the colours on your communicator. To turn the equipment on or off just press the appropriate button, you'll find it's all self-explanatory, and there's a guide in your room. Residents have a choice of an app or having a key card, but this is more fun, so we use this system for hotel guests.'

The mayor smiled. 'Well unless you have questions, I will leave you to explore, and I will go and check on preparations for this evening.' With that he headed back to the building.

Sam looked at ner watch, one forty-five, a snack was needed, ne said goodbye to the prime minister and headed back to the building. The prime minister and entourage wandered off in a different direction, no doubt to make calls and talk to reporters, who were still milling around the entrance.

Sam headed in and bought something at the deli, people knew ner face, and ne was being treated like a celebrity. Sam asked if there were bicycles or Segways to hire on site. Ne was told there was and that ne should ask at reception. Ne hired a bike and decided to see how far the land stretched, but really ne wanted to go and have a close look at the wall, the defences that made this site so different from any residential programme before.

Ne found a series of paths that led into the woods, ne noticed that almost every tree was different, oak, ash, beech, even palm trees were represented. Ne was deep in the woods now and stopped, there was complete silence, ne was in a small clearing, ne got off the bike and listened. Ne heard a ruffling and movement in a nearby bush at the foot of a huge chestnut tree. Ne crouched, a head poked out from the bush, a deer of some sort, its ears twitched, they looked at each other and Sam picked a handful of grass and held ner hand out. The deer approached, took the grass and stayed. There was something magical about this moment, Sam couldn't fathom what, but it was as if this was the first meeting between human and deer, in this Eden-like place. Sam's love of the place started to grow. The deer contented itself with more grass around Sam, and within a few minutes other heads appeared. Sam sat on the ground and soon ne was surrounded by deer, ne was being sniffed by some, ignored by others, all were at peace. Sam thought back to the tranquillity centre and wondered why they bothered, this was the most at peace

Sam had felt in a long while. Both parents had now died, Sam had struggled with loneliness, acceptance, inner calm, and here in this small clearing in this strange place ne felt at one with everything. There were other mammals within the forest, a self-sustaining eco system, with wild boar, badgers, foxes, as well as nesting sites for all sort of birds from sparrows to sparrowhawks. All thought to be relatively harmless to humans, although Sam had heard that wild boar could get quite aggressive if threatened, but luckily it was said they are clumsy creatures and if you don't hear them traipsing through the undergrowth, you'll hear them grunting!

Slowly Sam got up without disturbing ner new quiet friends and pushed the bike out of the clearing. Ne mounted the bike and continued in the same direction as before, it was another fifteen minutes of riding, so perhaps two or three miles, before ne came across the wall. The trees came to an abrupt end and a strip of tarmac created a harsh barrier as a signal to the green landscape not to outgrow its environment. Between the tarmac strip and the wall was a prairie-like area, full of wildflowers and on closer inspection, rubble. It was just waste land that nature was trying to conquer. The wall itself was both terrifying and magnificent, a concrete windowless edifice, like the side of a 1960's car park that didn't need any natural light. There were no signs whether it was hollow or solid, no signs whether it created ramparts or was just a barrier. Sam looked left and right, it continued for as far as the eye could see in either direction, seamless, solid, impenetrable. Sam put ner hand on the concrete, definitely real, definitely solid. Sam decided to cycle along the barrier for a while, soon ne came across more rubble. This time, larger chunks, and less overgrown. Ne got off ner bike and investigated, it turned out to be a demolished house. From the look of the wallpaper and the way the heap was left, Sam could not help conclude that actually it was half a house, ne wondered if the other half was on the other side of the wall. Ne decided to wander around, and soon enough ne found some other buildings, smaller and some wooden, a few, brick. It seemed that maybe the wall was built through a farm and the rubble was all that was left of the farmhouse, but the outbuildings, including a small brick farmworker's cottage, appeared untouched for what seemed like decades rather than years. Sam had a poke around, optimistically flicked a light switch, which made a noise but no light, there were old chairs in the front room and rickety stairs going up, at the back there was a room dominated by a large wooden table and then a small kitchen to the side. Outside there was a more modern structure to the side, with a sign saying 'Plant Room', maybe the home battery or a ground heating system, but it suggested that someone had lived here until quite recently. Sam wondered if they left of their own free will, or did they just live on the other side of the wall, that's probably where the fields were for this strange farm. Sam took a look at ner watch, retrieved ner bike and turned inwards and back towards the tower, glimpses of which were visible as trees cleared and small glades appeared. Back at the tower, or, Sam corrected ner own thoughts, back at New Horizons, Sam handed back the bike, and found ner way to the allocated hotel room.

The technology worked just as expected, one of the TV channels was a live broadcast from the radio station, who were now broadcasting from the roof, and talking to whoever would talk to them. It seemed to Sam that although referred to by the mayor as a radio station, it was doing a good job of impersonating a TV broadcaster. Sam checked that there was no camera looking into the room, and left the show running while ne ran a bath. Lots to contemplate. Ner bathroom was minimalist and practical, there was a sign on the side which explained that the splash backs, bath and toilet seat were made from recycled plastic, and that when replaced could be melted to a resin that could be used in the 3D printing laboratory. There were pictures of school age children holding up pieces of furniture and kitchen equipment that no doubt had been 3D printed, the leaflet went on to say that, if needed, everything in VV6 could be repurposed and reused as tastes and needs changed. Sam thought that all the leaflets might need changing now the new name was known, ne also thought about how bad things would have to get in the country for New Horizons to need to be completely self-sufficient. The answer to that thought was: 'Very Bad',

46

and furthermore in a few years' time the circumstances in the country would indeed be Very Bad.

**

The drinks were laid out in the roof garden and lights were strung between pillars ready to be illuminated. From here it was possible, Sam noticed, to see the wall, but it looked low enough for a horse or even a dog to be able to jump it. The timing of this event could not have been better planned, as Sam looked over to see the mayor in full swing, making changes and giving instructions to the staff. It was dusk, and the most amazing view of the sunset was being afforded to all the guests and residents. The size of the roof terrace was impressive, Sam wandered around and noticed that some areas were themed, Japanese, Italian, child-friendly etc… There were fully grown trees, and even a pond with fish in it. Through an archway were the beginnings of climbing plants clinging to the lower rungs. Sam walked past raised beds for planting and flower pots.

'Impressive, isn't it?' A voice ne recognised from behind ner, interrupted ner thoughts.

'It certainly is.'

'Follow me,' the mayor said, and they set off in what Sam knew now was a northerly direction. With the setting sun on their left, they crossed from one tower over a void which thankfully was not too obvious from this level and made their way onto what the mayor described as the North Tower. It was a corridor of fencing, with gates on either side. He opened one such gate into a private space, with fences on three sides, planters full of soil but no plants and a door incongruously in the middle of the square of rooftop. It was almost like a magic door you see in sci-fi programmes that open up into another world. On closer inspection it was a well-disguised access door set into a rectangular box. The fourth side of the 'garden' was a glass balustrade, that mercifully was head height to avoid any feeling of vertigo, but the view was spectacular, the sun was dropping in the sky and the colours were changing.

'Sam,' said the mayor in a very serious tone. 'If you choose to live here this would be your roof terrace, your apartment would be directly accessible using the stairs, completely private, complete peace. No need to answer now, or even this evening, just wanted you to have a look. I'll arrange for the apartment keys to be delivered to your hotel room tomorrow.' The mayor smiled. 'Now let's get back to the party before the sun goes down and the champagne gets opened!'

The drinks went with a bang, fireworks were set off in the grounds and lit up the night sky as they looked down upon them from the roof. It would have been misleading to say that the display also went off with a bang, as these were all silent. Sam guessed that it was to acknowledge that the grounds were shared with nature.

Although the fireworks went off with a fizz and a swoosh, they were none-the-less, spectacular. Sam learned that the population capacity for New Horizons, which was getting the seal of approval from everyone, was approaching ten thousand, but that currently there were only six hundred families who had moved in. So only about ten per cent of the units had been taken, the forecast was that it would be full within two years. Sam met teachers and scientists, accountants and more scientists, doctors and yet more scientists. One of the scientists, Dr Susan Durum, spoke to Sam for some while, Sam wondered whether they were flirting with each other but after many small canapés and almost as many glasses of champagne, ne couldn't be sure. The evening went on beautifully and also Sam was fairly sure ne'd been offered a job. And so it was, that by the end of this amazing day, Sam had agreed to move to New Horizons and within two weeks had started ner new job at Porton Down.

Sam's Story

Samuel was born in New York in 2003, to Andrew and Abigail Brown. His parents were lecturers at Columbia, his mother in theology, and his father in philosophy, they were both successful and were starting to write and become known outside the walls of the campus. Abigail was beautiful and statuesque; she was delighted to be having a baby and in no way did she think it would affect her career and her freedom. Andrew was different, he worried that their lives would be restricted and that their futures would be less successful. As the birth of their son approached their thoughts became more entrenched. According to articles written since, it was common knowledge that the pregnancy had torn them apart, Andrew doing more and more travelling. People around the couple thought that Andrew and Abigail would separate shortly after the birth. Abigail had strong family connections in and around New York and apparently had set up childcare arrangements in readiness for the new baby. Andrew was British and was widely believed to have been offered a position at Oxford University. There were tensions.

The birth was difficult, the baby was breach. Andrew was late to the hospital. Abigail died on 12th

April 2003. A lawsuit had started as Andrew had indeed accepted an offer to return to the UK and Abigail's family sought to fight the removal of their American relative. They failed. Andrew came back to the UK and, with nannies and boarding school, Samuel grew up to be independent and self-sufficient. Samuel and Andrew grew together over time, but mostly since Samuel left school, and forged his own path. He attended presentations by his father and even gave a presentation at Oxford University on gender identity. The two of them had in fact become inseparable in adulthood, neither of them were in relationships, both focused, serious and respected, but it was felt that both were traumatised and uncomfortable with their place in the world. Sam had often wondered if he had been allowed to stay in New York, whether his life would be different. He gradually became more and more uncomfortable, identifying as male, it didn't seem to fit, perhaps in an attempt to deny his father's interpretation of the duty of a parent. In any event Samuel became Sam, and He became Ne, and ne was alone now. Ner father had only one relative, a sister, Sam's aunt, who never married and who had no children herself. She worked for a charity and was often overseas, she never contacted them, so for all intents and purposes, they were alone. Sam's American relatives had been trying to reach out both privately and publicly, but somehow Sam felt any contact would be a betrayal to ner father, so, as yet, no stateside trips. The community that New Horizons offered might just give Sam the sense of belonging so desperately needed. Ne could start ner new job and continue with the book that ne was writing. Moving to New Horizons would in itself be a story. A story of development, of challenges and ultimately of survival.

Happiness and serenity typified Sam's first few years at New Horizons. Susan Durum, the scientist from Porton Down and Sam grew close and at times Sam thought a relationship might start. Sam even at one point considered re-engaging with ner biological maleness, ne still had all the equipment, so to speak, all the tubes and biology, and Susan was a very attractive and intelligent person. Then Susan met someone at work and he ticked all of her boxes apparently, or so she had said. There was a time when Sam thought the mayor himself might be on ner wavelength but again nothing came of that either. Sam to ner knowledge was the only non-binary person at New Horizons, quite a few openly gay people, some of whom flirted with Sam, but ne had not made any deep connection. So hopes of a relationship were slim, it was difficult in a closed community where everyone seemed to know everyone. One of the unforeseen consequences. Most people came into New Horizons as a couple or a family. Not Sam.

The mayor was still single though and he had a strength which Sam found attractive, maybe something would come of it after all, but then the mayor's term of office came to an end. Would the mayor have the same appeal if he was no longer mayor?

The existing mayor got the job by application and interview, but it was a fixed term contract for four years after that there are elections like a city mayor. Susan and the LGBTQ group were urging Sam to stand. The post came with a significant budget and decision-making powers. New Horizons was set up so that the local taxes more than covered the services provided, and Sam knew that the County Council was delighted to have New Horizons within their area and saw the towers as a source of income to be spent in other districts. Sam was increasingly aware of frustration within ner neighbours about the small number of County Council services they used and the cost of the local tax they paid. New Horizons had their own incineration system, their own wastewater management, their own library, the roads within the complex were all maintained by the population themselves, or by the MOD if there was seen to be a Porton Down implication. This was going to be the major election issue this time round. The word amongst Sam's closest friends was that Sam was a dead cert, because the existing mayor had negotiated the current level with the council, some hardline voters were calling for backdated refunds and zero local taxes. Sam had thought that the local tax should be phased out over time, and ne thought this was something that ner neighbours might vote for. So, Sam put ner hat in the ring, ner job at Porton Down was mostly administrative, and hadn't given ner the chance to spend as much time with Dr Durum as ne had hoped, so politics here we come!

A week before polling day and Sam and the mayor were sat opposite each other in the school radio station for a live streamed discussion on the election. They were the only two candidates, and the informal polling suggested that Sam would win the election quite comfortably. Sam did not realise that actually the current mayor was secretly hoping Sam would win, as he had already accepted another job, although the details of the new role were unknown, but that would depend on the result.

The debate, designed to be informational rather than confrontational, questions had been submitted to both candidates before the debate. There were over forty different questions, the candidates themselves chose which questions to answer. The candidates then took it in turns to cross-examine each other.

The mayor went first. He chose an easy question. 'The school uses the gym most days, but they always leave it in a state, so the gym is never ready when my exercise class begins, can you promise more staff in the gym or more control over the school?'

'Thank you, Mrs X,' the mayor started. 'We have tried to ensure maximum use of all the facilities at New Horizons, so timings were deliberately designed to limit down time, I will talk to the school and the gym and see what can be done.' The mayor looked at Sam to see if anything was going to be added. Sam cleared ner throat.

'Mr Mayor, in the early days you said that the first year was a trial period and that everything would be working smoothly after then. Why is it that things are not "Smooth" some three years after your "Trial Period" has elapsed?'

The mayor smiled. 'Thank you, Sam.' Again, a smile, not a politician's smile, but almost a proud parent smile, almost patronising but not quite. 'As we all know New Horizons was the biggest and most complex challenge yet for my team and the designers, getting decisions right at the beginning was difficult not knowing how fast the towers would be populated and the demographic profile that we would have to accommodate.' The mayor looked at his sheet. 'There is a question later in the debate about decisions made before completion.' Again, the mayor smiled at Sam, then the young people hosting the debate and then at the camera. 'I have been adjusting our way of living and made many decisions during my time here, making sure that everything is in a position to…' There was a pause, and for a second Sam thought the mayor was going to say that he was simply getting the towers ready for someone else to take over. Everyone waited for the mayor to finish his sentence. 'What I mean is, there are different decisions to be made in the first term of the mayorship than in subsequent years, schedules and gym use in particular can now be more confidently resolved, now that our population is known, and the demands and busy periods have settled into a routine.' Again, the smiles. Sam saw an opportunity.

'Well, thank you Mr Mayor for leaving me something to do!' Sam smiled. The mayor smiled and almost laughed.

The questions went on, around garden maintenance, dog walking areas, maintenance contracts, and eventually with about twenty minutes to spare the candidates put forward their proposal for the local taxes. The mayor's position was to honour the original agreement and to keep them at their current level. Sam presented ner proposal for a renegotiation with a phasing out of the local taxes within the next mayoral term of office.

The debate finished amicably, and based on the comments coming through on the internal message board, Sam's lead had been extended. In fact, within the week, it was clear that the actual voting was hardly necessary and with a last minute, 'Make sure you vote, even if you think you know the outcome' message being sent out by both candidates, most people did vote using the app, and Sam won with seventy-eight per cent of the votes, sixty-one per cent of the total population.

Sam sat in ner new desk a few weeks later after clearing ner calendar of other commitments, ner new team of three, visible through the glass, finance, maintenance and personal assistant, ner strategy agreed, ner commitments made and everything under control. As the outgoing mayor had said in his handover statement, all the big decisions had been made, now it was simply a matter of administration and welcoming new residents. That turned out to be quite true, for the remainder of 2036 at least.

2037

Everything Changes

New Year's Eve 2036 was a fantastic party, fireworks and the beginning of a year of hope and positivity for the whole community. The final negotiations had been completed with the County Council and it was agreed that indeed the local taxes would be scaled back. Currently they were paid monthly over a ten-month period, it was agreed that each year the number of months would reduce, to eight, then six, then four and so on, the monthly payment staying the same but freeing up more and more income each year. What's more Sam had negotiated a contribution to the community from the council which has alleviated many of Sam's budgeting challenges. This contribution was 'in no way a refund', politics was a game that Sam was enjoying. In fact, 2037 looked promising, Susan had recently separated from her boyfriend of three years and the party gave the perfect setting for some romance, lips were touched, hormones had surged and sparks flew. Happy Days.

Sam's routine involved a weekly spot on the internal radio show, representing New Horizons at regional and national events and opening the school fair, new restaurants, new businesses. Ner contacts at the MOD were also close and ne had access to a fair few briefings. Increasingly these briefings had fewer and fewer people invited. There were concerns over Russian attempts to develop more sophisticated biological weapons, like Novichok. There were new ways for countries to wage wars, some allegations that countries were sending Covid-19 infected patients into ill-prepared countries across the globe. The UK, and Porton Down specifically, were also helping with outbreaks and lockdowns in parts of Africa and South America. Conflict had increasingly become underhand and subversive, the days of tanks and bombs seemed to be fading into the past, we now lived in a world of infections and radar proof drones.

Sam was privileged that ne got updates sent regularly and this was the year that they came thick and fast.

Change was starting.

*** News Update ***
23 January 2037
CONFIDENTIAL
A new sickness is being detected in countries in Europe, Ukraine, Azerbaijan, Belarus and Armenia, all reporting Corona-like symptoms. Death occurs within twenty-four hours of symptoms. Widespread testing being undertaken.
*** Update End ***

Sam read the update and put a call into Susan. She was always a support and provided comfort. She explained that her boss would be calling on the landline. The landline rang. Sam had almost forgotten ne had one, then remembered it wasn't really a landline as such, it was a closed line between Porton Down and ner office, impossible to intercept, apparently. The ring was old school and loud, Sam jumped.

'Your Honour, we believe there may be circumstances coming our way that will put New Horizons to the test. We'd like you to consider a lockdown drill, for one week, effective immediately.'

'Excuse me? Immediately?'

'Correct, it should be your decision, and in this regards we are only offering advice, we suggest you say that as newly appointed mayor you want to test that the towers still operate as intended.'

'Do I have the authority to close the site?'

'Yes, you do, you should be aware that although we have recommended this action and fully expect you to carry it out, we will deny that we have been involved and may well publicly complain about the action, as it will cause significant inconvenience.'

'How do I do it exactly? What do I tell people?'

'Your Honour, I have no more to add, good luck.' Click.

Sam sat there listening to the dial tone for ten whole minutes, ne knew this because ne stared at the clock watching the seconds and minutes hands move.

Sam's mobile rang.

'Sam, are you OK?' It was Susan, confusion in her voice. 'Gemma my boss has just walked in and suggested I call you, why would she say that? Are you OK?'

'Yes, I'm fine,' the clock ticked. 'I'll see you tonight, hopefully.' Sam heard Susan's voice as ne ended the call, wishing ne hadn't said that.

Sam called in ner team of three and asked them to close the door.

***

Lockdown involved closing the station so no trains could stop, three train companies to call. Closing the road through the tunnel: Highways, council and AA to call. Announcement on the internal news feed and an automated press release to be prepared for the outside media. Sam knew ner phone would not stop ringing. A call for volunteers was issued to answer questions and help anyone with queries. Security was despatched to the quarantine area in the foot tunnel which would allow residents to return. They were told that the testing kits were dummies but in fact they were MOD Coronavirus kits. All external food sources were banned for the period of the drill. No one leaves without specific permission from the mayor. For good measure the mayor even deployed the anti-drone gun.

*** *New Horizons News Flash* ***

The mayor has today at 16.00 instigated a no-warning drill of the site. With immediate effect the community will act is if there is a Level One emergency. All entrances have either been closed or heavily guarded. No one is to leave the site without express permission from the mayor, all external deliveries will cease with immediate effect. A record will be kept at Reception in Main Tower of all impacts of this decision. The drill will be in place for one week.

*** *New Horizons News Flash End* ***

The message automatically sent to all devices connected to the village app. Sam could imagine the impact. Sam had no control over the underground pedestrian link between Porton Down and New Horizons, not all residents even knew of its existence, it wasn't a secret as such, but it was not discussed. Sam waited to hear if the link was going to be kept open, for all Sam knew, the request might simply reflect an outbreak of something terrible at the labs, and that the drill was simply to give them time to quarantine.

Ner mobile rang — Susan.

'Sam! What have you done?'

'I'm just performing a drill, we can talk later. Have they closed the link?'

'Ah, no, I don't think so, people with children are going home, they have asked anyone who lives off site to stay at the hotel, paid for by the MOD. People didn't see this coming.'

'Susan, that's kind of the point of a no-warning drill.' Sam tried to smile but failed. 'So are you coming back to the towers tonight?'

'Yes, of course, well at least I think so.'

'Do you want to come to mine?' Sam ventured

'I'd love too, should I bring a toothbrush?' Sam could hear the smile, and Sam smiled too

'Better safe than sorry! Love you.' It was out before Sam could stop it.

'Ah, oh, ah, OK? See you later.' Click. Sam panicked, it was too soon, did ne even feel it, how did Susan feel? A crazy day when things happen for a reason, maybe.

The drill happened without too many issues, people adjusted and after day three people felt reassured that they could in fact live cut off from the outside. Susan had come round with her toothbrush and in fact stayed for the whole drill, it was amazing, they worked. They also worked, she helped with communications and back massages, she was a tower of strength, this really was new horizons. Sam's list of requests for movement, included a few children being reunited with their parents and a few medical staff who needed to go off site to get to hospitals. Sam was pleased that the list was surprisingly short.

*** New Horizons News Flash ***

Congratulations, to all. New Horizons has successfully completed its first full shut down test, thank you for your help and understanding. The mayor has today at 16.00 released all restrictions.

*** New Horizons News Flash End ***

It was not long before the stakes got higher.

*** News Update ***

01 February 2037

REUTERS

Russia has announced that their Sputnik vaccine is effective against the new disease which has been confirmed as a new variant of the coronavirus. Their treatment programme used in 2020/2021 is also effective against the new variant.

*** Update End ***

Sam knew that the Russians had been frustrated by how much European and American vaccines were used in the first pandemic, robbing the Russian state of significant revenue and prestige, maybe this was a time when that imbalance could be rectified. Sam hoped it would mark the beginning of the Russians being more welcomed by the rest of the world, because surely that would lead to a safer world all round. The following days proved how naïve Sam was.

*** News Update ***

12 February 2037
Washington
The US Government has issued reports of Russian troops amassing around European neighbours. Military hospitals have been set up on the borders of Finland, Ukraine, Georgia and Azerbaijan, as infection rates increase in all these countries and new cases are found in Germany, France and Turkey.
*** Update End ***

Notifications were coming thick and fast and soon Susan was spending twelve hours a day at work, Sam found nerself cut out of more and more briefings, concern levels within the community were low, and Sam wanted to keep them that way. Sam decided to launch a project for anyone who wanted to partake which would turn part of the gardens into a petting zoo. It attracted lots of support from the school and also from nearby Whipsnade Zoo. For a few weeks Sam was in very positive meetings and there was a buzz around the community. Sam was not aware of the patients being taken to Porton Down, or the tests that they were undertaking. It wasn't until Susan and Sam were sharing some drinks in a rare break that Susan shared some disturbing news.

'Darling, we have been together over a month now, and I think there shouldn't be secrets between us.' Sam looked back seriously, they both had jobs which caused a lot of stress, but recently Sam had a spring in ner step, this felt like it was going to change. 'What I'm going to tell you is covered by the Official Secrets Act, but I have had special dispensation to share it with you, given that it will affect you.' There was a long pause, the beauty of their surroundings melted into the background, it was as if they were in a dark room only able to see each other's faces. The expressions would lead a bystander to think they were having a staring competition. Susan took her time to find the right words.

'OK, so here it is, we believe that this new variant has been developed in a laboratory, we believe that the Russians have allowed it to spread knowing that they have the only treatment and that Western treatments are at least a year away. We believe that it has a very long incubation period, that the virus spreads without symptoms into all key organs. By the time symptoms are visible, it is too late.'

Sam sat back and took in the information. 'So why haven't we closed borders?'

'The thinking is that it is too late, the incubation period is two months, we have sampled people all over the UK and we believe that around twenty per cent of the population may already been infected. In a few days, Porton Down will be asking you to close New Horizons again, and to test everyone, anyone who tests positive will be moved to Porton Down to be quarantined.' Susan paused. Sam was concentrating, thinking, churning ideas over in ner head. Susan went on. 'We are currently testing key members of the government and royal family, the hotel is due to be requisitioned, to house VIPs. As yet, to avoid panic, we are considering lower profile individuals, but those who could, if our worst forecast unfolds, run the country.'

'What is your worst-case scenario.'

'Well, Sam, the very scenario that these communities were designed for, the world outside the walls is uninhabitable.' Sam sank in ner chair, the enormity of this conversation, the weight on ner shoulders, the heaviness of the beautiful sky above.

'Anything for me at this point?'

'The original mayor, James, has been working with us to get people safe, he will be making sure the VIPs are taken care of, if you could reinstate his access rights. He has suggested that you close the hotel and empty it of non-residents, the only people who can stay are those who are using it, maybe while they are having work done on their own apartments or those who work on site, we understand there are quite a few who fit in this category. James wants to use it to house the VIPs.'

'Yes, there are about twenty or so, I think. Oh my god Susan, what are we facing?'

'Hopefully, we can modify our own treatments and vaccines, quicker than the Russians think, but there are military personnel at work who think that Russia plans to invade all its neighbours.'

'They'd never get away with it.'

'Well think about it Sam, we're waiting for them to start saying, 'Let our tanks in and we'll bring treatment and vaccines'. There are countries who will be tempted, some of them have quite pro-Russian populations and their governments may be in a position that they can't say no.' Susan paused. 'For now Sam you can't say anything, you just need to find a pretext to close the hotel.'

'OK, I'll think of something.' They sat in silence looking out into the darkness, they held hands. They had had plans, hopes, positivity.

All that had changed.

*** News Update ***
29 February 2037
Moscow
The Russian Federation is pleased to announce a cooperation agreement with a number of countries to support them through the latest pandemic. Support includes governmental, medical and military support until the resolution of the pandemic. Countries include Estonia, Latvia, Lithuania, Poland, Belarus, Ukraine, Georgia, Azerbaijan, Slovenia, Serbia, and Nigeria.
*** Update End ***

Western news outlets went mad, reports were coming through denying the associations. Within hours Russian tanks were seen on the ground, sources in Copenhagen were showing pictures of medical ships leaving Kaliningrad on the Baltic Sea, bound for who knew where. One by one, presidents and heads of state from all the countries listed were shown shaking hands with Russian diplomats. NATO was convened. The European Union couldn't decide whether member states who had been pictured should be supported, punished or expelled. They were, after all, unable to find a vaccine that worked, and the death toll was rising. In France and Germany, the infection rate was close to fifty per cent and people were on the streets protesting, quarantine adherence was poor, and unlike with the first pandemic, without hope, all that was left was despair.

*** *News Update* ***
03 March 2037
Beijing
Reports are coming out of Beijing that Chinese troops are patrolling the streets in western China, in Mongolia to the north, as well as Myanmar, Laos and Vietnam to the south. Reports that China is close to its own treatment programme, are being verified.
*** *Update End* ***

*** *News Update* ***
04 March 2037
Brasilia
Reports are coming out of Brazil that a treatment centre and vaccination programme is being introduced. Countries from Uruguay, south of Brazil, to Cuba and Mexico are talking to the Brazilian state as the death

toll globally tops one hundred million and continues to increase. The effectiveness of the treatment has not been verified independently.

*** Update End ***

By mid-March, Sam was ordered to lockdown New Horizons; it came as no surprise to anyone. The death toll in the UK was reaching one hundred thousand and for some weeks now people entering or leaving had to be tested. There had been ten fatalities amongst the community from those who had been quarantined at Porton Down. Sam hardly saw Susan now, even when she did stay over, she was taking calls well into the evening and off out before seven a.m. The only joy in the community was found in the new farm, which thanks to the locals, even included a young giraffe and a pair of gazelles. Maybe Noah's Park would have been a more suitable name after all.

*** News Update ***
16 March 2037
London
Reports are coming through of Russian Tanks crossing the border into Germany. Unclear whether this was a mistake by tanks patrolling on the Polish border or whether this is an act of war.
*** Update End ***

*** News Update ***
16 March 2037
Berlin
Germany, with the support of the European Union, declares war on Russia. Short range missiles have been launched, sites in Moscow, St Petersburg and Kaliningrad have been hit.
*** Update End ***

*** News Update ***
16 March 2037
Washington
United States of America amasses troops in Alaska and on the Mexican border. Washington refuses to confirm that this is the beginning of World War III.
*** Update End ***

*** News Update ***
16 March 2037
Tokyo
Japan announces that it has reached a non-military deal with the Russian Federation. In accordance with its constitution, it will remain neutral, but has secured medical supplies and vaccinations.
*** Update End ***

Today it is with regret that the Greek government announces that southern Cyprus has agreed a reunification treaty with the north.

Sam sat looking at ner screen in ner office, as each announcement hit, ne had the responsibility to issue local updates and reassuring words. Large parts of the United Kingdom were deserted, schools had been closed and Nightingale hospitals had been reinstated and were fully staffed by the military, volunteers, current NHS staff and retired NHS staff. Sam was communicating with the other Vertical Village Communities, of which there were now seventeen, and many were experiencing break ins. New Horizons was different, the wall was holding, and the community was safe. The UK government had yet to decide whether to rejoin the European Union; UK military numbers were depleted and there had been many casualties in the battalions based in Germany, Cyprus and elsewhere in areas of high infection rate. The government focus was to find a vaccine and to organise treatment. The other question was an increasing part of the population were urging a Japanese-style pact with the Russians. March 2037 would go down in history as the month the world changed. As Sam lay in ner bed remembering ner father and his vision, that was all based around the climate risk to the world and Mother Nature, and here we had what looked like a completely human act of self-destruction on a scale even Sam could not have imagined. Forecasts were coming through suggesting that sixty per cent of the world population might have died before the year end, mass crematoriums were being created and governments were in turmoil. There was no room in anyone's head for positive thoughts, the only thing keeping the community from losing their head completely, was the wall. But it had its strongest test yet to come.

The Rule of Three

It is difficult to pin down when the myth started, that bad things all happened in threes, but so far with the pandemic and now a war ranging in Europe, it was about to be proved true.

On the 20th March the rain started, there were thunderstorms far out in the Atlantic, the first lasted for three days, it hit land on the third day, bringing two months' worth of rain in one day. The rivers couldn't cope, the River Severn was the first to breach, followed by the Avon in the West Country and then the Thames. The Thames barrier had to stay open because of the weight of water coming down stream, which only complicated things a week later. The land south of Manchester had been completely saturated, the land north and east of the Pennines was ravaged by hurricane force winds, bringing down communication networks, bridges, buildings and tearing roofs off any building with even a bit of damage. As emergency services failed to cope, the demands on the communities like New Horizons grew, helicopters started arriving and people were ushered into the hotel. Sam was not even informed of who was arriving. Susan had not been seen for days and Sam was receiving no communication with Porton

Down. Sam's control and ability to reassure residents was slipping.

*** News Update ***
26 March 2042
Madrid

*** Translated ** The Islands of the Canaries are today being evacuated. The Cumbre Vieja volcano on La Palma is at imminent risk of eruption and possible total collapse into the sea. The island of La Palma has been subjected to more lightning strikes in one week than in the previous three years and this has destabilised the volcano. The fracture created in 1949 is showing signs of opening. All African and European countries with an Atlantic coastline should be prepared for a surge which may cause destruction. Bermuda, the Azores and Cape Verde Islands are strongly recommended to evacuate. America and Canada should expect significant coastal erosion.*

*** Update End ***

Sam read the update and tried to contact Susan. No answer. Sam remembered an article ner father had shown ner when discussing tsunamis and why they only happened in Asia. It was at least twenty years old and Sam was sure that the article said that a complete collapse of Cumbre Vieja wouldn't just cause a 'surge' but a full tsunami and that where natural funnels existed the devastation would be enormous. Sam opened up a map on ner computer in order to view the closeness of the volcano. The first delta to be hit would be the entrance to the Mediterranean, the English Channel and the Irish sea would be the next hardest hit. Depending on whether the Isle of Wight created protection or increased funnelling would dictate whether the whole area around New Horizons would be under water. If only ner father was around he had a modelling tool which would answer that very question.

Sam looked at the clock on the wall and watched the second hand, tick, tick, tick, time had not stood still but it sure felt like it.

*** News Update ***
26 March 2037
Met Office
Severe Weather Warning. A volcano in the Canary Islands has erupted causing the whole mountain to collapse into the sea, early models suggest this collapse will create a tsunami-like event affecting the western coasts of Africa and Europe and the eastern coast of North America. Evacuation protocols will be announced shortly for affected areas.
*** Update End ***

*** News Update ***
26 March 2037
London

Evacuation has started of all conurbations along the south coast of England and Wales, including the complete evacuation of the Isle of Wight. Towns and cities up the Severn Estuary as far as Bridgnorth are also being evacuated. Contact your local emergency services for more information. Given the global pandemic, all citizens should consider making their own way out of these areas if no assistance is forthcoming in your area. May God be with you. Your Prime Minister.
   *** Update End ***

Sam checked in with ner assistant Mary. Mary was a stoic sort, now widowed, and saw the move to New Horizons as a fresh start. She was in her late fifties, but tall and slender, she made quite an imposing impression and was excellent to check ideas with and would always answer honestly if Sam wanted to know what ner predecessor would have done in a similar situation.

'Mary, come with me, let's walk and talk.' They walked out at quite a pace, Mary hesitated as to what to bring with her. Sam noticed she prioritised a notepad over her coat. Mary was a real asset. Sam updated Mary on the events, allowing time for it to sink in, explained that ne wanted to check on the hotel. Helicopters might start coming thick and fast with refugee requests and Sam wanted to know how many VIPs they had actually taken in.

John Mathews was the hotel manager.

Sam rang the bell at reception and John came out of the office.

'Sam, shit, am I glad to see you.'

Sam looked at Mary and back. 'I've come up to see how many VIPs you have taken in, and to see how many rooms you have given the newcomers, I assume you've seen the evacuation orders.'

'Yes, my family are all based in Southampton, it's chaos, the hospital is full and they're trying to move patients. The roads are gridlocked and the word is that there is no support; the prime minister has effectively said to them all, "Good Luck, no help from me".'

'I know, but we're in the safest place, the towers were designed for this, maybe not all at the same time, but we have everything we need, so John, how many rooms have you got available?'

'It's really odd, Sam, you said that these would be VIPs, I thought, ministers, maybe royals, but I haven't recognised any of them. There is no registration, there is a guy from the MOD who is bringing them in, he collects the keys from me, and they go straight to their rooms. There was one guy who arrived and it looked like he has taken over three of our suites, he looked strange. I went over to introduce myself and the guy turned to the MOD chap and they spoke in what I thought was Polish. I had a neighbour who was Polish and I learned a few words, me and my team did a bit of digging and after a while we found out who he was.' He lifted his phone and there was a picture of a man who indeed had a very serious face, that looked as if it had never smiled. Underneath was a name Ivan Kuznetsov, Russian Ambassador, London.

'What the fuck!' Sam blurted out before thinking. 'Let me think.' He turned and beckoned Mary over.

'Thoughts?'

'I've absolutely no idea!' They looked at each other,

Sam turned to John, 'so, John, let me get this clear, you didn't recognise any of the VIPs, they've not spoken to you directly, and the only one you have heard speak, was Russian?'

'Correct, there's something not right going on, Sam.'

'My thoughts exactly, John. Where's your wife?'

'In the flat.'

'Go get her and come with me.'

John stopped in his tracks,

'Now, John, NOW!' John moved. 'Mary get Steve and Simon from the office and get some things. Meet me in reception in ten minutes.' Mary shot off in the direction of the lifts.

'Mary, wait,' Sam called. 'Do we still have those communication devices the mayor gave me when I arrived?'

'Yes, shall I get them, there are six of them.'

'Yes, please, and am I right that they are on a closed network?'

'Yes, it was a gadget the mayor thought would impress you!'

'Well, it did! Thanks Mary.' Sam picked up ner mobile, glad that the towers had their own receivers and transmitters, ne called Susan. With huge relief, she picked up. Before Sam could say anything, she spoke clearly and fast.

'Sam, don't say anything. I am coming through the tunnel at the moment, meet me at your end in ten minutes. Do not use your phone.'

Click.

Sam's mind was whirling. What did it mean? Why was the Russian ambassador here? Who at the MOD spoke Russian? Surely military Russian speakers would be based at GCHQ not Porton Down, what should we do?'

Sam took the lift to the school floor and told the headteacher to close the school and for all students to be with their families until at least the weekend. By the time ne got to the lift, the New Horizons app had been updated and the students were leaving the classrooms. Sam took the lift to the underground car park. Though a door marked 'Elevator Maintenance' ne waited, it was a small room with just two doors, the one ne had just come through and another with retinal security, which Sam had only been through once with Susan. This was the underground access to Porton Down, it had the feel of an older tunnel, that had been there many years. Sam wondered what was on this site before that it needed an underground tunnel. The door buzzed, clicked and swung open, Susan came through with at least six other people, but that was not the surprise. They were each pushing two large trolleys of equipment, and medical fridges.

'Sam, we need somewhere to hide this!' Sam ran through all the various places ne could think of in New Horizons. 'Not in the towers, there are cameras everywhere.'

'Are there?'

'Yes, there are and not all of them are controlled by you and your team, but we can discuss that some other time, don't you think! Any ideas where we could go?'

Sam thought through the tunnels, the possible exits and then remembered. 'There's the abandoned farm, do you need power?'

'Yes, but we can get round that.' Sam drew a map as best ne could of the farm ne had found what seemed like a lifetime ago, and the abandoned cottage.

'Perfect. Let's go.' Susan clicked the keys in her pocket and a truck nearby unlocked itself.

'Susan wait, I can't leave, the building, my responsibilities are here, in any event my team are on their way to reception to meet me.'

'Sam, you have to leave they are coming for you, so meet us at the farm as soon as you can.'

Sam stood shaking while they sped out of the car park taking the ramp on the right to get out, as the outside tunnel had been closed for what seemed like weeks. Ne took the stairs and went to reception. Mary wasn't down yet, Sam looked around and remembered ner first look at the building and the plaque they unveiled. Ne remembered ner name on the plaque. But it wasn't ner name that caught ner attention now

New Horizons named by Cz Sam Brown
in the presence of the mayor, James Lebedev

Mary came out of the lift with Steve and Simon, but also Steve's wife and child and Simon's girlfriend. They came out bewildered and confused. Sam looked at them and decided to update them now. They stepped into the office behind reception, where the bicycles and left luggage was kept. As they opened the door it was clear that many other things were being stored in the room, the table was now in the corner and acting as its own storage area. They stood around. Sam looked at Steve and his wife.

'Do you want your child here for this?'

'Yes, no secrets here, she'll soon be sixteen so I'm sure she'll want to stay,' said mum, and the daughter nodded her agreement.

'Sam, what did Susan mean when she said said, "they are coming for you,"?' asked Mary.

'What did she mean?' asked Mary

'I think it means we need to be careful and watch our back.'

'It makes no sense,' she muttered. 'There's so much happening, so fast. Have you seen the latest?' Mary asked. Sam shook ner head. 'The wave has hit Portugal and there is devastation, Faro has been wiped off the map, and Lisbon is looking more like Venice. The motorways and main roads along the south of England are all gridlocked.'

'Thank you, Mary, it seems inevitable that people will look to be let in to New Horizons. Let me grab Joseph, we need our head of security here for this discussion.' Sam stepped out into the lobby and called Joseph over who was talking to a group of residents, as Joseph turned the residents saw Sam and started to approach. Sam put up ner hand and they stayed where they were. Sam wondered how easy it would be to keep people calm over the next few weeks.

Joseph was ex-army and huge, he filled the already cramped room, and closed the door behind him.

Sam started, 'Thank you all, there are more people who should be here for this but it seems that time is of the essence.' Sam paused, all eyes on ner. 'It seems that we are now in a position for which New Horizons was designed, so firstly we should all be reassured that from a tsunami perspective we are well protected, and even if the tunnels are breached by water there is sufficient underground areas to mean that the risks can be managed. The challenge we have to face is that this complex was designed to keep the residents safe, it wasn't designed as a safe haven for evacuees, so soon

86

I'm going to ask you to vote by a show of hands to see whether you feel that we should allow some people to join us, as I am conscious that you and others here have relatives on the outside. But before I put that to the vote, I feel I should raise a concern I have. It has come to my attention that some or all of the VIPs who have been flown in during recent weeks because of the German/Russian crisis, are in fact Russian.' There was a gasp around the room, the only person to remain impassive was Joseph. 'It seems that we have some senior Russian diplomats upstairs including the Russian ambassador. We also have three Russian families who have been living here quite legitimately since the beginning.'

'The previous Mayor was Russian too,' said Mary

'I did wonder.'

'Yes, and he's back,' said Joseph

'When did you last see him, Joseph?' Sam exclaimed

'Joe, please,' he corrected. 'Yes, he came last week before the lockdown, he just popped in to see a friend, but I never saw him leave. He is marked out in the register, but I checked the CCTV this morning, he did not leave at the time on the register, he has been going through to Porton Down on a regular basis, so my guess is he's still around. Last time I saw him was about two days ago with Susan, sorry Dr Durum.'

They all looked at Sam. 'It seems our old mayor has been leading key people down the wrong path.'

'But how did he have access to all the exits?' asked Steve

'I reinstated his privileges,' said Sam. 'Long story!'

Suddenly a memory popped into ner head, ne had had a good relationship with James, but there was one moment that seemed a bit sinister, they were discussing card games and dominoes, and the subject got on to chess, James had said he was good at chess, and had added, "When you play a strategic game like chess. The important things are patience, making sure all your pieces are in the correct place and to know when to strike." At the time Sam was surprised at how seriously James took chess, but what if it wasn't about chess at all, what if New Horizons was part of a bigger picture.

'Okay, so in summary, we are sealed from the outside world, but within our walls we have some residents and some non-residents who might in the coming days be our enemies. If the government do join Germany, which seems likely, then we will have our own potential for conflict within these walls. There is one added complication, there has been movement between Porton Down and New Horizons, there is as yet unknown disturbances at the MOD site, and some people have in the last hour come and sought refuge here, this may mean that we have viral risks to contend with.'

Sam took a pause. 'So what do you think, shall we look to find a way to let more people in?'

The room erupted with noise and discussion, there were some people who were in the definite 'No' camp like Mary and Joe, and others in the definite 'Yes' camp. Sam took a moment to listen and absorb, ne kept eye contact, as people started trying to persuade each other to their point of view. Sam tried to recall some of ner late father's tricks for managing such a situation, but Sam thought with a smile, that ner father would not have chosen this room to have this discussion, it would have been a lot more choreographed. Mary saw the smile and looked across puzzled.

Steve came over to Sam. 'Sam we're not going to agree. I'm going to propose that you make the decision.' Sam nodded, and Steve clapped his hands, too softly at first to get any reaction and then possibly too loudly as people jumped, but the objective was achieved. 'Look everyone, I'm sure Sam was hoping for us to agree, but that doesn't look likely. Sam is the mayor, and the only one of us with an electoral mandate, I think ne should make the decision.' Nods around the room.

'OK for the moment, I say we keep the gates closed, Joe and I will check on them from this side to see if they are holding as the decision may be taken from our hands, so we need to be prepared. Mary and Simon, can you find a place where we could move our office to that's not that obvious. Let's each keep one of the communicators handy and charged, we should be able to talk to each other without being heard. Sorry to be so clandestine, but we need to be careful.' Sam saw Steve look at his wife. 'Steve, you go with your wife and child, and we'll call you if we need someone on the inside.'

Simon looked at his girlfriend. 'Jess you go with, Steve, I'll be back soon, love you.' A quick kiss and she joined Steve and his family as they left.

'Sam, shouldn't you make an announcement on the app to let everyone know what's happening?'

'Good idea Mary, let's draft that now.' Within a few minutes an update was issued to the New Horizons app.

*** Update from the mayor ***

You will all no doubt be watching the news releases; we are all keeping an eye on the briefings as they happen. New Horizons has been built with this in mind. My father had many adverse scenarios that he considered when he helped to design our community and we seem to be facing quite a few of them at once. Our stock levels are good, and if needed we could be self-sufficient. I would ask you all to stay in your apartments for the time being and I will keep you updated as things change. You can ask questions in the comments and my team and I will answer as many of them as we can. Just for the moment we are closing all community facilities until such time as the situation beyond our walls is clear.

Sam

*** End ***

With that posted, Sam and Joe headed off down the tunnel. The shutters had come down at the tower end of the travelators, huge steel shutters that rolled out of the ceiling and then steel joists come down vertically to reinforce the shutters, designed to keep water at bay in the event of the tunnel flooding. Also, in the event of the towers being flooded from another source, or an excess of rain water, the tunnel could in fact be used as a reservoir to store excess water. Sam banged on the metal grill and the sound reverberated, meaning there was a void on the other side. No return bang suggested there were no people on the other side so the barrier at the other end was still intact, or undiscovered. Sam remembered that the only easy way to the other end of this tunnel was by train and the few trains that were operating were no longer stopping at their station. Sam gave the nod to Joe to open the shutters, the control board on the side was sealed, and took an eye scan, only a few people in the community had access, luckily two of them were present here. Once inside the control panel, there was the simplest of buttons, one with an up arrow and one with a down arrow. Joe pressed the up arrow. The first noise to be heard was the vertical girders as they disconnected from the fasteners in the concrete floor, the echo reverberated around the concrete chamber bouncing off the metal shutters and slowly fading into the distance behind them. Then the grinding of the steel columns as they rose slowly into the ceiling above, each weighing half a ton, it seemed to take forever. Then the final stage as the steel shutters automatically started to rise. What greeted them, was to shock them to their very core.

Trapped

With their ears still ringing from the girders, the next sense to receive an onslaught was their sense of smell, it hit them like a wave, and both took a step back. It was nothing like Sam had smelled before and immediately ner thoughts went to very dark places, and none of the places ne visited in ner mind matched the horror that greeted them both as they crouched to meet the rising shutters and to get a glimpse of what lay behind.

What lay in front of them were row after row of dead bodies, but Sam knew these weren't just any bodies, they were fellow residents, adults and children lined up neatly but not in a respectful way. They were lined up, like in a storeroom, as if someone was about to audit them and check on them. They were one step short of being labelled, one thing was clear their humanity had been completely stripped away. Sam noticed that some of them still had their eyes open. Sam vomited. Joe followed suit. Once the two of them had recovered, they walked along the line of bodies, the automatic lighting clicking on as they walked revealing more and more bodies. There were hundreds of bodies, how had Sam not noticed? But in fairness Sam only really saw people on ner floor in the North Tower and those people near the office. With shame Sam realised ne hadn't been in the South Tower since running for mayor. The North and South Towers only had accommodation and separate services for the use of that tower only, all the main public spaces were in the main tower. They came to the first travelator and it leapt into life in stark contrast to the line of death along the wall. Now as the speed increased the magnitude of what they were seeing increased, there weren't hundreds of people here, there were thousands. All brought down here and lined up against the wall, but by who? Sam needed to speak to other Vertical Villages and soon, and for that Sam needed access to ner office, but first they needed to see if the external wall was secure. Sam started to run, partly a reflection of the escalating nature of the situation but also to get past the gruesome sight on ner right. The ventilation was designed to cope with people traveling through the tunnel in a flash, it wasn't designed for this intensity of sensory overload. They were past the horrors now and the smell was gradually returning to a level where breathing did not create nausea. They kept up a steady jog as the travelators changed speeds, and soon they were at the external barrier. The same metal fortifications met them and again the panel to the side. As they both stepped off the final travelator they looked with horror, in fact not horror, because that would imply this was the same level as the feelings a few minutes previously. More accurately they looked on with resignation as they stared at the charred remains of where the control box used to be. They looked in silence, and then Sam watched as Joe banged the shutter with his fist in frustration. To their surprise there was a flurry of return bangs from the other side. They looked at each other. They knew there were forces at work that did not want them to leave, they knew they were trapped, they could provide no help to those on the other side. How they could tell them was less clear. Sam shouted that they were trapped and couldn't help, but the banging continued, they couldn't hear.

Sam stepped up to the shutters, the only communication method ne could think of was SOS in Morse code. Ne banged on the shutter three quick bangs, three slow bangs, three quick bangs. Ne repeated the message hoping it would be heard, understood, and even if they weren't in a position to help, at least they might conclude that neither were they.

The banging stopped on the other side. Sam counted to ten.

'Let's go, I need you to check the road tunnel, take someone with you, if that is blocked then our only ways out are by air or through Porton Down, neither of which is going to be easy. I need to check with the people to see who is missing and why no one has been reported as missing.'

***

Once back at the towers, Sam clicked the communicator to speak to Mary. 'Mary, have you found somewhere?'

'Yes, behind the shop there is a staff room with everything I think we need, what's more it is through the storeroom, so well hidden.'

'Excellent, I'm in reception now, I'll join you, is there a landline there?'

'Yes.'

'Good.' Click.

Mary had done a fantastic job, not only were there chairs and sofas in the room but she had arranged the table to make a work station, a map of the site was laid out and two computers set up. Sam also noticed tea and coffee making facilities which indeed made this an excellent choice.

'Impressive Mary, thank you.' One of the advantages Sam had noticed of being non-binary, was there were potentially fewer risks of being seen as sexist or patronising. Sam had noticed some of the extra care ner male colleagues had needed when dealing with their female counterparts. Sam just said it as it was, complimenting and chastising male and female colleagues in exactly the same way, people had found it refreshing, or so they claimed. You never really knew with people.

Mary and Simon looked at Sam expectantly. Sam decided to choose ner moment for full disclosure. 'The tunnel has been sabotaged and the far end tunnel shutters are no longer openable. Joe has gone to investigate the road tunnel. Our first job is to check on the residents, Mary, have there been any comments or questions on the app?'

'Quite a few and we have been answering them as best we can, maybe twenty or so, I would have expected hundreds though, so we should consider ourselves lucky.'

Sam didn't add anything, it wasn't luck.

'Simon, take a communicator to Susan, do you remember her?'

Simon nodded

'She has set up a new lab in the woods.' Shocked faces looked back. 'I'll explain later, but it is an abandoned farm by the perimeter.' Sam pointed on the map to the point where it was although the buildings themselves weren't shown, just paths nearby. 'I just need more information about how accessible Porton Down might be if we need to go there.'

Simon left. 'Mary, could you get me the school headteacher's mobile number, please.'

She logged into the computer and wrote down a number on a piece of paper.

A quick phone call later confirmed there were quite a few absences, all saying the same reason, that they were worried about the virus being present in the community and wanted to keep the children at home. The head confirmed that yesterday's attendance was down seventy-five per cent.

'Mary, have we got access to any security cameras from here?'

'No, we'd need to be in Joe's room for that.' Sam hadn't realised Mary was already on 'Joe' terms with Joseph, and added to the softness of tone when she said it, Sam did wonder.

'OK, let's go, there's something I need to check.'

They set off to the security desk. The reception area was again deserted, except for one person by the lifts. Sam did not recognise the person, but was nervous about accusing everyone as yet. As they approached the security office Sam went to check the door and noticed that Mary had a key. As she inserted the key Sam thought that ne heard movement inside, maybe Joe was back. The door opened. Two men were sat in the office watching the screens. James Lebedev was one of them.

'Hello Sam, you've been busy. You've been into the tunnel, that was a mistake, you're trapped here, so what's your next move Sam?'

'What's going on James?'

'Oh, please call me Yakov, although you can also call me Lieutenant Colonel of the Western Military District of the Russian Federation. I think no more lies are needed are they.'

'My question still stands.'

'Well, Russia is fed up with being marginalised and treated unfairly by the West, even when we can help you turn us down. There is no peaceful way to end your view of us as second-class citizens. Europe will be Russian soon. We thought the UK would rather die than submit, so that is what will happen, and we will be here to run things when all dissidents have died.'

'The British people aren't dissidents.'

'Alas as of now they are. Your government has been offered treatment and vaccines, and they refused both, on your behalf. Porton Down was close to finding its own treatment, but that has also now been closed down, the question now, for those of you here, is whether you resist or join us? This is after all our New Horizon is it not?'

'You'll never get away with this.'

'I think you'll find we already have. By the way, did you hear that Finland has agreed to receive the treatments, and over the next few days there will be more, just you wait.

'You are safe here, Sam, there needn't be any further casualties. As you know we have made room for some of our compatriots. All Russian citizens in the UK and Ireland are now here in the South Tower, the hotel is being used to house other key people, but I think you already know that, Sam.'

Mary looked at Sam, Sam nodded back.

'Well, it seems we have few options,' Sam said with as much confidence as ne could muster. Ne took Mary's hand and left the office, luckily, they were not stopped from leaving. To Mary's surprise they didn't head towards the shop but rather down to the car park.

'Let's find Joe.' They headed down using the stairs and into the carpark. The car tunnel also had two barriers, one at either end, Sam ran towards the tunnel, as they approached, they heard the shutter mechanism engage. In unison they both shouted out. Sam shouted, 'Joe!'

Mary calls out, 'Joe!' No response.

Sam ran to the control panel, but it had been overridden by security. Again, Sam called out, the sound echoed down the tunnel, the shutters continued to drop.

'Mary, we need to stop the shutter, otherwise Joe will get trapped.' They looked around the car park, there was nothing lying about that they could use to jam open the ever-descending shutter. The tunnel height was three metres and already the headroom had reduced by a third. The grinding of the mechanism echoed round the garage.

'Mary, have you got car keys on you?'

'No, sorry.'

'No problem, help me out.'

Behind them was a row of cars pointing directly at the tunnel entrance. Sam had seen this in the movies and tried to elbow the window, it didn't break. The shutter ground slowly. Sam tried a karate kick, it didn't break. Sam stood on the bonnet and tried to jump on the windscreen, not only did it not break, but the angle almost knocked ner backwards. Two cars down there was a car with a sunroof, Sam thought this might be their only chance. Ne put everything into it, first jumping roof to roof and then, with both feet planted in the middle of the glass, Sam jumped.

The roof shattered and Sam cascaded into the car, one foot caught the gap down the side of the front passenger seat, the other foot hit the hand break. The motion sensors went off and the alarm echoed round the garage. The car moved and Mary got behind and started to push the car towards the descending grinding wall of steel. The car wasn't going to make it, Sam's plan to wedge it under the barricade wasn't going to work. Sam grappled to get a footing within the car, climbing up the seats and onto the roof, bits of glass everywhere. Sam jumped down and between them they pushed, the car gathered speed, the shutters ground their way. Joe was nowhere to be seen, then they just heard him. The words were barely audible above the din echoing around their concrete chamber. Sam thought Joe was screaming, 'Hold the gate, hold the gate!' It flashed through Sam's mind that it might equally have been, 'Close the gate, close the gate'.

The car was moving under its own momentum now, Sam and Mary just keeping it moving, it was close now, the grinding steel mechanisms still whirred. The bonnet of the car made it under the descending steel gate just in time. Joe was still a long way away down the tunnel, his shouts echoing screams just perceptible through the din of the alarm, still blaring and the grinding of the mechanisms. Crunch. The steel of the shutters met the

101

steel of the bonnet and it buckled, and crumpled. Sam and Mary watched as the car was being dissected. The rear of the car rose up as the bonnet was being sliced in two, the car alarm succumbed and left only the grinding of the shutters to fill the ear drums. The steel shutters made it look effortless, and for a minute they both thought their efforts were in vain. But as the tyres blew out and the car seemed destined to be decapitated, the grinding of the shutters grew high pitched with strain and then silence. The engine block of the car had refused to yield, and the shutters gave up their fight to the floor, leaving a two-foot gap below. Silence echoed around the space, Sam and Mary experienced the sound-lag ringing in their ears, and then they too got to experience the silence, but not for long. Soon they heard footsteps getting louder, and echoing, then breathing added to the new noises. They looked around nervously, waiting to be caught, but the noise came from the other side of the shutter. Joe scrambled underneath and out. He ignored Sam and went straight to Mary, they embraced, such that their relationship was no longer a mystery. The embrace was long enough for Sam to feel awkward standing there.

'We need to get out of here,' Sam broke the silence. 'We need to find somewhere safe.'

'I'm not sure anywhere is safe now.' Joe looked at Mary, and then over to Sam. 'We need to find somewhere to go now. he emphasised the *now*. May spoke up, 'Is the farm safe enough, Sam?'

'It's not on any map that I've seen of the development, but it would probably have been on a map that pre-dated the development work, it was part of a village from what I could fathom.'

'OK, let's collect some stuff and head out there, I can then tell you what I found in the tunnel.'

Sam desperately wanted to know what Joe had found, but Joe took Mary's hand, and they ran to the base of the North Tower. Sam followed them, deciding to recover some things from ner apartment before the opportunity was gone.

Ner apartment was untouched, and the hallway was empty just like any other day. As Sam opened the door, a number of apartment doors opened, and a barrage of questions greeted Sam, crowding ner in, worry and annoyance written all over the faces of ner neighbours, not yet panic.

'Look, it's a rapidly changing situation, best advice I can give you is stay in your apartments.'

Sam didn't want to lie and to say any more would have meant creating panic or barefaced lying.

Sam got into ner flat and shut the door. Ne looked around for things to pack, ne packed some clothes, some toiletries, some shoes into a rucksack, then stopped. 'What are you doing?' ne thought to nerself. 'You're not going on a weekend break to Paris.' Ne unpacked everything, repacked the rucksack with chocolate bars, bottles of water, some tins, a tin opener, and a selection of kitchen knives. Ne remembered there was a wind-up radio in ner bedroom cupboard. Ne surveyed the items, and put the washbag back in. Ne was ready to leave, just did a last sweep of the apartment, and then Sam stopped as there was a crackle behind ner.

The TV screen popped into life. The logo of the internal broadcast station appeared on the screen. Sam, like almost every other resident of New Horizons, sat and stared at the screen.

It flickered and then there he was, James Lebedev.

'Hello residents of New Horizons, most of you know me, my name is James Lebedev, Sam Brown has had to take a leave of absence, as I was here working with Porton Down on special research, I have taken over on an interim basis.' There was a long pause for effect, Sam could only imagine what was going through the minds of the other residents. 'There has been an outbreak in the South Tower, so we have had to quarantine that tower, but for your safety, even if you are in the North Tower, we would ask you to stay in your accommodation, and food deliveries will be made regularly.' The screen clicked and the logo appeared. Sam grabbed ner rucksack and went to open the door, ner electronic key did not work. Ne tried to force the door, but nothing, the central override had been triggered. They were all locked in. Sam slumped to the floor, back to the door, looking into the apartment. From here ne could see out into the distance, there was no noise, just blue sky and treetops and a solitary plume of smoke, that could be as innocuous as a bonfire, but Sam was fairly sure it wasn't. At this point who knew what the future held, and for the first time in ages Sam recalled ner father's phrase when discussing the future. He would often add, 'if indeed there is a future' and here sat on the floor, Sam started to wonder. Even if there was inevitably a future, was it a future Sam wanted to be a part of? It wouldn't be long before Susan and ner team would be found, that seemed inevitable now. Joe and Mary were trapped like ner, hopefully for their sake they were trapped together. Maybe it was just a waiting game. Sam eventually got up, ne wasn't sure how long ne had been sat down, but ner legs told ner that it was a very long time. Ne went into the kitchen and made a cup of tea, what the heck, ne got a cake out too, then as ne put the milk back in the fridge, ne saw the cream and added that to the cake. Ne sat alone, in silence in ner luxury apartment with spectacular views and every mod con ne could wish for, and smiled at the irony of watching the end sat in luxury, eating cake. Ne started to cry. 'Dad, did you see this coming? Did you know James was in the Russian military? Did you plan this?' Crazy thoughts went through ner mind. Ne had started a mental downward spiral, that blocks out all rational thought, left unchecked, it was only a short journey from here to slitting ner wrists in the bath. Luckily it got checked.

The shrill noise of ner communicator made ner jump and the remains of the cake and tea were splayed across the kitchen floor.

'Yes, Sam here.'

'Sam, it's Joe.'

Sam sat bolt upright and darted into the living room to pick up the rucksack.

'We're getting out of here. Can you get to the roof?' Sam hadn't even considered that

'I'll check,' Sam clicked ner security key on the door leading up to ner private garden — it opened.

'Yes, I can.'

'Excellent meet us up there, they've only locked down our tower, I think we can get out.'

Sam took the spiral steps two at a time, slipping several times on ner way up. It was only later that ne realised ne hadn't picked up the rucksack. Out in the fresh air, it was easy to think ne was free, there was no one up here, the glass balustrade looking out gave a sense of freedom at least, but freedom was an illusion, maybe it had always been an illusion. Ne let herself out of her back gate which ne had not used since the mayor had let ner through all those years ago. In the gap between the gardens, there was no one to be seen, it reminded Sam of a back alley between old Victorian houses like the ones ne had seen on *Coronation Street* or *EastEnders*. Nothing ne had experienced first-hand, and ne wondered what city people would be doing right now, were they panicking, looting, hiding? Ne suddenly realised that ne had not seen any news broadcasts for some days now, only small snippets of information, maybe it had all been staged. For a split second ne wondered whether it was all a conspiracy and that outside these walls the world was carrying on as normal, maybe the volcano hadn't collapsed, maybe there was no tsunami, then ne heard it. Somewhere in the distance a massive explosion, followed by a couple of smaller ones. Sam looked up and down the alley, there was no sign of movement. Sam made ner way towards the centre tower, when a gate opened behind ner and out came Joe and Mary.

'Sam, follow us,' Joe and Mary squeezed past and set off towards the main tower.

'Wait, what's the plan.' Sam stopped them. Joe was about to insist on moving immediately but saw the look on Sam's face and set about explaining his plan.

'The North Tower is in lockdown, there are guards at the bottom stopping anyone who might be able to leave their apartment from leaving the tower. I don't think they are intending to reason with people, their Russian weapons would suggest otherwise. At the moment the main tower is their centre of operations, and there are more people moving about, if we are careful, it's our best chance of making it into the woods but we have to be quick. I have made some copies of my pass, it should get us access, that is until they realise that my security pass is working, they'll be looking for us and will be able to track our movements.' Joe took a handgun out of his bag. 'Here you might need this.'

Sam looked at the pistol, and hesitated, then with reluctance took hold. 'Is there a safety catch?'

'Yes, here and it's on.' Joe showed Sam and together they shared a moment of realisation that this was where they were, any plan made from now, would start from the premise that they wouldn't choose this as their starting point. Any possible plan of action was flawed purely by the fact that so many of the cards were stacked against them, in fact to think of it as a plan, was also stupid, thought Sam. The next steps could at best be considered a series of actions, some of which would no doubt bear no consistency with the previous actions. They no doubt would be taking one step forward and hopefully no more than one step back for the remainder of this situation. A game of cat and mouse. It suddenly hit Sam that they might be living like this for the rest of their lives, which at the moment looked like months at best. Sam looked around from their vantage point, the sound of the explosions had faded away and the blue sky and birds above showed no signs of the human chaos that seemed to be everywhere. A true global war whose enemies were human, viral and Mother Nature herself.

And so, they set off trying to get out.

Back to School

The three of them made away across the skybridge to the main tower. Here the space was open, and Sam reflected back on the drinks' reception laid on for ner by the mayor. All that preparation, when all along the mayor knew that there was another plan. Sam wondered whether in fact the mayor just hoped that this would be the outcome, or maybe the mayor had hoped that this wouldn't be the outcome, maybe the mayor was just obeying orders. Sam thought back over the conversations they had had together to try and remember any clues but came up blank. Sam wondered whether it might be worth trying to get the mayor/Yakov on his own, just to check. Sam had a gun now after all. Sam remembered that Yakov was a colonel in the Russian army, not a good idea that. Anyway, to stop the leadership you'd need to be able to stop the ambassador as well.

Sam looked over as Joe and Mary opened the door to the lift lobby, and only then realised the almost fitting nature of their names and the fact that they were so clearly a couple. Maybe it was destined that they would be the only survivors in all this, Sam smiled. They looked back. 'Glad you have found something to smile about Sam,' said Mary.

'I was just thinking if you are Mary and Joseph, what does that make me?'

They all laughed, a moment of humour. Hopefully not the last.

Sam followed through into the lift lobby, they could see that all the lifts were being used, at various floors going up and down.

'It's going to look suspicious if we call a lift to the roof, if anyone is watching, and I'm not sure I could do that many stairs.' Sam looked at the other two for inspiration.

'We could use the service lift; I use it quite a lot if there's a queue at the main lifts,' Mary offered.

They went through into the service area, empty plant pots and various gardening equipment littered about, the lighting here was also functional. Concrete walls and dirt marks on the floor and walls, all gave a feeling that was somehow closer to the reality of the situation than the resident friendly lobby next door. Joe pressed the button to call the lift, there were no cameras in this area , but Sam couldn't remember if there was a camera in the lift. Susan's words came back to Sam. 'There are cameras everywhere, and not all of them controlled by you.' As if reading Sam's mind, Joe looked at them.

'There's a camera in this lift but it is above the door looking inwards, so when you get in, as soon as the doors close, we should stand with our backs to the door, as tight as possible.' They got in and followed Joe's lead. The lift ground and clattered, and for a split second, Sam was cast back to the tunnels earlier in the day. Ner mind went to the car, the crushing and then the bodies, only hours had passed and already Sam's mind was starting to doubt the pictures in ner head. Sam collapsed and tried to stifle another bout of vomiting.

'Are you OK?' It was Mary

'I'll be…' started Sam

'Come on, Sam, you can do this.' Joe grabbed Sam and pulled ner up, Joe might well have retired from the army a few years ago, but he was still strong and Sam felt weaker as a result, but managed to compose nerself.

'Just thinking once we get out of this tower, it's unlikely we'll get back in, is there anything you two think we should collect?'

Sam thought aloud: 'I had a rucksack packed, but left it in the apartment. Sorry. But if we're trying to get to Susan, we need to think what we might need there, food, supplies, or maybe medical kits, in terms of potential trouble, maybe weapons?'

Sam looked at Joe, who nodded. 'We also need to think if there is anyone we should take with us?'

Mary replied: 'Well most of those people we have left in the North Tower.' Sam wasn't sure if it was a recrimination or just regret.

'Agreed, but for the moment those people are relatively safe, if we take the mayor, sorry, Yakov at his word.'

'That's one enormous "If" Sam!' said Mary.

'Again, I agree, but if extermination was their plan, they would have done it by now.' Sam looked over to Joe with pictures of bodies in both their minds, this was not the time to share that memory. 'I was just thinking if there was a resident in the main tower, they might feel even more scared.'

'But if we're going to make assumptions, then they are probably confined to their apartments like in the North Tower,' added Joe. Or like the people from the North Tower, Sam sensed that they were both thinking the same.

Mary said, 'So are we saying let's just get out.'

'I can't think of any one we should endanger by bringing them with us, can you?'

Joe pressed the B for basement and the lift clanked into action.

'Sam, you said earlier that the farm is not on any map, are you sure about that?'

'There may be older maps with the hamlet on, and I guess that would include the farm buildings but I don't know of any. I know roughly where it is, but that would be fine if we had a truck like Susan, but I'm not sure whether we'd find it on foot, even if we did. Without a map it would take us ages.'

Mary interjected from her position between them. 'Isn't there a set of prints on the wall in school reception, I think one of them might be a map of the area before and after?'

'Oh my God, Mary there is. Joe, press two.' Sam turned and looked up, hopefully out of the view of the camera, they were at floor fifteen, a few seconds later and the lift started to slow. The three of them turned to face the door. Sam saw that the other two had turned inwards and were facing each other, they stared at each other for a second and then turned away, Mary looked at Sam and smiled, with a wink. Sam winked back. It was great that this situation had clearly acted as a catalyst for them. The doors ground open, and the clang, as the doors reached their fullest extent, sent an echo in the concrete space they were now in. They stepped out, each only taking one step, staying in formation, while the door closed behind them. If their movements were being tracked, then they would soon know about it. Joe put his hand up, and they all waited. Sam put ner hand down and held Mary's. She squeezed Sam's hand, and for a split second Sam felt a stirring inside, a rush that Sam recognised. It wasn't affection, on the contrary it was loss. Sam suddenly felt very alone, even though the gesture was one of support. Sam knew that Mary was probably also holding Joe's hand and Sam knew which one Mary would let go of first. Sam turned, faked a smile, and let go. Sam needed to get to Susan, to make sure she was all right.

At that moment they heard a noise, and immediately Mary grabbed Sam's hand once more. Joe put his hand to his lips, and they waited. It seemed like forever, then Sam realised, followed quickly by the other two, that the lift had been called, the mechanism above them whirred into action and they waited. Sam looked up, the lift was going down. It was probably just the automation kicking in. Each lift had a home floor, so when not in use it went back to its own floor. Two defaulted to the ground floor, one to the restaurant floor and one to the hotel, the other two main lifts just stayed where they were last. The service lift defaulted to the basement. Sam smiled as ne thought about how people naturally waited near the lift that is most likely to come first depending on which floor they were in relation to the default floor of each lift. It reminded Sam of passengers on a train station platform standing ready for the perfect carriage that would be near the exit at their destination station. The lift disappeared beneath them and so did the noise.

Sam looked at Joe and then led the three of them through the door, into the main lift lobby. The school children weren't supposed to use the lifts unless they lived in this block, they were supposed to use the stairs, for exercise and to avoid the lifts being clogged twice a day, so the stairs were twice the width from this floor to the ground. But Sam knew that most students disobeyed, and a few even stayed on in class for up to half an hour, just to be able to use the lift without a queue. Kids will be kids! They stepped out into the main area, with classrooms around the edges and the headteacher's office on the other side of the lifts. This space served as reception, and school hall. Opposite them was a large desk, which looked more like a company reception desk than a school, maybe a tech company or advertising firm. It had a minimalist white marble effect counter behind which sat the school secretary and a receptionist, their chairs currently empty but behind them a brightly coloured wall of red and blue horizontal block stripes, with an oversized clock above and in large letters the school motto, "The future belongs to you". To one side, was a series of bookshelves with a school library of sorts and then a bank of a dozen computer cubicles. On the other side of reception there were a few sofas, strictly, 'Not for students' as the sign so clearly stated, and sure enough above the sofas there were a number of framed photos and prints. the first was a photo of the head teacher at the opening of the school. The second was also a photo, and reminded Sam how far they had come. It was a special non-binary day celebration. Sam had given a talk as one of the most high-profile non-binary figures, and this was a photo of a group of young people for whom gender was not something defined at birth, but something to discover as biology and psychology battled within them, to create an identity that enabled them to find their way. Sam was glad we had moved on from predetermining peoples' futures from birth. Birth operations were now carefully monitored so babies born with various elements of gender identity, were allowed to develop without surgery. Biology and psychology in harmony. Next to the photos, exactly as Mary had said, the first contained a map of the area. They took the frame down and took the map out, and then decided to hide the frame behind the counter just in case.

'This map's not great, I think the farm is here.' Ne pointed at a grey area about a mile from where the towers were marked on the map, with the proud statement saying "Site of New Horizons". He continued, 'But without the wall being on the map too, it's difficult to tell. Mary are there any other maps here?'

'Hold on you two,' said Joe. 'Won't there be maps in the geography room?'

They looked around, not knowing if indeed there was a geography room. They walked past a maths room, science lab, language room, round all the building.

'We must teach geography, right?!' Sam asked

'Of course, we do, the school only goes up to sixteen, but there is definitely a geography GCSE available, I didn't see any sign of any of the social sciences.' Mary replied

'Social science?' perked up Joe. 'I found that room it's over here.' Mary and Sam smiled at each other, and they followed Joe across the hall. There were in fact two rooms dedicated to social sciences, one covered business, economics and politics, the other psychology, law and geography. Sam thought history was missing but anyway, that was hardly important at the moment.

At one end of the classroom there was the web-enabled whiteboard, and then each subject had a wall to itself. The wall facing them was for law, and had all the windows. it was unclear whether this was a reflection that studying law made you contemplate the meaning of life and maybe whether to jump out of a window, maybe just less wall space was needed. Not that the windows opened on this level. The wall at the end opposite the whiteboard was dominated by a graphic showing all the areas of the brain. For some reason the amygdala area of the brain seemed to be highlighted, this is the area that controls subconscious, emergency reactions, like when you jump out of bed, when you hear a bang, even before you've properly woken up. It's there to react faster than your brain can process information. Sam hoped ner amygdala was in working condition. That left the wall opposite the windows to cover geography. As they turned round, it was obvious that this was the geography area with a complete wall of a map of the world. Sam smiled as ne noticed that this was a European map, with Europe in the middle, Americas on the left and Asia on the right. Ne wondered whether the teacher taught perspective, and that not all maps are drawn like this, even the terms East and West are a very European construction. This was Sam's favourite subject, particularly as it also included lots of climate change topics, which this map didn't seem to acknowledge. And then on closer inspection Sam noticed that it was a map of the year 2100 and Sam was shocked to see how many islands in the Pacific had gone, the Thames estuary was very wide, and then on second glance, Sam realised that the whole of East Anglia was gone, what seemed like islands were remains of cities that were currently inland. The island of Norwich, the island of Ipswich, Cambridge was on the coast, and whoever drew this map clearly didn't think Great Yarmouth was worth saving. Sam quite liked Great Yarmouth, although ne remembered the wax works museum there being one of the worst things ne had visited. Sam looked around to see Joe and Mary hard at work opening drawers, and looking in folders. One of the drawers opened and crashed to the floor, it was heavy and made a significant noise. All three of them held their breath. Quietly they continued their search. Mary, a few storage units down from Sam, picked up a selection of maps and waved them at Sam. Sam nodded and they walked quietly towards the door, listening out for any signs. They froze.

There was a noise of footsteps. Definitely footsteps. Multiple footsteps from multiple owners. They listened hard, as the footsteps started to move faster. Sam looked round the door and caught sight of a person disappearing towards the headteacher's office end of the hall, but there was something not quite right. It all happened so fast, Sam couldn't work out what it was.

Joe motioned that they should follow and Sam noticed he took out his gun and looked down at Sam's waist, gingerly Sam took out the pistol from ner belt. Joe unclicked his safety catch and motioned that Sam should do the same. Sam shook ner head. Joe immediately made it very clear that 'No' was not an option, his eyes blazed, his nostrils flared and for a split second, Sam was scared of him. Sam unclicked the safety catch and immediately ner hand started shaking and ne was incredibly conscious where the gun was pointing. Ne decided to point it at the floor, rather than forward. They made their way across the hall, down the side of the lift lobby round the back. More of the classrooms had glass on both sides, so the natural light down this end was greater, the age groups were younger too, so, although the desks were the same, adjustable desks as elsewhere, the chairs were shrinking, and the window sills getting closer to the floor. They were all on alert, but no sign of anyone. All the classrooms were empty, the only room they couldn't see into was the head's office. The blinds were down on the glass walls and the glass in the door. Sam turned the door knob gently, expecting it to be locked, but it wasn't, the door opened slowly. There was a sound of movement inside. Sam froze for a second, without thinking, note to self — amygdala is working just fine. Conscious brain clicked in, and Sam continued, this time gun pointing forward.

The door opened silently, there was silence inside the room. Sam could hear breathing behind ner, but nothing in the room. Ne silently stepped into the room. The headteacher had a spartan office, no personalisation on the wall, only a couple of photos of the family on the desk. Sam remembered that James had told him this role had been particularly difficult to fill, not just because all the year groups were mixed up to allow for the numbers, but also because many headteachers, and in fact teachers, apparently try to live outside the catchment area of their school. At New Horizons, it had been a requirement that the head teacher lived on site. In fact, all the teaching staff lived on site and all of them in this tower. At least at the end of the school day when children travelled down by stairs, the staff could travel up in a lift. But for some applicants, this wasn't far enough away from the children. Sam had never considered being a teacher, ne had after all been a pupil, and Sam had never understood how a child, having been a pupil could ever imagine that teaching was a good option. There was very little furniture in the room, just a large desk, all the daylight was borrowed from the building, and the office, much, to the surprise of some of the parents, had no external windows. The head always remarked, 'Well, I try not to be in my office very much, and when I am, I like to avoid any distractions.' Sam smiled at the thought of ner own headteacher, an old man with a wicked sense of humour. It was always a surprise that he had recruited such miserable teachers, but maybe it was the students that made the teachers miserable. So often in life the behaviour you get from others is a reflection of your own behaviour, a bit like dried ketchup on the side of your mouth, you might get smiled at, or even laughed at, it's only when you look in a mirror that you can understand their behaviour. The silence in the room had built, and now all three of them were standing side by side. Sam lowered ner gun and turned to Mary.

'No Russians here then!' and smiled. Just then there was movement from each side of the desk, two young heads appeared around the sides and looked up. A boy and a girl no older than ten, either of them, at first look, their eyes wide and scared, amplified by their youth and innocence. Sam did not recognise either of them, ne looked at Mary. Mary smiled and crouched.

'Hello there, who have we here?' There was a pause and the children looked at each other.

With a hesitancy bordering on a stutter, the child nearest to Sam, looked up.

'My name is Samantha, and this is my younger brother Bastion.' Sam smiled too, mostly because the situation seemed to require it, but also because the name Samantha brought back so many memories.

Sam was given the name Samuel at birth, but at the age of seventeen chose to live as Sam, and in fact started at university as Samantha. Ne started dating boys for the first time, with some lovely connections made and some disastrous encounters, being Samantha allowed ner to explore a new side of ner, but it felt like just another mask. People ne met, felt almost misled when they got to know ner more. Ne graduated as Sam, short hair, slim, mostly jeans, it was as Sam that ne felt most comfortable. If ne did get questions about gender or sexuality at least now it was mostly from a position of not having presumed or prejudged. Sam had got used to drunken questions like: 'So what are you, really, I mean, you know, which bits do you have, luv, can I call you luv or should it be mate.' With laughter that followed, Sam used this to reinforce ner identity, ne didn't want to fit in to a set of binary boxes, and if that created short circuits in the brain processes of a few Neanderthals then that was fine by ner.

Sam bent down also and held out ner hand. 'Hello, Samantha, I'm Sam.'

'Er, yes I know we've seen you on the telly and you came to an assembly at the beginning of the year.'

'Yes, of course I did, this is Mary she came to that assembly too, although, I think you stood at the back'

'Yes, I watched at the back, keeping an eye out for any misbehaving.' Mary forced a chuckle, and grinned. The children smiled too.

'So Samantha and Bastion, how come you are sat in the school?'

'Well, we were due to leave, but Daddy won't let us go home without him picking us up, which he does every day, we waited behind reception, then the call came to close the school and everybody left. Daddy didn't come.'

'So where do you live then?'

'Our apartment is S408, in the…'

'Yes, we know' Sam looked over at Joe, they both knew what the S stood for. 'Well for the moment would you like to join us and get out of the school?'

'Yes, please, Mr Mayor.'

'Please, call me Sam.' Sam didn't react to the Mr, and reminded nerself how easy it was to forgive children and yet so difficult to forgive adults, why did we always think that adults made mistakes on purpose and yet children made mistakes by accident? Sam had not had much contact with children, but at school ne felt the opposite was true, children can be really cruel sometimes, as flashbacks to school started to fill ner head.

Joe cleared his throat, pointedly rather than out of necessity. Sam looked over and did a half shrug, as if to say, 'What else do you expect me to say.'

'Excellent, then that's decided, you two, Bastion you're with me, Samantha, you go with Mr Mayor, Joe you lead on, I think we've all had enough of school for today.' Mary emphasised the Mr, and then winked at Sam, and luckily for her, Sam smiled back. Over the few years they had worked together they had had a few conversations about gender, mostly on the back of a letter wrongly addressed or a resident checking with her how to address Sam. Sometimes they got confused and they would refuse to speak to Sam and Mary had to deal with it. Mary had joked once that Sam was mayor of

New Horizons and she was mayor of Neanderthal Town.

'Daddy's not coming, is he?'

Sam was also amazed at how perceptive and wise children were. People often talk about wisdom as though it increases through your life. That hadn't been Sam's experience, Sam had come to the realisation that wisdom increases astronomically in children, and peaks at around thirteen, from then on it is a gradual slide down to ignorance. Ignorance in Sam's mind typified by an increasing polarisation, a reducing level of empathy, a clouding of moral judgements and a shrinking world view. Obviously, there were many high-profile exceptions, but that only seemed to prove that the majority of people become less wise and more dogmatic as they age. Sam could even feel this change within ner.

Sam started first. 'Look, there's a lot going on at the moment, the first job is to get out of the headteacher's office, we'll have answers soon.' Sam hoped that provided enough reassurance without actually lying to the children.

'Everything will be fine, you'll see.' Smiled Mary, taking a slightly different tack. Sam thought that if a doctor had said that, then Sam would probably have expected a very painful procedure.

In any event, the children stood up and held out their hands, Sam took Samantha's small warm hand, smiled and led her out of the room and back to the service elevator. As they walked through the main elevator lobby, they stopped in front of an old, black and white photo of Sam, on a poster, with some Russian writing below.

'Looks like a "Wanted Picture" if you ask me,' said Joe. 'We might need a change of plan.'

Sam stopped for a moment and thought maybe about leaving the other four to go on ahead, but if ne was honest, ne quite liked having Joe close by.

'Wait a minute, I'll be back.'

Sam disappeared off, and then immediately, came back in, 'Samantha, can you help me?'

At first, she looked worried and looked at her brother, who was now being carried by Joe. She then smiled as if glad to be doing something.

'Sure.'

Sam and Samantha set off. As the door to the lift lobby closed behind them Sam turned to Samantha and said:

'Two things, can you direct me to the drama department and how are you at make-up.' Sam smiled conspiratorially, and Samantha smiled back.

'This way, and I love make-up!' She gleamed, in a way that Sam wondered whether maybe she wasn't allowed.

They found their way into the drama section, which had a huge cupboard, within it an Aladdin's cave of wonder. They soon found some make-up, some wigs, and a few dresses. Unfortunately, the only dresses anywhere near adult sizes were from a pantomime or something similar.

Between them they found a mirror and set it up back in the classroom. Samantha had the job of holding the mirror.

'So Samantha, time for a transformation, do you mind if I transform myself into a Samantha too? I haven't done this for years.'

Samantha, didn't hesitate. 'That would be wonderful,' she said with a smile. The wisdom of children.

And so, the transformation began, Sam chose a brown wig, for maximum disguise, and it needed a lot of brushing, then Sam applied the make-up, lipstick and a bit of blusher went on fine, the eye-liner took a bit of remembering. Sam added a beauty spot on ner chin, which made Samantha giggle. Sam looked at nerself in the mirror and loads of memories were instantly unlocked in ner brain. The early days when ner make-up was so clumsy, it had been three weeks before ne had progressed from putting make-up on and then taking it off again before leaving ner room, until ne had had the courage to go into the lounge and show ner father. He had known ne was experimenting with make-up, but even so, it took all ner courage to open the door and step out. Another two weeks had passed before Sam could leave their apartment. Other memories fought for space, having ner wig come off on the bus, when the person behind caught a few hairs when they grabbed a steadying pole. Then the time when a guy stormed out of a date, leaving ner in tears and alone in a busy restaurant. Then the summer ball when ne wore the most beautiful taffeta dress, and heels.

'Samantha, let's forget the dress, but there might be some nicer shoes in the cupboard, size eight, and maybe a necklace?' Sam thought, with the jeans ne had on and if ne took off ner shirt, it left a plain T-shirt underneath.

Samantha didn't come back for a few moments, so Sam went in to help. Together they completed the outfit with shoes and a jacket.

'Ta da!' Sam even surprised nerself. 'Let's go!'

Back at the lift, and the surprised faces carried on. 'So where to next?'

'Er Sam?' asked Mary, in the shortest question ever asked of Sam, all the layers and depths of the question were conveyed in the expression in the tone, a few years ago, it might have been an even shorter question 'WTF?' Sam knew ne looked better in make-up. Sam could turn heads dressed like this. Sam always walked taller literally and metaphorically dressed like this. There was a period as Samantha, when Sam considered becoming a full-time drag queen, but then that was before, drag queens hit the mainstream. With their positivity and glamour, they soon were presenting everything. In the early 2020s comedians were everywhere, presenting chat shows, panel games, quiz shows, travel shows, even news programmes by the end of the decade. It seemed the only route to becoming a presenter was through the comedy circuit, and then Drag Queens took over. When the BBC appointed a full-time drag queen as entertainment correspondent on the ten o'clock news it was something to behold. Not a transvestite you understand, not simply a gender presentation change, this was full on drag. Glorious and uplifting for all but a tiny minority. A shrinking minority, but the problem with a shrinking minority is that they were increasingly marginalised and increasingly violent in their protests. Sam didn't know this yet but this group of marginalised, mostly white, mostly male dinosaurs, had taken the expansion of Russian ideology as an opportunity and were welcoming this new more conservative outlook with open arms, and forming alliances with other groups who preferred how things used to be.

'You like?' was all Sam could say.

'Ah yes, but it'll take some getting used to. Just help ne out, I'm lost on pronouns now.'

Sam smiled at Mary. 'I'm still me, so pronouns, same as before, but I'm guessing that others will use female pronouns, and probably safer if we meet anyone else that we all use female pronouns, just so we don't send any accidental clues.' Mary stepped across and gave Sam a hug.

'So while I've been making myself glamorous, has anyone come up with a plan?'

'We need to contact Susan, I have tried the communicator, but it doesn't work,' Joe chipped in.

128

'How about the community app?' Sam looked at Mary, who had released her hug and now had gone over to stand very close to Joe.

Mary checks. 'I have no signal.'

They all checked their phones in unison, and both data and network were showing out.

'OK looks like they have taken charge of communication.' Sam sighed, as the odds of creating a plan were reducing, well at least, the odds of creating a plan that might actually work were decreasing. They looked at each other as Mary slumped to the floor.

Help from Within

'The school computers are on a different network.' The words came from somewhere, not a voice Sam had heard before. For a split second, Sam wondered whether it was a voice in ner head, but it wasn't, it was Bastion, quietly listening.

'Bastion, you are right, there is a separate school's network, with its own connection to the outside. Sorry about this, but we need to go back to the headteacher's office!'

Sam grabbed Samantha's hand with a new sense of optimism, and they all ran back to the office, like they were changing zones in an episode of the *Crystal Maze*, from the underwater city zone, to the lunar outpost zone perhaps.

Sam logged in, using ner own log-in details without thinking, the screen didn't accept ner credentials. Sam looked at Mary for help. 'Do you know the head's log-in details, by any chance?'

Mary shook her head.

'I could log in!' said the small voice, Bastion again. Of course all the pupils have their own log-in.

Bastion took up a seat at the headteacher's chair. Sam helped out by raising it to its maximum height, it was still a bit of a stretch.

'That suits you,' says Mary. 'Maybe this is a career option for you Bastion!'

'I'm going to be a pilot,' retorted Bastion immediately

'Earth or space?' Mary was quick to ask. All children wanted to be a space pilot, it was the new firefighter or policeman.

To everyone's surprise Bastion said 'Earth, of course, the new hydrogen propulsion system, will make flying easier than ever before and Mach 5 aeroplanes will be commonplace by the time I leave university. By then they will mostly be taking people to the three space ports, but that's what I want to do.' Samantha rolled her eyes, she had no doubt heard it all before. Sam smiled but ner mind went elsewhere. This was possibly another reason why Russia had felt marginalised, there were now three space ports under construction. America and China both had space ports built for missions to Mars, and NATO, working with space agencies across the world, approved a third passenger space port. Everyone thought it would go to Russia or India, in the end, a dubiously funded Australian bid, was awarded the contract. Russia was furious, it was like the world was saying that none of the space faring history of the Russian Federation was being acknowledged. Russia was being squeezed out of yet another history making opportunity.

Bastion had logged in. 'What shall I look up?'

'Do you mind if I take your seat now?' Sam asked with a smile.

'I'm not allowed to let anyone use my log in account,' said Bastion quickly and started to log-out again.

'Wait, Baz.' Jumps in Samantha. 'It's OK, no one is going to tell anyone.' Nods all round. Bastion slowly gets off the chair. Sam settled down and lowered the seat again. A child's access rights were less than a teacher's access but still there was SchoolNet which was a social media for schools, and a secure email account.

Sam logged-in to both. There was not much in the email folder, it was the email folder of a boy after all, an announcement that all schools should close and a return to electronic teaching, for all age groups. A suspension of exams and tests. A message from the headteacher at New Horizons to all pupils giving them information and links to their teachers and explaining that the school was not accessible and that pupils should stay in their apartments wherever possible.

SchoolNet proved more useful.

There were lots of comments mostly about the tsunami rather than the Russians, in fact Sam had to scroll to find anything about the Russians, all ne could find was relating to the German offensive and all the other messages were of vaccine rollout in Russian allied countries, mortality rates getting under control. Lots of photos from France, Poland, Sweden showing people going about their business. Propaganda no doubt.

Then there was a simple message saying,

'Hello'

Just 'Hello'. It was from a user called 'Amadeus' Sam wasn't sure whether it was the simple message or the username, but something rang a bell. Sam clicked, thinking it would just open the message, instead it opened up a whole new window on the screen. Sam was aware that ne had a lot of eyes peering over ner shoulder as everyone looked over, little Bastion was being marginalised. Sam looked around for him. Ne leant over and dragged a chair over so Bastion could be front and centre, it was his access and idea that had got them here after all.

They were now looking at a message site, with updates from all of the Vertical Villages. Of course, Amadeus was the project name all those years ago. There was a lot to read, and many updates, almost all the villages had closed their doors, this time more messages to Red Curtain which Sam thought was probably a way of avoiding detection from the AI that now controlled the internet monitoring of what was being said and removing data. Its aim was to remove fake news, but in truth whoever was in power never seemed to be the subject of AI correction, funny that. If the Russians were in control, then information would need to be spread with care. Lots of messages around food storage and transport limitations, then a message with thirty-five comments below. The message simply read:

'VV6 are you there?'

Sam scrolled through the comments. People were repeating the question from Vertical Villages across the country, and some users were simply putting emoticons, some thumbs up, some prayer hands, some sad faces.

Sam needed to be careful, but also this was an opportunity to get the message out.

Sam grabbed Bastion and returned him to the floor, with a sigh he slouched off and found a seat in the corner. Sam drew ner seat up to the desk and started typing.

Comment: *VV6 here, thank you for your messages. Lots has changed here in the last few weeks. The Red Curtains have been drawn. We have new residents, and lost some existing residents, the gates have now been closed. Tunnel three is still open, but concern there too.*

Sam knew that all the other villages only had two tunnels, if they had any at all, so hopefully people reading this would look it up and, if they didn't know already, would know that Porton Down had been compromised. Sam was hoping the message was clear enough to be understood but would evade the AI mechanisms. Sam then added for completeness of message:

Food supplies adequate, water, electricity and heating all working although no access to computer or telephone networks.

Sam hovered over the 'submit' button and looked round. Nods all round.

Sam clicked Submit. They all looked at the screen in silence, as if it was going to self-destruct, or reply immediately. But that's exactly what happened, not the self-destruction, but a message appeared on the side of the screen, like a DM, direct from User Amadeus. The message read:

VV6, Which mobile network are you on?

Sam typed:

Ethernet

The response came back with a code.

Sam looked at the code, puzzled.

Joe understood first. 'Open up your phone and go to settings, then network, then advanced settings, then emergency network, then preferences, then security code.'

'Hold on, hold on,' said Sam, but noticed that ne had in fact kept up and was now looking at a screen on ner phone which said, 'enter code' and a space. 'How is anyone supposed to find this?'

'They're not, that's the point,' said Joe with a smile.

Sam entered the number from the computer screen in front of ner.

The phone came alive, 'Searching contacts…' The wheel of dots appeared on the screen, reminiscent of the days before 8G data. Data so fast that nothing was now stored on a mobile phone, everyone had a data block in their houses which backed up instantly from any device. Ten years ago, the explosion in data had started, the power needed to keep data storage facilities grew so large, that a solution was needed. The amount of data being handled was exceeding the storage available. A Dutch company then launched a revolutionary new heating system for the home. All your data storage needs in one unit, the excess heat produced was recycled to heat water in your taps and in your radiators. Tap water was no longer scalding, but it meant that you only needed to turn the hot tap on to wash your hands, mixer taps had effectively been made redundant. It had spurned a new industry of bath heaters though, as most people found the new 'hot' water not hot enough to bathe in comfortably. Sam looked at the wheel, it was still whirring.

After a few minutes the screen changed, and as a list of contacts started to load, the phone rang.

'Hello,' Sam answered the phone cautiously.

'VV6?'

'Sam Brown here, mayor of New Horizons, so yes VV6.'

'OK this is a secure line, but we still need to be careful what we say, just in case. Are you alone?'

'No, I have…' Sam was about to give the details of the people all staring at ner. Did ne trust them all, surely, yes? Mary definitely, and Joe most certainly, and Mary certainly seemed to be trusting him, the children also. Obviously. Everyone trusts children, don't they? Sam looked at Samantha and Bastion. Yes, of course Sam trusted them, '…friends with me, but I trust them all.' Sam clicked the phone onto speaker. 'I've put you on speaker.'

'I am honoured to talk to you, Sam, I knew your father, he was a great man and would have been a huge help in the current circumstances.'

'Thank you, it is good to speak to someone who can help us.' Sam looked at ner friends and they all nodded.

'Well, to be honest, we are hoping you can help us.'

'We will try, sir.' Sam surprised nerself by saying 'sir' and wished ne hadn't, what was it about this person's voice that made ner say it? I suppose it

137

conjured up a vision of a man, probably white, probably over fifty, probably military.

'Please call me Amardeep.' Probably not white then. In fact, Sam thought back, possibly of Sikh heritage, double e's featured quite a lot in Sikh names. Sam had found out from a friend at college an interesting fact about Sikh names. Sam was discussing whether to change ner name, and the friend had said, 'Shame you're not Sikh, all their names are gender neutral.' Something that Sam had not known and found fascinating. Religion for Sam had always been very binary, Adam and Eve, Mary and Joseph. It wasn't a lightbulb moment for Sam but it had left a door to religion ajar.

'No problem, Amardeep, how do you think we can help, because quite frankly we're kind of trapped here.'

'Well, you mention red curtains, so we need to know exactly what's going on, it seems you have different problems from the rest of us. Most of the villages are shielding because of the virus. The ones in the south are dealing with attacks from displaced people trying to get in, who have been evacuated from flood hit regions, added to that we have a growing militia that is causing havoc in towns and cities across the country. Casualty figures are no longer being issued by London. I am trying to coordinate a doomsday scenario where, to be frank, is the catastrophic scenario where only the Villages survive the unrest.'

There was silence in the room, as the thought that chaos outside the walls was so intensive that this might be the end of the country. Sam didn't know what to say.

The man on the phone continued. 'Just to be clear, we're not there yet, the army are on the streets of most towns and although there are skirmishes and a bit of looting most people are staying in their homes, reminiscent of 2020. There are hot spots for the virus, it seems that there have been a number of targeted super spreaders set loose across the country. London is particularly badly hit, casualty numbers are high, but as I say figures are no longer being reported.'

'So where are you?'

'I can't say, but not that far from you.' Sam wondered GCHQ, that's quite a long way, but to Londoners or anyone living north of Manchester it probably might fit the description of 'not that far'. Sam hoped it was GCHQ.

'Sam, sorry, I'm sure you have lots of questions, but we haven't got long, I need an update.' Sam looked at Mary and the children, and she got the message and took them out of the office. Sam went through the sordid details, the residents of the hotel, the Russian citizens, living in the complex, the murdered residents in the tunnel (although ne downplayed the number and left out that they were probable all South Tower residents), the lockdown, the lack of communications. It took some time and the man on the end of the call listened, asked for pauses as notes were taken no doubt or maybe others were invited to come and listen. Sam took a breath.

'Thank you, Sam, I'm sorry for what is happening to you. In your message you mentioned the third tunnel, what can you tell us about Porton Down?' Sam was surprised with nerself that ne hadn't started with this information. Thoughts of Susan suddenly filled Sam's mind. Sam hoped she was safe and managing to do whatever she was trying to do in the farm. The thoughts of Susan, gave Sam's subconscious brain a chance to process the information the man on the phone was giving, and suddenly alarm bells started ringing. Sam was about to divulge very sensitive information, in fact ne had already said a lot. Sam thought. Sam knew nothing about this caller, it could be anyone. Sam in ner desperation had divulged a lot. Sam thought back to the times before encrypted phone lines when someone simply armed with your phone number could phone you and claim to be from your bank, or your employer and get you to divulge information. Encryption put an end to that, an algorithm ran across the encryption codes looking for patterns, if the same phone was used to make two similar calls it was automatically blocked. So any fraudster either had to buy a phone for every different call made or had to find another way to make a living. Unfortunately, many of them found their way into betting scams, leading eventually to the wholesale banning of all gambling across the western world. Sam remembered the impact on the stock market as many share dealing activities were inadvertently caught in the legislations, options, futures, hedging, whatever they all were, were caught by the legislation, but once resolved, they were now living in a gambling free world. Well at least on the surface, like many things, the practice went underground, in some countries literally. Sam stopped and looked at Joe, then spoke to Amardeep.

'Tell me something about my father that only I would know.'

'We don't have time for this Sam.'

'We need to make time, I'm not answering anything until you tell me something that proves you knew my father.'

There was a pause.

'He had a birthmark on his bottom,' Sam laughed, indeed he did, he also had a birthmark somewhere even more private, but Sam didn't expect his father would have told anyone about that, even when drunk. Sam's laugh broke some tension.

'He also had a birthmark on his…'

'Yes, well I don't think any of us need that amount of detail.' The small group in the room smiled, and a tension valve in all of them had been released. Mary had come back into the room and had actually sat down in a comfortable chair, almost looked relaxed. Sam looked over and realised that she was on the verge of falling asleep.

Sam looked at ner watch. Six p.m. What a day. Sam explained that a small group had left Porton Down through the tunnel, Amardeep asked questions about the equipment and they answered as best they could. He was particularly interested in Susan and her qualifications and role within the centre, and what she was doing at the farm. Yes, she was trustworthy. No, she didn't have any foreign connections. No, Sam had not known her long. The call went on for a few more minutes, then Amardeep said, 'You seem to be in control, keep safe, it seems that you are in one of the safest places at the moment, although it probably doesn't feel like it. If I were you though, I would collect some provisions and join your friends at the farm you mentioned, it seems that might be safer, still. Good luck.'

'Amardeep...' But the line was dead. Sam closed the call ner end and looked at the others.

Sam pocketed ner phone. 'OK, next stop we need provisions.'

They all nodded, and searched for bags and things. Sam remembered that ne saw rucksacks in the dressing up room, and so it was that they were all back at the lift, all of them with rucksacks as large as they felt they could comfortably carry. Sam caught a glimpse of nerself in the reflective metal of the lift door, it looked like someone getting ready to go to Glastonbury.

They took the lift to the restaurant floor. It seemed to be the logical choice, and should be OK, particularly if they tried to leave the place as if it had not been raided, the new authorities, they assumed, still thought they were sitting tight in their apartments. The restaurant floor was quiet, maybe all the chefs were staying in their homes. Sam led the team to the store cupboard and whispered that they should take light dry food where possible. Sam emptied tea bags into a packet in ner rucksack and coffee bags too. Ne found powdered milk also, and cereals, some bread, biscuits, and then breaking ner own rules, picked up some baked beans and jam with the children in mind. How long will we be there, how many of us are there? Sam tried to count Susan's team. Ne looked around and saw that the others were filling their rucksack with carbohydrates, rice and pastas mainly! Sam went looking for other food stuffs, ne came across a cupboard full of dried fish, ne took a load, and then another cupboard with dried peas, mushrooms, and kale.

Then next to it, another cupboard. Sam opened the door, a series of drawers that triggered a memory from ner first days at New Horizons. Emergency rations for anyone needing to do an excursion beyond the wall in the event of an extinction level catastrophe. Astronaut type food, in vacuum packs. Sam called the others over and got them to fill any spare space in their rucksacks with these packs. They all looked at each other, looking like they were about to go on an excursion. However, this was no school outing, if they met someone now it wouldn't be to ask for directions.

'OK, shall we do this?'

They nodded.

'Joe, would you mind leading on, and see if we can get to the farm before nightfall, I'll stay at the rear, and try and keep up.' Sam looked at ner drama cupboard shoes, ne was going to regret the change of footwear. It was now approaching three p.m.

Escape

Joe, nodded and looked at them all. He held his fist high up.

'This means freeze.' He flattened his hand out and sliced it through the air. 'This means forward, if I crouch, you do the same, if I run you run, try and stay together, if I go like this, then we separate in different directions,' He threw his arms out sideways, Mary looked at Joe and then at the children. Joe added, 'Bastion you're with me, Samantha you stay with Mary.' Mary nodded. Bastion seemed pleased and stepped past his sister to position himself right behind Joe. Sam noticed that Bastion found it easier to let go of his sister's hand than she did releasing his. Sam wondered what a difference a sibling would have made in ner life, and whether ner journey would have been different. Another question to add to the list of questions to which the answer will never be known.

Joe looked at them all, making eye contact, the chain of command had changed and everybody knew it. Joe looked taller all of a sudden. Instead of heading out of the stores into the main part of the kitchen, he went the other way. Sam was about to say something then remembered, ne was not in charge!

Joe led them to a rear lobby area with a special lift for food deliveries, it was chilled but hopefully reduced their chance of being intercepted. Sam's spirits started to rise. Sam was at the back and out of misplaced optimism, doubled back and picked up a bottle of cooking brandy, and dropped it in ner rucksack.

The lift doors clanked and echoed around the lobby, but hopefully not throughout the building. They all got in and Joe pressed one of only two buttons in this fridge-like lift. The doors shut and for some reason the lift felt incredibly claustrophobic, maybe it was the temperature, maybe the fact that it looked like the inside of a fridge. Maybe it was just the thought of getting stuck in there. The clunkiness of the doors was replaced by a smooth hum, as the lift started its way down, very slowly, and very steadily. They waited in silence. The doors opened and they were in an unfamiliar place, Sam didn't recognise it at all. Ne wasn't sure whether ne had never been here or just that it had changed. There were trolleys everywhere, shopping trolleys but the tall ones that looked like cages on wheels. There was even some stock down here, one of the trolleys was stacked with tins, which would have been helpful to take except the wheels were so small that they would never cope with the terrain ahead. They were assessing whether any of it could be used. There was a clang in the distance. Joe's fist shot up in the air and they all froze. Joe crouched and one by one they all crouched, only Sam was left standing. A stare from Joe and ne crouched also. Joe put

146

his finger to his lips and they all knew what that meant. Joe crept around the edge of a pillar and looked towards the source of the noise. Now they were all listening, they could make out voices and movement. Sam mouthed at Joe as best ne could, 'How many?' Joe held up all ten fingers with a shrug. The only exit from this end was across an area of open car park, and there was no way they were going to be able to make it. They could see the exit across the way, right next to an emergency stairwell. Joe looked at the group, as if calculating the options. Sam hoped he wasn't planning to leave some of them behind, how well did Sam know Joe anyway? Most of the trust earned was on the back of the relationship that Mary and Joe seemed to have. Sam looked at them both. Joe retreated from his lookout point and stood up. He had clearly made a decision. He pointed to the lift.

So here they were making their way back into the freezer lift and up to the restaurant. They retraced their steps out through the store area, only this time there were noises in the kitchen, one step forward, one step back. All of a sudden the weight of their predicament swamped Sam, again Joe stepped forward, he peered round the door and saw people in the kitchen. He looked worried and then called Sam over.

'We need to cross to the lifts on the other side of the building to get out. Do you know the people in the kitchen?' Sam looked round where Joe had been looking. With excitement and relief Sam did and was going to go over and talk to them. Joe held her back.

'They won't be here alone. We need to call one of them over to create a distraction.' Sam looked round and tried to catch the eye of a young kitchen porter whose name was Carl, or Craig or Kyle, he couldn't remember. The young lad was head down and focussed on something. Sam looked at Joe to get guidance, but his face seemed simply to be saying 'Do something!' Sam coughed. The lad turned, Sam quickly waved him over. Sam used the international sign for 'in silence' and the lad theatrically tiptoed across the kitchen, amazingly it didn't seem to arouse suspicion in any of his colleagues.

'Hi,' he said.

'Hi, I'm Sam.'

'For real! Sam Brown? You look…' He didn't finish that sentence, thought better of it. 'I'm Connor.'

'Hi Connor, we're trying to meet up with some friends, by going down the stairs across there.' Sam pointed through the restaurant beyond the kitchen. 'Are there any non-residents with you?'

'I'm a non-resident, well I was until you called the lockdown.'

'Sorry about that, are there any guards or strangers with you?'

'Yeah, we're preparing to feed loads of them, there are two miserable guys sat in the restaurant, you'll not get past them without saying hi.'

'Well, we need to, can you distract them at all?'

148

Connor looked at the children and Mary and seemed to resolve to help, although his manner made Sam worry that his problem-solving skills might not be what was needed at the moment. Sam needn't have worried.

Minutes later they got a wave from Connor having at first disappeared from sight and now waving from the far end of the kitchen. Following non-verbal instructions from this young lad, they crept along in silence following his directions. A door to the right had been propped open, no doubt it was a squeaky one, they were now in the corner of the restaurant and they could see the door they needed along the wall. Joe back in the lead, followed along the wall. Sam was back in the rear, had ne not looked to ner left, ne wouldn't have realised the jeopardy they were in. To their left, only ten metres away at most, were two massive men sat at a table with guns alongside cutlery. Connor was in front of them holding court, he looked up over the heads of the two bruisers and saw Sam. Connor watched as Sam's group crept silently past. Connor looked down at the table and Sam caught a bit of what he was saying. 'So then, you both prefer the lasagne to the hot pot? Well, I'm glad I asked for your help. What about puddings, I'll get you some to choose.' And so it went on. Connor kept the two men happy and distracted with food. Straight out of a 1950s housewives' manual. Not that much had changed in almost 100 years. They made their way to the stairwell. Sam was careful not to let the door slam shut and closed it as quietly as possible, leaving it held by the latch. They started their way down the stairs. The door behind them clicked loudly as the latch retracted and the door clunked shut, it was no doubt a fire door, which had been designed to lock under its own weight. The noise inside the stairwell was loud, they hoped it hadn't been heard in the restaurant. But just in case Joe picked up Bastion and started down the stairs at an increased pace. They were out of sight of the door they had come through, when it opened above them. Joe flattened himself against the wall of the stairwell and they all followed suit.

A man spoke in Russian, then in English said, 'Anybody there?' There was a pause, they didn't move, but it seemed that the Russian just out of sight didn't move either. Then in the distance Sam heard Connor.

'Puddings are served.'

Silence. Then the door shut. They all breathed.

Mary turned to the children and told them both, well done. They both looked back, their faces blank of expression, reflected in their eyes was the weirdness of the situation they all found themselves in. Sam wondered whether as a child ne would have found this all an adventure? As a child, surely, you'd be able to enjoy the 'doing' without the 'knowing', but the answer lay in the eyes of these two orphans, a status still unknown to them. This was not an adventure, this was an ordeal. Sam felt a chill, perhaps the cold in this concrete tower, perhaps as yet subconscious exhaustion, maybe even hunger. Bringing the thoughts into the conscious brain made all three feel more pressing, they must all be hungry. Sam removed ner rucksack and found the biscuits, took out a pack and handed them first to the children and then everyone else. With a nod towards Joe, they carried on down the stairs.

At the bottom of the stairwell, Joe's fist rose again, they waited. He carefully opened the door marked 'Exit', it opened outwards. As expected, this was the slowest evacuation this door was ever designed to deal with. The door was designed to open wide and at speed, not slowly and silently. Luckily, they held their breaths and the door made no sound beyond the initial click of the locking mechanisms. Joe held it ajar for a few seconds, listening intently for movement on the other side. From memory, Sam knew that they'd be in full view once they left the relative security of this concrete stairwell. As if reading ner mind, Joe whispered:

'OK, listen up, the door we need is close, we need to exit this door quickly but silently, Sam you're in charge of closing it without making a sound. Suggest you wedge something soft to stop it shutting. I will go out and open the other door, if they see me and run over then you retreat up the stairs, if not when I give my signal you will run through the next door. Shoes off, everyone. Understood?'

The nods were difficult to see as they were all removing their shoes, an act which made it all seem more real somehow, not the guns, not the bodies, not the world seemingly falling apart. Shoes being removed. Maybe this was the level that the brain could make sense of. Here they were all now holding their shoes with heavy rucksacks on their backs waiting, as if performing some strange military exercise. Joe opened the door and slipped through, taking away any more thinking time. Sam stepped forward and held the door. Sam could see Joe make his way to the other door, he managed to open it, then he signalled.

Mary and the children ran through quickly and quietly, Sam jammed the door with the leftover biscuits ne was still holding, and set off after them. It was only about ten metres, but it felt a long way. Before Sam reached Joe waving him on, ne heard it.

'Oi, you get over here!'

Sam froze, but Joe just waved with more urgency. In through the door and into the fresh air outside.

Joe carefully closed the door, not to make a sound.

'They saw me,' said Sam. 'We need to run!'

'No panic, Sam, they weren't looking this way, they must have been talking to someone else, but just in case let's make our way to the farm. Sam?'

All of a sudden, Sam couldn't think where the farm was, which side of the building they were on, adrenaline was supposed to make you perform better, think more clearly, fear does the opposite. Fear was winning. Luckily Joe had kept the map from the school reception area.

With the map in hand, they decided to get far from the towers as quickly as possible and then change direction once in the woods. The map wasn't ideal for this as there weren't many paths or points of interest in the land around the towers. Although the towers were marked, the wall around the site wasn't, but the grey buildings which hopefully were the remnants of the farm were clear, and a stream which hopefully they could find. Shoes back on, they set off. It would be getting dark around eight so they only had a few hours. Sam looked up, it was cloudy, so no moonlight, they had about an hour ne reckoned to get to the farm. They kept their formation, although this time they were much closer together. Sam's shoes were starting to rub, they weren't designed for this but ne struggled on. Glances behind made ner even slower and soon a gap was developing between Sam and the rest. There was nothing behind. No movement. No sounds. But Sam couldn't help regular glances. The trees were ahead, but before them a ring of dense bushes, no paths that could be seen. Sam had been looking back, thought ne saw movement, crouched and observed. There was a vehicle moving near the far side of the building. Sam watched, but it was doing something unconnected to them, Sam turned to follow the others. There was no one.

Sam looked back, they had run maybe five hundred metres and only about twenty metres to go, straight ahead looked impenetrable and undisturbed. Sam scanned for faces, probably Mary, waving him to a path into the woods, but she could not be seen. Sam made ner way in a straight line away from the tower, and reached the undergrowth, it was mainly brambles, surely, they didn't make their way through here. Sam was conscious ner clothes weren't exactly subtle. Camo always seemed like a style choice that had no practical uses, but now at this distance Sam would have been very grateful for camouflaged clothes. Left, or right? If the woods ahead were as dense as the undergrowth here, they might not find each other before nightfall. Left, or right? Sam stood up tall and tried to peer over brambles. Looking back the car had been joined by another car and what looked like some guards.

'SAM.' A loud whisper down low. Joe.

Sam looked at ground level and at Joe's head sticking through the brambles.

'Sorry, Sam, thought you were closer to us, we found a badger route or something, crawl through!'

Sam crawled through picking up leaves and mud on the way, nature's camouflage. It was quite dense and reminded Sam of tunnels found in children's indoor play centres, although no slide at the end of this tunnel, just a relieved Mary and some expectant children. At the exit of the tunnel, Sam's rucksack got caught and they all helped ner out.

'Ours got caught too.'

'I vote we take a break,' said Mary. They all agreed and sat down. Another packet of biscuits was opened.

'I'm thirsty,' said Bastion.

154

They all looked at each other, Sam and Joe both feeling they should have packed some water, life's most vital substance. You can survive days without food, but without water, was it days, hours or minutes? It surely couldn't be minutes! Mary delved into her rucksack.

'Apologies, Sam, I didn't follow your instructions back there. She brought out two bottles of water.'

'What else have you got in there?'

'Quite a lot of tins, and sauces, baked beans, even some jam.'

'Mary, your rucksack must weigh a ton!' Joe picked it up and raised an eyebrow.

'Well, I picked up a few things that weren't on my list!' Sam showed them the bottle of brandy.

They smiled, thinking the worst was behind them and safety lay ahead. But their story was not yet completed.

***

Snacks and water consumed, Joe laid out the map. 'I think we are about here.' He drew a remarkably large circle with his finger on the map. 'We need to get here.' Pointing at the point that Sam had indicated. 'Two options, we either head in roughly that direction, towards the farm and look for any paths or water that might be on the map, but given the rain we have had lately there could be a lot more water about than is on this map, or we could head in that direction,' he pointed

155

at a direction heading directly away from the towers, 'and keep going till we meet the wall and then turn right towards the farm. Didn't you say the farm buildings are visible from the wall?'

'Sort of, there wasn't much undergrowth when I last saw it, but I think I'll recognise it.'

'You think?' said Mary in a tone of disappointment rather than accusation.

'I'm sure, anyway, when we are close, we should be able to see or hear Susan and her team.'

'True, true,' said Joe. 'Let's make for the wall.' He grabbed Mary's rucksack and put it on, '*Vamos*!' He smiled.

'*Si, Senor, Vamos,*' said Bastion, Spanish being a compulsory language now, having replaced French a few years ago. Maybe Russian would have been a better choice, thought Sam.

They set off, it was a whole lot darker under the cover of the trees, but soon their eyes adjusted and it was manageable. As before it wasn't long before the towers were no longer visible, but they kept on, hoping they weren't making their way in a big circle, the trees thinned and suddenly they were in a small clearing, small and with a pond, or puddle, in it, with rabbit droppings all around, and tracks through the vegetation. Ivy and grasses everywhere, no flowers, no colour here, and in the late afternoon light, it seemed almost fairy like, as if in the corner there should be a toadstool large enough to sit on, or at least a stone formation shaped

156

like a toadstool. Instead, just this ethereal light from all around, rather than from above. Sam looked up, the clouds were dispersing, maybe moonlight would give them more time. Joe was looking around as if trying to get his bearings. None of the group offered to help. For some reason he chose to leave the clearing at a different angle from where they came in. Had they taken a turn to the left? As they reached the edge of the clearing, they heard it.

A grunt, and then what seemed to be a grunt in reply, low angry grunts, not human, definitely, well, certainly not female human. The grunts were followed by twigs breaking, and a sound of movement, hooves maybe. Horses? Deer? Movement in the undergrowth.

Joe swept up Samantha this time, Sam grabbed Bastian.

'Run,' called Joe

Sam looked round. At the far side of the small clearing three wild boar appeared, they stopped, they assessed the group of humans and then they started towards them. The humans ran.

The priority now was running where it was easy to run, gaps between vegetation, clearings, paths, they twisted left and right, the adults running as well as they could, again Sam being the slowest, the children holding on. They ran for what must have been five or six minutes, Sam was exhausted. Joe's fist went up again just as Sam could take it no longer, and they stopped, and listened. Sam could hear nothing above ner own breathing, but Joe seemed to be able to get a sense of whether they were still being chased. He seemed satisfied.

'Let's hope they were just protecting their territory.' Mary glared.

'We're safe now, they're not following us any more,' he added looking from child to Mary and back.

Joe looked around, no hope of deciding a direction, not in this light, not knowing which way was north, south, east or west. The light was bouncing around between the trees, for a second it looked like Joe was contemplating trying to climb a tree but decided against.

'I vote we camp here for the night.'

Mary and Sam looked at each other and their respective clothes. There was nothing in their bags for this eventuality. Nothing to protect them from the elements.

And so here they were, huddled together on the ground, feeling colder and colder as evening led to night and the temperature dropped. Hearing woodland noises echoing around. Sam did not expect to sleep. They ate some bread each, and soon the children fell asleep, Samantha in Mary's arms and Bastion in Sam's. They talked and reminisced, at a whisper. Joe opened the brandy and they all had a swig. Mary was the first to sleep. The next thing Sam remembered was being nudged.

'Sam, sun's coming up, let's make a move.' It was Joe. No sleep for him. They stretched out their aches and pains, and set off in the direction they thought the wall would lie.

***

The early morning light filtered through the branches creating shadows and reflections like starlight. There was a dewiness in the air and the freshness filled their nostrils. The children had clearly slept well and were running up ahead. It was a beautiful morning. The serenity that surrounded them was complete when the children stopped still just ahead, they looked back at the adults who caught up. Up ahead there were two deer grazing quietly. They stopped and waited. Sam grabbed a clump of grass, and showed Samantha how to hold it, like a bunch of flowers with leaves aplenty. Ushering her forward, Samantha silently stepped forward with her brother behind. The deer head up, watched. Samantha hesitated but the adults urged her forward, she got within two metres of the animal and was instructed to stop and wait. Her patience was admirable, and soon rewarded, the closest deer took a cautious step forward, it was like a dance in slow motion, as the deer approached, Sam realised the height differential. Bravely Samantha raised her hand almost vertically in the air, but she kept watching. For the next few minutes all the stresses were melting away, like a therapy dog in a hospital, this deer was calming them all and bringing them closer to what it was to be human. Caring, sharing, helping. For some years now humanity seemed to be transitioning from Exploiters of Earth, to the role of Guardians of Earth, and this simple gesture seemed to embody all of that change. Sam was not sure how long they all stood there, but they stood until the deer decided there were other things to eat. They carried on heading east.

At this time of the morning there were lots of animals about, lots of birds, and here they were deep in the woodland. For a moment Sam thought maybe somehow they had got past the wall, but ne knew that not to be true. They found a stream, with rabbits everywhere, but could not find the stream on the map, they found a ruin of a hut or outbuilding, but again checking the map they could not find anything. It was a shame that trees weren't on the map, some of these trees would have been much older and more permanent features than any of the man-made objects on most maps. They'd seen the rise and possibly now the fall of the industrial age, from ideas, to production, to mass production, to competition, through envy and then finally destruction. The have-nots finally rising up against the haves. Although this time it was at a government level. Sam's father had been to Moscow once and had been impressed at the way it coped with being the global bad boy. Is it surprising if someone is accused of bullying enough times that they become a bully? Who are the West to judge a country for expanding its territory, surely colonisation was a

European invention? Sam reminded nerself this was the twenty-first century not the fifteenth. Had we learned nothing in over five hundred years? There was something so permanent and stable here in stark contrast to what was no doubt happening beyond the wall. There was a bit of Sam that just wanted to sit down here, make a rudimentary shelter, last out the self-inflicted human chaos all around.

They carried on, they walked for only another fifteen minutes or so before they reached the wall. They stopped, the wall here looked very different, a tree had fallen touching the wall and ivy had started to make its way up the face of the wall, like a *Jack and the Beanstalk* show, not climbable yet, but maybe one day. They stopped and checked the map.

'I reckon we head south,' said Joe and they all agreed. 'How far do we think it is?'

'I reckon about half an hour on foot, maybe an hour at best.' Sam checked ner watch just past six a.m. 'We could make it to the farm in time for breakfast!' Ne smiled, and the thought of food prepared in the kitchen, spurred them on.

They headed south with the wall providing comfort on their left, and keeping them in the shade. When the wall was built, they had felled and removed trees either side so that although they might touch the wall if felled, they wouldn't damage it, which left a wide avenue space, tree-lined on one side and wall-lined on the other.

There were tracks on the ground where New Horizons' gamekeepers had patrolled over the years.

'We're looking for rubble up against the wall,' Sam called forward to the others. They had naturally fallen into their formation of Joe, Bastion, Samantha, Mary and Sam at the rear. Single file for no reason except habit, they could easily have walked five abreast swinging the children between the adults and laughing as they did. But although everything around them looked like they were on holiday exploring a new path, they weren't.

It was barely another ten minutes when they saw signs of rubble, upon inspection Sam recognised the rubble. They'd only been up about half an hour, they could easily have made this trip last night.

'OK, we're here, the farm just over there.' Sam pointed towards the trees. But there was nothing there. Just dense overgrowth, a wall of vegetation. 'I'm sorry, I thought this was it.'

Dejected they set off, all except Bastion who had already followed the direction that Sam had identified. Bastion disappeared through the bushes.

His head popped out. 'It is here! Sammy come, come'

Samantha followed her brother through the bushes, as did the others.

They were now standing in a man-made clearing, from this side it was clear that the vegetation behind them had been put there, branches and uprooted bushes all piled up to create a barrier.

There was silence, no welcome party. Joseph pointed at his watch, reminding them all of the time. They hesitated, what was the etiquette, it was like a large family camping trip, and you are the only family with young children, trying to stop them waking the uncles and aunts all of whom could sleep for another two hours.

'Do we go in?' asked Mary.

''I suppose so!' said Joe.

Sam stepped forward. Ne needn't have hesitated, people were awake inside, working on equipment and talking quietly, all men, no women to be seen. One of them looked up. 'Susan, you'll want to see this,' he called out. From a doorway at the back of the cottage Susan appeared. She rushed across and gave Mary a hug, and then hesitated looking at this tall woman in full make-up. 'Sam?'

'Ah, yes, long story.' They hugged. It felt good. Sam introduced Joe and the children, Susan bent down, and said, 'Hello, would you like something to eat, we've not got much'.

'We have,' said Bastion taking off his rucksack and opening the top.

'You clever young man. Will you help me unpack?'

They took their rucksacks through the doorway into a kitchen lost in time.

'We were very lucky you found this, Sam, it has an Aga for solid fuel and, although no water supply, the water butt outside has been collecting rainwater, so we have managed to boil up some water. We have crockery and cutlery, it's as if people left without taking anything with them.

'Would anyone like a cup of tea?' Sam said and it was like ne was offering to make them all millionaires. Teas and coffees were made, cereal for the children and they even managed to toast the bread on the stove without burning it. Once the food was unpacked and they had all had something to eat and drink, Sam took out the phone.

'We have spoken to someone outside, on a special network, do you have a charger for this?'

'Yes, we probably do, but power is limited here. It doesn't look like this farm was ever on the electricity grid, there is a generator out the back, but not much fuel. We have some solar panels that Malcolm over there brought with us, but the tree height means we can't get much direct sunlight. I have started to set up a lab next door.'

'Have you checked the plant room?' asked Sam surprised ne remembered.

'Plant room?'

Sam led Susan outside and walked to the side where the plant room had been. It wasn't there. Sam turned and looked at the cottage, it was definitely the same cottage. Ne turned and checked down the side of the building, and there it was, but completely covered in ivy. A tree had come down, maybe in the same storm that had caused the earlier tree to collapse, in any event, nature was trying to reclaim the plant room. They opened it up and it was a battery store with cables and mobile emergency solar panels piled up to one side. Susan gave Sam a big kiss.

'I'll get the guys to set this up, we've been using the truck's power up 'til now.'

They went back into the cottage and through into the room that Susan had set up as a lab. It was very impressive, the massive wooden dining table was the only piece of furniture left, the rest of the room looked like it had been cleaned. A tower of empty crates in one corner, and a science laboratory had been set up all around the table with room for at least four people to work.

'Everyone will be down soon, now that we have good enough daylight.' There were cables running across the floor, but those seemed to be going to fridges rather than any lighting. 'We're trying to replicate doses of the vaccine we created, but it's proving difficult. We haven't got much time.'

'At least the vaccine might be a solution.' Sam said with a grimace. 'I'm not sure they'll be many left, after all the rioting that seems to be taking place.'

'Well, I can't do anything about that, but I can get the vaccine replicated.'

'And then what?'

'I suppose then we need to get out of here and get the vaccine up to London.'

'I'm not sure that will work.'

'Well maybe your contact can tell us where to take it, can you phone ner?'

'No, they phone me, their number isn't stored in the phone.'

'Well, how about you leave me and my team to carry on the work we were doing before we had to evacuate, and you get some rest, charge your phone, and let's be ready for when the call comes through! Sound like a plan?'

Sam nodded. Ne went back and joined Mary and the children, who were sat with Simon telling him stories of how they got to the farm. By now the wild boar had grown enormously and they sounded more like human-eating angry bears rather than protective pigs. More tea was served.

'I think we'll be here a few days, maybe we could look at sleeping accommodation.'

Simon pointed upstairs. 'There are rooms up there but they're not as watertight as the barn, so we moved all the bedding to the barn, I'll show you.' He showed them a makeshift dormitory with four beds and a number of makeshift beds made of straw. Simon and Joe made up some more for the new arrivals, down one end. Sam went back to the cottage front room and sat for a while. It wasn't long before Sam fell asleep, this time deeply.

Over the next few days there was a hive of activity amongst Susan's team, Joe was helping out the technicians, the solar panels had been positioned for maximum sun, trees had been felled, one of the barns had now been completely rain proofed, and beds had been improved using materials found around, some cushions and a few extra mattresses found in the attic which were allocated to women and children first. Each discussion led to an awkward look in Sam's direction. In the end, Sam was deemed 'male' for allocation of resources. Make-up and wig gone, Sam was back. A rhythm had developed where Sam and Mary had taken charge of the kitchen, Simon and Joe were in charge of making the farm work for them — security and maintenance now the most important skill sets they had. Susan and her team rarely left the lab, which now was looking more and more like it had been purpose built. Lighting was now available, the solar panels had been supplemented by a heat exchanger, which Sam did not understand, but it sat next to the Aga and they had instructions not to touch it. It meant that the Aga had to be permanently on. The children were in full log collecting duties. Breakfast was served at seven thirty each morning, and the day went from there, roles were clear and people took their responsibilities seriously. Every day Sam checked the phone to see if it had rung and was charged. It hadn't. It was.

It was after a few days, might have been two, maybe three, when Sam was lying on his bed of straw, but comfortable nevertheless, ne heard movement in the dark. Slowly ne raised up onto ner elbows to see through the darkness, others were sleeping around. No pyjamas here, and the washing facilities were rationed, due to water being in short supply, it had hardly rained since they arrived. The noise was gentle, careful. Sam was trying decide whether it was friend or foe, when ne felt something touch ner leg. Ne froze. Thoughts of everyone being slaughtered in their sleep, went through ner mind. Was everyone else already dead? Why was everything so quiet? Sam's breathing must have changed, maybe louder, maybe quicker, panic was rising, plans tumbling through ner head, had they been found, was this the end? Options: run, scream, play dead. Prognosis: Death, slow death, painful death.

'Sam, shh, is that you?' It was Susan.

'SUSAN!' Sam hissed

'Sorry, did I scare you?'

'No, you think!' retorted Sam still hissing but definitely calming down now. A nervous laugh started to build from deep down in Sam's throat, but ne swallowed it.

'Didn't mean to spook you, but didn't want to wake anybody. Fancy sharing a mattress?'

Irrationally, Sam's first thought was, 'Oh, so you have time for me now!' Again swallowed.

'Well, that would be…' Sam couldn't think of the word. Sam wasn't sure what was being offered, they were in an open barn with lots of people. Somehow, it felt strange, the thought of sharing Susan's mattress.

'Don't worry if you're comfortable on your straw.'

For a second Sam felt like defending the straw, making excuses for it, in reality, now given an option, the straw wasn't nearly as comfortable as ne had been trying to persuade nerself.

'That would be lovely, thank you, you lead the way.' Sam held out ner hand and touched flesh, not ner own, but beyond that not sure, Susan's leg maybe, or her arm. There was the faintest crackle of energy created, was it chemistry, or physics, whatever it was Sam was thinking it might lead to biology. In the dark, Susan led Sam across the barn like some management training trust exercise. But trust had already been established. Sam followed without concern, just optimism and something else, maybe it was the stress from the past few days, maybe it was the horrors, maybe it was the fact that yet again, like in 2020, they were living in the plot of a Hollywood movie, but Sam was thinking this was love ne was feeling. Susan stopped. The darkness changed, it was no longer an empty void, now it was a cocoon, wrapping round them and erasing everything else. Sam felt they were alone, not only in the barn, but in the world, it was as if nothing else existed except the two of them in this moment. Time no longer existed. Space no longer existed. Just the two of them. Susan turned, and they kissed. Hands moved as in slow motion, reacquainting themselves with each other, stroking and calming each other. The lead role changed imperceptibly, and soon Sam was leading the slow ballet that they were creating. Susan let ner take charge. Susan needed to be held. Their mouths still connected, but Sam tasted salt. Susan was crying, her eyes washing away emotions, no shaking, just flowing. The kiss turned to an embrace, they held each other, Susan lowered onto the mattress and ne lay in her arms, a puddle of tears growing on Sam's chest trickled down, being absorbed by the T-shirt ne was wearing. They must have both fallen asleep, as the next thing Sam was aware of, was a shadow passing. Sam opened an eye. It was Mary. She looked down and smiled. A flood of emotion filled Sam's whole being. Sam knew then that ne would follow this beautiful, intelligent woman wherever she wanted to go. More people were stirring, and so as not to become an attraction for onlookers, Sam stroked Susan's hair and whispered gently.

'Susan my lovely, people are waking.'

She responded with a squeeze, and a stretch.

'Morning, Sam.' Her smile lit fireworks in ner heart. And then she was gone.

Twenty minutes later, toast and dry cereal were served, Sam and Mary had been busy. Sam wondered whether Susan would treat Sam differently now that she was in work mode. Ne needn't have worried, Susan came in for breakfast, asked Simon to move, and took up his seat next to Sam. She took ner hand, squeezed it and said, 'This looks delicious, I just want to say thanks to everyone, we're making good progress in the lab, we have quite a few samples now. Simon, how are you getting on with the drones?'

Sam looked up. 'Drones?'

'Yes, we brought four drones with us, but only one of them was working properly. Simon's been using the parts to make three working drones, so we can hopefully get the vaccines out there.'

All eyes were on Simon. He smiled at Susan, and Sam realised that they both knew that the news was good, she was just giving Simon a moment in the spotlight.

'We now have three working drones, I finished them last night. I have tried to get them so they will fly autonomously beyond the range of the remote control, just waiting for coordinates to set them off, depending on the wind. I reckon we could get them maybe forty kilometres, in theory they have a top speed of eighty kilometres an hour and batteries should last thirty minutes. But really, it's a guess, if you want it to deliver the vaccine to somewhere specific then you'd be safer picking a destination within a thirty-kilometre range.'

'Thanks Simon. Sam, I assume your phone hasn't rung?'

'No, still nothing.'

She put her hand out, Sam handed the phone over. She searched in settings, pressed a few buttons, and like a computer she ended up with a black screen with computer code showing and a prompt saying, 'Input'.

Susan typed some more. 'Pen and paper please,' she said seemingly to the phone, but Sam realised it was a general instruction. Ne moved to get up, but realised that one of her team was already on the errand, they must be used to it by now, always listening for her instructions, much like a surgeon in a complex operation, fully focussed, in charge. Pen and paper appeared. Susan wrote something down.

'OK, I have the number that we can call, but let's get things ready here, tidied up and ready to leave at a moment's notice, and then at midday today, if we don't hear from your contact, Sam, I propose we call them. If that doesn't provide some extra insight, I think we should release the drones. Comments?'

Sam had no comments, and realised, the question wasn't aimed at ner. The scientists raised questions and clarifications, but it was clear no one had any intention to contradict the plan.

'Good comments, agreed we need to fix where to send them, Joe, you have a map?'

'Oh, yes, let me get it.'

'Excellent, I'll leave you in charge of finding sites that Simon is confident the drones can reach, I guess hospitals, or medical centres would be the logical choice. We also need to find someone good at communication, to write a message on each sample with instructions, that will be succinct but comprehensive. Sam, could you work with Ian on that?'

Ian put his hand up to identify himself, a short man in his fifties maybe, always in the background, never really part of any activity or discussion. And so new roles were allocated, a renewed spring in everyone's collective step. Susan took Sam's hand, gave it another gentle squeeze and disappeared with a fresh cup of tea into the laboratory. Just over four hours until drone release.

***

Everyone completed their roles, rucksacks were packed, drones were readied with their cargo, in polystyrene containers, coordinates were chosen. A hospital, a nearby medical centre, and interestingly, the house of the local MP, on the basis that it might not be overrun and likely to reach someone who had the contacts to do something with it. All evidence they were there was packed away.

In the back of people's minds there was a plan to somehow return to their apartments. Sam found out that Simon's girlfriend was pregnant, so was keen to rejoin her as soon as possible.

Joe had planned it out in his mind and took Sam to one side.

'Sam, I'm thinking when Susan has released her drones, we'd all split up into smaller groups, some want to get back to New Horizons and face their fate with their families. I think we should try and breach the wall somehow, and I think Susan is planning to try and get back into Porton Down, what do you think?'

'I don't know, Joe, are you sure the wall is breachable? My instinct tells me to provide Susan with any support she needs, shouldn't we all head back to New Horizons, if we do breach the wall, and there is a flood of people coming in, are we not opening up the prospect of mass slaughter?' Sam paused. 'We might be able to go unnoticed but if a thousand people start to get into the complex, then we'll leave the Russians with no real choice. Who knows how many weapons they have, it seems to me that they are likely to be heavily armed.'

'That's true enough, we've also got Bastion and Samantha to think about, Mary has grown quite attached to them.'

'Maybe two groups then, one led by Susan, and one by you. You can try and start a resistance group ready to react if an opportunity arises, and I'll help Susan and her team get into Porton Down.' A plan was set. Sam set about duplicating Joe's map with a mixture of free hand and tracing. They marked on doors that they thought might be good access points into New Horizons, and both made a mark on the map that showed the location of the farm, but which hopefully wouldn't be recognised as such if they lost either map. The watches ticked on. At midday, they all convened in the laboratory, which like some time travelling trick was now back to being a dining room with a bookcase, some random chairs and a cupboard in the corner, the only clue that there was anything amiss was that the cupboard was filled with modern crates. One of the team closed the door and the illusion was complete, people appeared with chairs and stools from around the farm, and soon they were all sat round the table like a war briefing, which in a sense it was.

Sam put ner phone on the table, and Susan picked it up and got past the encryption, so the call could be made. It rang and rang, the loudspeaker on the phone echoed the ringing tone around the room, and they all waited. Bastion was the only one to lose concentration and was now sat in the corner with some biscuits. As everyone listened, the sound of the boy munching his biscuits was the only noise between the rings. After eight rings. The call was answered.

'Hello?'

A quick eye conversation took place between Sam and Susan, each encouraging the other to speak. Susan won. Sam started. 'Hello, is Amardeep there?'

'Who's calling?'

'Sam, VV6.'

'Please hold.' They all looked at each other and waited, even Bastion was waiting, there was complete silence in the room.

'Sam?'

'Speaking, is that you, Amardeep?'

'Yes, it is, surprised that you called, this is not supposed to be possible.'

'We have some very clever people here and hoping for an update so we can compare plans.'

'Interesting, let me know your news.'

Sam looked at Susan for confirmation, she smiled and nodded.

'OK, so we have a base away from the towers, which we think has not been discovered, we have scientists here who have been able to create copies of a vaccine, which they believe to be effective against the new strain of Covid, although clearly no human trials have been undertaken…' Susan put her hand up.

'Susan Durum here, we have tested the vaccine on a few humans and they were able to fight off the new variant, it's a single dose, and crucially can survive several hours at room temperature, Sam, continue.'

'So yes, eh, we have a number of samples, and three drones ready to send three samples to specific sites, the details of which I don't think I should share with you. We are planning to split our team into two groups, one is looking to re-infiltrate the towers and one is planning to get back into Porton Down and see if that can be taken back from the Russians. We are all packed up and ready to go this afternoon, just wanted to speak to you for fresh information, to make sure our respective plans were compatible.'

Silence at the other end.

'Have you explored trying to leave the compound?'

Joe perked up but did not speak. Sam replied.

'We have discussed it, but felt that if we breached the wall, then we might not be able to stop the flood of people coming in and there might be a bloodbath.' Susan looked surprised, as did many of the others in the room. 'In any event we're not entirely sure how we would breach the wall, it was designed to withstand a tank, so not sure if we have the equipment to either scale it or smash it down.'

'Fair enough, Sam, how many are you?'

'Twelve plus two children.'

'Children!' exclaimed Amardeep. 'Whose children?'

'Not important, they heard our last call, from a few days ago, so you can continue.'

'Firstly, that was last week, secondly, I'm not sure they should hear this, we should carry on this conversation privately, have you got a room you could go to?'

Mary stood up, to take the children out, but instead, Ian gestured her to sit down, and he took hold of a reluctant Samantha, but delighted Bastion and they left the room. Sam looked at Ian, and wondered whether he didn't really want to hear this either. Certainly, as they had worked together writing their messages a few hours ago, it seemed that Ian was finding this whole situation very difficult, it seemed he didn't like group situations. The door to the room opened and closed and they heard the kitchen being raided for any snacks that they had decided not to pack into rucksacks.

'OK, the children are next door.' What they heard next changed things yet again for this small team.

'Firstly, let me start by updating you on what we think is happening globally, then the UK and finally what that means for the Vertical Villages, in particular yours.'

He started slowly, and although first instincts from the group were no doubt that the order was wrong, and that he should start with what impacts them directly, this was soon forgotten when details were shared about the wider situation.

'Germany and Russia are technically at war, but this has become complicated by the fact that parts of the country that were in East Germany, had started receiving vaccinations, and importantly a new treatment for those infected. The old Iron Curtain was returning and countries like Poland, Hungary and Romania, were effectively back behind it, any war with Russia now meant lining up against countries who were still, on paper, within the European Union. The Union was unable to keep up with the speed of change. France, also largely lost out in the Covid 19 vaccinations race, has promising results, but Russia seems poised to invade. Added to the fact that France is coping with having lost almost all their cities on the west coast from the tsunami. Africa is trying to cope with biblical levels of migration from highly populated countries in the west to the east, and whole infrastructures are collapsing. Across Asia, the Chinese vaccine has either failed or at least is not leaving China, and more and more countries are following Japan's lead, signing deals with Russia. The death toll in India is no longer being reported. Case levels across North America seem to be under the greatest control, with total lockdown being put in place almost immediately, and being enforced by the military. Alaska has become a critical location as the global map is being redrawn. Canadian and American troops are heading there every day. There is talk of a counter-attack, but without a competitive treatment, countries are unwilling to put up a fight. In terms of the UK, the BBC are still broadcasting on local frequencies, based out of Manchester, and the seat of government has a temporary seat in an undisclosed location, using the BBC to communicate. Refugee centres have been set up across Oxfordshire and Warwickshire. The water is receding, but flooding is still everywhere and building foundations are being swept away as the water recedes. Looting has settled down and people are pretty much staying in their homes. The broadcasts are currently telling the story that the UK focus is on treatment and tsunami relief, the Russian situation is not seen as an issue. Your situation has not been shared, although the government do know about it.'

There was a pause for breath, or maybe water. Sam took the opportunity. 'So might a rescue attempt be made to rescue those of us trapped here?'

There was a pause, and for a second, Sam thought the connection had been lost, but after an interminable, few seconds, Amardeep carried on.

'So that brings me to your situation, I mentioned that the US are focussing their activities on their own soil, but that does not take account of the full story. As you know, we have a number of American military bases here in the UK but they have instructions to take any action which might help protect the US. We shared your information from the last call with them. I'm sorry Sam, all of you, but we think the Americans are planning a strike.'

'Excuse me?'

'The information is not clear, and they won't share full details of what they are planning, but there is a chance that they plan to bomb VV6, I'm sorry, you have to get out.'

There was no screaming in the room, no tears, the shock had just drained all the faces of their colour, as if turning the room to stone.

'But what about the vaccine?'

'I'm sorry it is out of our hands; you need to find a way out of the complex and fast.'

'When were you going to tell me this?'

'Had you not phoned, then, probably never,' he hesitated. 'But you have, and I can't not tell you. I'm sorry.' Amardeep lowered his voice. 'You've been categorised as collateral damage, I will of course deny any of this was said.'

'OK, here's what we'll do, we'll send the drones up now, but we need two days, I don't mind how you do it, but Amardeep, get us forty-eight hours.'

'I'll try, good luck.' Click.

Sam looked at the group. There are two types of people in the world, those who are paralysed by fear and those who use the adrenaline to attack. There seemed to be only four of them ready to take charge. Susan, Joe, Simon and Sam. They set about forming a plan.

First, they released the drones, which went without a hitch. Simon could see them on his screen, as they flew over the wall and set off towards their destinations. Then, much to the disagreement of many of the group, they ate and drank, to give energy but also, they weren't sure when they would eat again. Then they were told to rest, and they would leave in four small groups at dusk.

No one slept. People talked about life, once the case had been made to only operate at night, the doubters came round, a packet of cards was even produced by one of the scientists and the time was spent. Sam and Susan went for a walk.

'Susan, when this is over, can we talk?'

'We can talk now!'

'Maybe not, who knows what the next few days will bring, I just need to know that we will talk about us, when we're through.'

'OK.' She took both of Sam's hands in hers, and looked Sam directly in the eyes. Her adoration was evident. 'Your father would be proud of you, you know.'

'Thanks, I hope so.' They walked in silence along the wall and then turned back as the afternoon wore on, the last few moments of calm before things turned crazy again.

'We'll need to make up more maps, for everyone.'

'Good thought.' She took ner hand and squeezed. Sam returned the gesture.

When they got back to the farm, it was all quiet, people were dozing in chairs and Joe was sat at the table already replicating the map, great minds think alike. Laid out on the table were also knives, and metal bars, as well as two more handguns, which no doubt came from Susan's team. It didn't look like much, but it was all they had, their chances were not good.

As dusk arrived, they split into their groups. Joe, Mary and the children left as one group, their aim to break back into the North Tower, and lay low, until an escape route had been found. There was some discussion about which apartment they would stay in, Sam smiled to nerself as they chose Mary's apartment even though it was smaller. Sam's group consisted of Ian, and two other scientists, Paula and Gavin. Their role was to get back safely following a different route to Mary to avoid being detected and then get the North Tower ready for an evacuation. It all hinged on Amardeep being able to buy them time, if he couldn't they'd all be gone anyway. Susan left in the truck with

Simon and two further members of her team, they planned to separate as they got closer to the towers. Sam's group was missioned with speaking to as many residents of the North Tower as possible and work out a plan to get them to Porton Down, once the route had been cleared by Susan. Simon had the tricky job of staying with the truck having first taken Sam and her colleagues as close to the towers as possible, and when signalled, to create a diversion. Susan had one of the guns, Simon the other, not much ammunition. Sam kept hold of the one Joe had given ner earlier. Joe chose to be armed with just a knife which he concealed in his pocket.

The plan was to leave during dusk, so that they reached the edge of woods as darkness fell and created a blanket of cover. Luckily for Sam, Ian had a compass, so they were going to leave with Joe and walk together to the edge of the woods.

They checked their maps, they checked their compass, they chose a route and they left. Sam looked back at Susan, and they smiled, she would be next to leave with Simon. The needle of Ian's compass bounced about bringing back memories from school, but they followed its course, trying to head in a straight line. Stories of animals that they had met on the way in were retold, with young Samantha telling most of them. Sam found nerself walking alongside Gavin. They'd not spoken much, he was about ner age, athletic, with manly features, more good-looking rugby player, than good-looking football player. Dark brown hair, and when they caught a glimpse of each other, he had piercing blue eyes. He smiled. His smile was disarming.

'So Gavin, tell me how you got into this!' Sam said with a smile. Gavin looked at Sam, as if for the first time, weighing ner up. It would have been easy for Sam to think that this was ner gender identity that was being observed, but Gavin's eyes were so disarming and genuine, that Sam was lulled into taking the look at face value. Gavin was just looking at ner, plain and simple. Sam wondered whether this was exactly how Gavin had got into this, he had just looked people in the eye and they had succumbed to his silent charm.

'Well, that's a story to tell.'

'Well, it looks like Ian is happy leading the way, we have time!' Sam smiled in what ne hoped was not a flirting way, although this man certainly had his charms.

'I was born in Dublin, and came to England when I was six. My mother is a scientist, and she worked in a laboratory in Oxford, then my father and I followed her to Germany, then back to Oxford. I studied medicine, to become a doctor, and then found the reality of being a doctor difficult, it's not all that glamorous in hospital, not everyone gets saved, and I found that challenging. The first pandemic we saw so many bodies, I was still training then. I felt I could save more people by working on vaccines, so my mother's team were recruiting and I joined them straight from medical school. When the truth came out about the Covid-19, Porton Down went into overload and I got a job there. Susan is amazing, I know she is our age, but she reminds me of my mother, she's amazing.'

'Have you and her ever...?'

'Oh no, God no, that would be weird!' Sam was relieved but slightly surprised, it seemed Gavin was one of those blessed individuals, who at school everyone wanted to date. Looking at Gavin, Sam wondered whether he'd been propositioned by the complete spectrum. Sam wondered if Gavin felt this was a gift or a curse. He walked tall and talked effortlessly. Sam was pleased he was on their team.

'So forgive me, I should know this, but do you live in New Horizons?'

'I got offered a flat, but decided to stay with my parents, Dad has effectively retired, so life is easy that way. It's made me lazy though, so when this is all over, who knows.'

'Where are your parents now?' A millisecond of composure loss flicked across Gavin's face.

'I don't know, when we did the drill and closed the site, what was it, last week, the week before? I spoke to them, and they seemed fine. Dad was busy getting in provisions.'

'Your mother would have been a perfect person to send a drone to, would she not?'

'Yes, I spoke to Susan, the distance was too great, the drone wouldn't have made it.'

'Shame.' They walked on in silence for a bit, thinking about all the lives that had been turned upside down beyond the walls. It was the not knowing that was the worst. Sam held back from platitudes, like, "I'm sure they'll be fine", or "You'll see them soon". Neither was likely to be true.

They came across a stream, perhaps the same one as before, they crossed, and Sam's thoughts went back to wild boar.

'This is about where we had our boar encounter, on our way to the farm!'

'Sounds frightening.'

'Well, it did make us run, and it certainly made us all a bit more cautious.'

'What else is in here?'

Sam smiled. 'Only the animals that were already here, so you'll be pleased no bears! Deer, boars, badgers, that sort of thing.'

'What about the zoo animals?'

'Well, yes, I have assumed no one would be stupid enough to let them out, most of them are young and thankfully, all of them are herbivores. They wanted to send some young lions, but I drew the line at that, it was supposed to be a petting zoo, after all. When we let them in it was a morale boosting idea because we wanted it to look like a drill.'

'Wasn't it a drill?'

'It was, it just was a drill that I was encouraged to arrange, at quite short notice. If it was a genuine doomsday scenario there was a plan with Whipsnade Zoo that we would take samples of almost all their animals including lions. My father had scoped it out in the event of catastrophic environmental destruction.'

'Worse than this?'

'He was really focussed on the wildfires that crop up, his view was that England is so heavily populated and the love of houses, and therefore, gardens, meant that a wildfire in England would hop from town to town destroying everything in its path. Gas pipes everywhere. He built these sites as refuges not only for humans but also for flora and fauna. We have the largest acreage here of any Vertical Village, so we were due to take animals, Manchester, already have a duplicate set of seeds and plant specimens.'

'Well, I'm quite pleased we don't risk meeting a rhino as we walk through the woods.'

They smiled at each other. Gavin was definitely a great person to know.

'So how well do you know Susan?' asked Sam, hopefully in a neutral way, rather than in a "Tell me about my girlfriend" sort of way.

'Well enough, we work together a lot, but the person who knows her best is Paula.' He gestured to the woman walking alongside Ian.

'Are they friends?'

'Yeah, they share an apartment on the Porton Down site, so yes I think Paula would be your best bet for info.' Gavin smiled, and nudged Sam with his elbow. A conspiratorial plan had been hatched.

'Maybe later.' Smiled Sam

'Oh, go on, as you said this might be our chance to have a chat.' With that Gavin set off and caught up with Ian, before long they were chatting and Paula was on her own.

'Hi, Paula, thanks for joining our group.'

'No problem. I see you've been talking to Gavin.' A hint of inquisition slipped through her tight smile.

'Yes, he's a nice guy, looks strong as well.'

'Definitely, him and his dad are doing lots of building work, and I think, from what Gavin says, his dad is just directing, and Gavin is doing most of the work!' They smiled.

'Have you worked with Gavin long?'

'A couple of years, we all knew of him, because his mother used to be a regular visitor back during the first pandemic.'

The group reached a clearing, and although they had only been walking about half an hour, Mary was suggesting they take a breather. Sam and Paula sat down. Water was being handed out, Joe and Ian seemed to be checking where they were on the map. Sam wondered if ne should help, but felt, sometimes, help equals interference. They seemed to be coping all right.

'I take it you know Ian as well, do you think he'd want me to go over and help?'

'No, Ian's happiest in small situations, he needs time to think things through, I think he'll like that you are leaving him to it. Susan does the same.'

'What's Susan like as a boss? Gavin says you know her most of all.'

'Well, I don't know about that, but we share a flat, when she's here, but she used to travel a lot.'

Sam wasn't sure from where this comment came, but ne found nerself asking:

'Has she talked about me?'

Paula laughed, and then covered her mouth, as if it wasn't allowed. The group in the clearing all looked round, they all smiled at them.

'I'm sorry how old are we, twelve?' Paula laughed some more.

'Yeah, OK, forget I asked.'

Paula's laugh subsided into a smile. 'I'll tell you about Susan if you wish.'

Susan's Story

Sam listened with interest and shock as Paula, shared
what she knew. Perhaps Susan had given her permission
to tell her stories, maybe it was the situation they were
in. It could also be Paula's attempt to matchmake. As
Sam listened ne did wonder whether Paula actually
didn't like Susan because there was lots of information
given out. Sam's feelings for Susan increased with
every word.

Susan was an ordinary girl from Kent, she had an
older sister, and spent most of her time as a small child
on the beach, collecting shells and looking in rock
pools, she had blessed early years. She enjoyed school
and passed her eleven plus to go to grammar school.
Family holidays always involved a beach. One such
holiday, Susan was twelve, her elder sister was about
fifteen. They were in Thailand. They woke up early for
a special trip in a taxi to go catch a ferry to a remote
island, with paradise-like beaches, where there were
interesting animals for Susan and the rest of the family,
but mostly Susan, to see. It started to rain and they were
all sat in the taxi wondering if it was a good idea. But
this was warm tropical rain, and it often blew across
quite quickly. Her dad was sat in the front of the taxi in

silence, as their local driver only spoke a few words in English, and Susan's father could only say hello, which sounded something like 'Sa wa dee', and thank you which Susan could never remember how to say. Her father watched the road ahead. Susan's mother was between the girls on the back seat. Susan remembered the colour of the taxi very well, it was what she came to call 'Thailand Pink', an iridescent mix of pink and purple, a colour she loved instantly and then hated forever.

The rain had picked up, and the road was now awash, it was like they were driving along a river. Her father was holding the dashboard now, and she remembered her mother taking hold of her hand. Nothing was said. In complete silence Susan had sat there and watched as the taxi hit something, possibly a pothole, or the curb, she would never know. Her sister's scream pierced through the air. The car slid and span sideways. The crash barrier on the side of the road would stop them. The driver's side hit the crash barrier, the rain thundered down, her sister screamed as her window smashed and her door crumpled against the barrier. Susan's door flew open, and the next thing she felt was her mother unclicking her seat belt and pushing her. As the crash barrier gave way, Susan hit the ground. It must have been painful, later, she spent two days in hospital, but she felt nothing. Susan looked around dazed. She got herself up, as the taxi stopped on the other side of the crash barrier. Luckily, there was no vertical drop at this point in the road, the verge was just green vegetation and was not deep, there were no trees to hit, the taxi sat there relatively intact. Susan watched as her parents were moving, her sister seemed motionless and her mother was bent over her. Her father opened his door to get out. This image is indelibly marked on Susan's brain.

Paula stopped and checked that Sam wanted more of the story before carrying on. Ian was signalling that they should continue walking so they got up and Paula carried on with the story.

It was then that Susan had heard the horn. A sickening feeling engulfed the teenager. A massive lorry overladen, no doubt, was careering along the other carriageway, a carriageway that was now blocked with a bright pink taxi. Seat belts were all undone. The lorry hit. The taxi shunted. The family screamed. The driver didn't as he flew in what felt like slow motion through the windshield. Her mother and sister got shunted down the carriageway in the taxi, only to see it explode two hundred yards down the road. Her father was nowhere to be seen. Susan got herself up and found him crumpled on the central reservation grass. The rain continued to hammer down. She held him, the two of them intertwined, drenched, motionless. The next few hours were a blur. Ambulances, police, lights, noises, incomprehensible voices. A day later, she woke in a room that was white and bright and clinical. A hospital room just like any hospital room anywhere in the world.

There was a young woman at the end of her bed looking at charts. Susan coughed.

'Ah you wake. Good. Eat?'

Susan nodded and looked for a drink which she saw on her bedside table. The young woman ran quickly round and helped her. Susan sat up with surprising ease. Then she noticed that there were no tubes, no medical equipment at all. In fact, she was not hurt. She sat herself up and went to get out of bed.

'Wait. Stay,' said the young woman 'English?'

Susan nodded assuming it was a question, but it hadn't been. The young lady left and returned with food, twenty minutes later. And again, simply said, 'English,' with a smile.

An hour later a man arrived. Geoffrey, from the British Embassy. He took her to see the only other survivor from the crash. Her father.

She stood numb, a fifteen-year-old, looking down at her father. In contrast to her room, this room could not have fitted any more equipment, his leg was in plaster and slightly raised, his head was bandaged. His face was swollen and taxi coloured. The machines were breathing for him and beeping. Lights and displays measuring everything. She looked.

'He's in an induced coma, while they do tests on him.'

'Is he in pain?' she asked

'No, he can't feel a thing, they are hopeful he will pull through.'

'Hopeful?'

'Yes, Susan, he has a serious head injury, he is very ill, your father, but I'll be here with you.'

Susan couldn't remember asking about her mother or sister, only later were they referred to as bodies to be brought back to the UK. Despite desperate pleas from Geoffrey, Susan returned to the hotel room that night, the hotel staff could not have done more for her. She slept in her parents' bed that night, by morning the pillow and the sheets were sodden. The following morning, she dressed smartly and carefully, no one would have known but she was wearing her sister's blouse, her mother's jacket and her father's chain around her neck.

Susan was different from that day on. She worked with Geoffrey, both sets of grandparents turned up a day later, but by then she had organised everything. The bodies were being flown to the UK. Her father still in a coma, they were trying to decide what to do. Twenty-four hours later he died also. His body was sent back alone. The embassy paid for flights for Susan and her grandparents. They didn't talk. She stayed at the grammar school to complete her GCSEs and while the house was sold. She moved to Leicester to live with her grandparents. She never visited a beach again, always blaming the accident on her need to visit beaches.

She studied the sciences, but not wanting to work in a hospital with constant reminders, set her sights on laboratory work. She went to Oxford and then

194

Cambridge for her PhD. She was headhunted by Porton Down.

Sam had listened and asked questions. 'That's a lot. Does she know you tell people this?'

Paula looked affronted and then relaxed. 'Firstly, I didn't tell people, I told you, Sam. Secondly, she has been wanting to tell you for ages and keeps asking me how she should tell you, she thinks you ought to know, but she is so focussed on not being defined by her past tragedy. She can't tell this story without it all flooding back, and you know Susan, sympathy is not something she wants to receive. So, there you have it.'

'Thank you, Paula.' In the absence of being able to give Susan a hug at this moment, Sam stopped walking and gave Paula a long and tight hug. They let go, tears in their eyes. They looked over and the group ahead had also stopped. They had reached the edge of the woods.

Rescue

It wasn't completely dark yet, but the lights in the towers had come on. Sam joined Mary, Ian and Joe looking at the map. They needed to split up now and find their way over to the towers. They looked to their left for any signs of Susan's group or Simon, but no sign. They stood and waited for Simon's distraction. The plan was that they would drive the truck close to the front so that it would be noticed, assuming Yakov would send people out to investigate. Simon would abandon the truck, hide, and if caught, surrender peacefully, his cover story was that he tried to get out, but couldn't get past the wall.

They waited, it was now, by everyone's definition, dark. The area in front of them was grassed, there was a playing field over to their right, but if they walked in a straight line towards the towers there should be no obstacles. Suddenly the lights of the truck were switched on and it made its way along the edge of the woods away from Sam's group. Joe's group left in a straight line across the grass, heading directly for the North Tower and the door they had come out of before. It was a different angle, so they would be going through the sports area, following the edge of the football pitch for most of the way, hopefully giving them some cover. Sam and ner small group ran diagonally left to forge their own route across the grass to the central tower through the vegetable garden. The grass was soft underfoot and they made good progress. They stopped and watched as noises appeared from the towers. Gun shots rang out to their left, amplified by the darkness. Sam looked over to check on the children, but they were nowhere to be seen. Gavin was the first to speak.

'Come on we need to keep moving,' he whispered, grabbing Paula's hand and urging them all to follow. Gavin now led the group as they crossed the grass, hearts pounding. Sam could not help but glance across. The truck was now heading back into the woods. Another truck left the towers and headed for the woods, as did a drone with a light attached. The drone headed for the woods following the truck. Then, to Sam's horror, four more drones appeared and were not heading in the same direction. Two headed away from them but two headed directly towards them.

'Come on we need to keep moving,' Gavin said again, with more urgency this time.

'But Susan.'

'She can look after herself,' whispered Paula. But they could all see that the drones would find Susan first, it was only a matter of time. They moved forward, everything inside Sam wanted to move towards Susan's position, but not being able to see her made that impossible. Then came a voice ne recognised.

'Come on you guys, keep moving.'

'Susan!'

'Let's outrun some drones, shall we?'

They sped up and ran low and fast, this whole area had been flattened to allow it to be used for activities, marquees, sports, storage, the ground was as flat as a cricket pitch. In no time they made it to the relative safety of the kitchen gardens, only a few hundred metres and they'd be at the base of the tower. They crouched as the drones flew past behind them seemingly making a perimeter inspection of the woodland. They ran the last stretch as if they were in the one hundred metres final at the Olympics. They stood up against the tower until the drones were out of sight. They walked along the side of the tower, until they found an access door. All the doors had been designed so that they could be opened from both sides. The idea was that the perimeter wall provided all the security they needed. Unless activated, all the access doors, from reception to doors on the roof, would be unlocked. Sam turned the handle and the door opened.

'Quick, quick.'

They piled through the door into the parking area, which spanned all three towers matching the footprint of the gardens on the roof. Susan made sure everyone was through, and then they heard it. A whirring sound echoing around the car park. The light above the door shone red. The locking mechanism had been activated. They were locked in.

'That doesn't change anything, internal doors are not affected so our master keys should still work. We'll head to the North Tower, get some sleep and then tomorrow we'll see if we can get people ready,' Sam reassured them all.

'Agreed, we'll head over and look at the Porton Down access tunnel now, while they are all busy out front. I'll come find you tomorrow to tell you what we have found out,' Susan replied and set off with her group.

Sam led ner team along the wall heading for the North Tower, hoping that Joe's group had made it in time. There was commotion to their left and they froze, cars were being started and heading out of the building. They carried on, there were still many cars in the car park, but over the years people had started using their car parking spaces for storage. Sheds had appeared in the space where residents might have parked a car or had available for visitors. They made their way along using whatever they could to stay hidden.

Bit by bit they got closer to the lift and stairs.

'Are you ready for this?' Sam said to the others as they walked past the lifts and entered the stairwell. 'Let's go.'

They started their walk up the stairs, shoes in hand, taking each floor one by one. Sam had told them which floor ne lived on, but still they had agreed to stay with ner. Step by step, level by level, they made their way up the building. It looked like Yakov had been true to his word, there was silence in the tower, no sign of his men at all. After an exhausting climb, they reached Sam's level and opened the door onto the corridor. The door made a sound but no one stirred. The corridor was deserted. They walked silently towards Sam's apartment, ne opened the door and all was exactly as ne had left it. They sat down at the dining table and looked at each other. Paula got up and put the kettle on. The sofa and cushions were rearranged to make more sleeping options. Votes were taken and Sam and Paula got the double bed, Gavin and Ian made do in the sitting room. They took it in turns to have a bath, which was a luxury indeed, bubble bath was used and lots of shampoo and conditioner. They were clean and refreshed. Gavin wasn't wearing much, as his clothes were in the washing machine, neither was Ian, but Gavin's torso was difficult to ignore. Sam had found pyjamas for Paula. They were raiding the slim pickings in the freezer, the fridge, the cupboards, and were relaxing at last, when there was a knock at the door.

Sam shushed them and quietly went to the door. Ne listened pressing ner ear to the surface, no sound. Ne looked through the spyhole. No one there. Then suddenly a face appeared close up. Sam jumped back and the group jumped up to be ready. Ian had to grab his towel as it almost fell down. The comedy moment was not even noticed. The tension, the reality check, the alertness was back in a flash. Sam looked again at the figure on the other side of the door.

'Don't panic everyone, it's Shamir, my neighbour.' Sam opened the door.

Shamir came in, laden with produce, and stopped dead when seeing the half-naked group in the room. Sam smiled.

'Eh, hi Sam, we heard movement and hoped you were back.' Sam looked at the armful of food, as Gavin came forward and started to unload Shamir's arms. 'Oh yes, we've been collecting your food parcels, so they didn't pile up in the corridor. Thought you might be hungry.' No answer was needed as Gavin and Ian were already tucking into the food.

'That's brilliant Shamir, how are you getting on?'

'Oh, we're fine, James has been updating people on a daily basis, he said you had fallen ill and were in the medical centre, apparently there was an outbreak in the South Tower, they have locked it down. He says he hopes to open the school again soon.'

'OK, anything else he's been saying?'

'That there is a state of emergency now in the UK, with the pandemic and that the UK government is refusing to accept Russian help, and apart from Germany, all other European countries are back to normal and have extensive treatment and vaccination programmes. Apparently, the Russians are also helping rebuild parts of France most affected by the tsunami.'

'How are people feeling do you reckon?'

'I think people feel safe in their apartments, they are worried about being infected. I have spoken to a few people in the corridor, but nobody is mingling. James has arranged disinfectant to be sprayed in the corridors twice a day.'

'Well that certainly will keep people in their flats. But you risked meeting us.'

'Well to be honest, I wasn't expecting you to have people here, and there's something not quite right about the information we're getting, it's almost as if…' he paused.

'As if?'

'As if James is a Russian sympathiser.'

'Shamir, James is Russian.'

'Yes, I know that, but not Russian-Russian, if you get what I mean.'

'No definitely Russian-Russian, Yakov Lebedev, Lieutenant Colonel of the Western Military District of the Russian Federation, were his exact words, I think.'

'So what does that mean?'

'It means we are prisoners, being held for reasons unknown, perhaps the Russians think that they can win the propaganda war, perhaps they have plans for us, at the moment it's not clear. But our biggest problem might not be the Russians, it might be the Americans!'

'Excuse me?'

'Well, before we had our little excursion, we found out that there are some very influential Russians living here, the hotel levels seem to be some sort of command centre. The Americans know this and seem to want to get rid of the Russians.'

'How on earth do the Americans know?' asked Shamir with concern rising in his voice.

'Well, I sort of told them, I have been in contact with the intelligence service, and they have shared the information with the Americans.' The look on Shamir's face looked like he was going to hit Sam. He didn't. 'That's why we're back, we need to evacuate.'

'People won't want to go. They feel, I feel, safer here, this place was built to protect us. It's impenetrable. You know that Sam better than anyone.'

'Not if they bomb it.' In hindsight more delicate wording would have been useful. Shamir collapsed to the floor, just as his wife appeared at the door.

'Shamir!' she yelled, assessing the situation quickly. 'Get away from him,' she screeched at the four of them. They might have been dressed in the least threatening way possible, but all she could see was her husband outnumbered and lying on the floor.

'He fainted,' spluttered Sam. 'He'll be fine, Jasmine, it was shock. Promise.' Ne raised both hands in surrender, stood there in ner pyjamas. Jasmine tapped her husband's face gently, and lovingly. He twitched and came round.

'What happened?'

'Apparently you fainted,' said Jasmine, looking at Shamir for confirmation.

'Oh, err yeah, it's just that…' He couldn't finish the sentence. 'Sam, you tell her.'

They collected themselves and sat around the table and sofa. Jasmine and Shamir listened while Sam and ner group talked and ate.

The decision was made that they needed more people to persuade the residents that what Sam was saying was true. That it would take at least ten minutes per household. After breakfast they would speak to everyone on this floor and recruit them as messengers to talk to each floor, everyone they convinced to leave would be asked to persuade two more people. Each floor would be reminded of the evacuation procedure and what the signal would be. They had just one day to persuade as many people as possible. The food got delivered between seven a.m. and ten a.m. It was agreed that Sam would talk to this whole floor at ten thirty in the morning. That would give them at least eight hours to get people ready for an evacuation the following night. Jasmine and Shamir left puzzled and overwhelmed.

An hour later Sam found nerself unable to sleep, lying in bed, Paula breathing smoothly beside ner. Gavin and/or Ian were snoring gently next door. All was quiet, it wasn't like a Hollywood movie, if it were there'd be chaos and noise, screaming and blood. Sam remembered clearly the 2020 pandemic, when actually, although it was described as a catastrophe, there were long periods of quiet, even boredom, to Sam nothing really happened. Ne remembered ner father being very agitated and busy with video calls at all times of the day and night, but Sam spent most of the pandemic being bored. As Sam lay there during this new crisis, which surely would be seen as the worst catastrophe since records began, ne tried to recall the known facts ne'd seen first-hand. The dead bodies in the tunnel, the Russians in the tower, the commandeering of the restaurant, drones tracking them. Then the information fed to them from outside, was any of that real? The tsunami, the war with Germany, the riots, the American plans? Was it propaganda? Who could you actually trust in times this crazy? Leaders often said one thing and did another, but that was never more prevalent than in times of crises, and always justified in terms of the public good. Maybe they were being encouraged to leave so that the Russians could have New Horizons to themselves. Maybe Sam had been talking to someone inside the complex. Maybe they had all been tricked. Sam closed down these thoughts and reminded nerself that the Russians were the bad guys. But what if they weren't. No, this time they definitely were. In the end, exhaustion beat brain activity and Sam fell asleep.

The smell of a cooked breakfast reached Sam's nostrils, and as ne came round, ne realised that ne was alone in ner bedroom. Noises and quiet chatter came from the kitchen. A quick shower, lots of antiperspirant, deodorant and perfume for good measure, fresh clothes and proper comfortable shoes and ne joined the others as they ate eggs and beans on toast. The meal the night before had been necessity food, they savoured the breakfast as if it was a Michelin starred meal. Orange juice, cups of tea, cereal with real milk were all laid out beside the eggs and beans on toast. As they sat there in the warmth and with food, Sam realised the challenge ne would have trying to get people to leave their apartments that they believed to be safe, and swap them for the outside which they knew to be dangerous. They'd be lucky if they managed to persuade even half the residents to leave voluntarily. Once the bombs start dropping the Russians would want to leave too. Sam hadn't wanted to allow these thoughts to enter ner brain, but the decision could well come about whether to close their escape route behind them to prevent the Russians following them, that assuming Susan had found one. Sam checked the phone, no messages. No missed calls. They cleared up the dishes, for no apparent reason, even so far as stacking the dishwasher and setting it off, as if it was just another day, going to work and then back later to a clean kitchen, but it wasn't just another day. They heard noises in the corridor, as if to remind them not to get too comfortable. They all went quiet, they heard a clattering of noise, and some banging on doors. Sam waved the others into the bedroom and ne listened at the door. Something was being wheeled down the corridor, it took a few seconds before Sam realised it was a provisions' run. Sam looked through the spyhole as two people he didn't recognise pushed a restaurant dessert trolley along the corridor, depositing provisions, tins and dried food, and each door seemed to have one item of fresh produce. Sam wondered how long they could've fed everyone here, the same thought must have occurred to the others. The spyhole didn't allow ner to see what ner collection included. Ne watched as all the deliveries were concluded. As the trolley returned to the lift, Sam opened ner door and collected ner package, one by one doors opened and passive faces picked up the parcels of food. No one interacted, it was as if hope was draining. Sam looked down, some pasta, some beans and mixed vegetables, both in tins, and two eggs. No fresh fruit or vegetables. Sam wondered whether no one had been sent out to the cottage garden, or maybe they were keeping all the fresh food for themselves, surely, they wouldn't be letting it rot. Ne closed the door and let the group out of the bedroom. They put the food away and finished clearing up the breakfast things. They sat and chatted. The clothes they washed were still damp in places, but they wore them anyway. The conversation slowed and then stopped, and the group sat in silence once more.

The silence was interrupted by a knock on the door.

Expecting to find Shamir, Sam only quickly looked through the eye hole. It wasn't Shamir.

'Morning, Sam, you look refreshed!'

'Morning Susan!' Ne smiled and almost kissed her. Susan looked over Sam's shoulder at the group behind. Sam watched as hidden women-only communication took place between Paula and Susan.

'Morning all, I have a plan!'

Susan's plan was very good and fitted in with Sam's own plans for the day. It was agreed that Sam and Susan would together talk to residents and start the cascade of information, the first at ten thirty. The evacuation was scheduled for twelve hours later. Answers were prepared to expected questions. What about the South Block? Why now? Why should we believe you? Can you guarantee we'll be safe?

At ten fifteen, Sam collected Shamir and Jasmine and they started gathering people in the lift lobby, the largest area they had on this level. A few came with masks on, a few neighbours refused to attend, claiming it was not safe. Most apartments were represented. Sam and Susan clambered onto chairs and stood in front of a group of curious onlookers. And so, it began.

The Speech

Motivational speeches were Sam's father's speciality, full of choreography and flair. Sam stood there on a random chair, with an apprehensive audience who wouldn't want to hear what Sam had to say. Sam thought this would take about half an hour, but they were already running behind, as a few more people joined at the back. Sam wished ne'd rehearsed this.

'Good morning neighbours, I'm Sam, but I am no longer your mayor. This is Dr Susan Durum from Porton Down she has been working on treatments to cope with the latest variant of the coronavirus which has spread across the world. We have grave news, which will require a leap of faith, and we also have a solution.' Sam paused for effect. 'We do not expect all of you to want to join us in this mission, but we hope many of you will.' Sam smiled and looked over at Gavin, what Sam wouldn't do to have even an ounce of Gavin's energy. Ne might ask Gavin to come up and act as a supporter, yes ne should definitely do that. Sam detailed the situation they were in, and the calls made to MI5, if indeed it was MI5. Questions followed, but not as many as Sam feared. In fact, people seemed more willing to take Sam's words than ne thought. A question came asking what they had been doing in the period since the old mayor had returned, and Sam saw ner opportunity. Instead of asking Susan, Sam asked Gavin to come up and talk from his perspective. It caught Gavin by surprise, but he obliged. There was definitely extra interest, Sam could hear ner father's words. 'Influence rule number one, people are more likely to be influenced by people they like.' Gavin was instantly likeable. Gavin stepped down.

'Any more questions?' Susan asked.

'Just one, what do you want us to do?'

Test one complete, commitment to action gained. Sam took a deep breath.

'We're looking for volunteers to help us save as many people as possible. Tonight, at around ten thirty after dark, we want people to evacuate the building and head to the relative safety of Porton Down. It is a more militarised location, that offers a greater prospect of withstanding an attack. If nothing else, more of it is underground. The challenge that we will face is that people will most likely BELIEVE that they are safer here and they KNOW that it is dangerous outside.' Sam emphasised the words BELIEVE and KNOW, and paused for effect. 'The problem we will face is that beliefs are stronger at creating action than knowledge. So, we need to harness all my father's tricks for getting people to take a leap into the unknown. He spent his career trying to get governments to behave differently in advance of predictions that they believed would not happen, in the face of a lot of scientific knowledge. So, I am going to remind you of his now famous three-point plan to get people to do what you need them to do.' Again, Sam paused, ne had their attention, even Susan had stepped down off her chair, leaving Sam the centre of attention. So, this was what it felt like to be the famous Andrew Brown. Deep breath. As ner father said, when delivering a key message, you must get it word perfect and rehearse, rehearse, rehearse. Ooops. 'The first part of the three-point plan is: TRUST. People will agree to do things for people they trust, so in a second, we will split the volunteers up so that you each start on a floor where there is someone you know very well. A relative or partner will work best, but close friend or colleague can also work. You will go to them first and persuade them, and then get them to contact two more people who they know well. There will be duplication doing it this way, but we need the cascade of information not to be diluted by nervous remainers.' There was a laugh, which surprised Sam, ne looked at Susan who was also grinning but encouraging ner to carry on. 'At five p.m. we will start the process of confirming the evacuation time and talking to anyone who has been missed in the trust cascade. You should each choose five people per floor to do this. The next point of the plan uses INFLUENCE. People are more likely to do what other people are doing. Please feel free to use my name as someone who is leaving tonight, also I suggest you use Dr Susan Durum's Porton Down Lead

Virologist. It is important in terms of influence, that you mention 'Dr', you mention 'Porton Down' and that she is a virologist. You can get her name wrong, if you do it doesn't matter, do not correct yourself. Just make sure it's a woman's name!' A hand went up. 'Yes, Jamie, is it?'

'Yes, it is,' he smiled. 'Why does it have to be a woman's name, isn't that sexist?'

'My father used to say it was gender specific, rather than sexist, which I have to say was a major problem for me growing up, but he had this story about discrimination being legal, it was always unfair discrimination that was outlawed. Jamie, you are right, these are mostly issues for the early twenty-first century. However, it is still true that women are more likely to favour finding ways to cope within a current situation and men are more likely to choose the riskier option if a better prospect is possible. Women, who are parents, will seek to stay and protect even more than parentless adults. If Susan had children, I'd be asking you to mention that too. Remember we need to use every opportunity to persuade in a very short space of time, so I am recommending we use every opportunity. It does need to be natural, I don't want any of you saying, "Oh, and by the way Dr Durum is a woman, Sam thinks you should know that". For this to work people have to make their own decision, and they have to feel it is their decision, and this way, if there're women in the building who favour staying, then they are more

212

likely to be persuaded, knowing another woman with more information than them, has decided to leave. We don't have guns to be able to force people to leave, and we can't afford to leave it until bombs start dropping.' Sam took a breath, Jamie seemed satisfied, he looked at his girlfriend, and Sam guessed that they may be discussing this at some stage. 'The final part after trust and influence is PERSUASION. Do not frighten them at your first meeting with them, I don't want anyone using the word bomb when you first discuss it, otherwise we will have people wanting to leave straight away, and our plan is to evacuate in an orderly and hopefully unnoticed fashion. So, we are going to use reasoning, the statement I want you to learn and say is as follows.' Sam took a pause to make sure they were all listening. Ne began, 'I met with Sam Brown this morning, good news the Americans are going to help the UK cope with the virus. They know about the outbreak in the South Tower, they are planning something, we don't know what. We have until midnight to get healthy people out. If you are healthy, you are eligible to leave, and we are taking healthy people to Porton Down for safety. So please be ready to leave at ten p.m.' Jamie's hand went up. 'Yes, Jamie.'

'But that's not all accurate why not tell them about the Russians.'

'Good question, we don't have time to bring in new craziness, you'd spend too long with each person and the mission would fail. We need to use logic which fits in with the propaganda that has already been fed to people. I spent time with Shamir last night discussing what our neighbours and friends might find easiest to believe. For this to work they need to believe the message. Not everyone will agree and some people who you know will not want to follow you. Those people will change their mind if and when the Americans show their hand, and hopefully they will then at least know where to head.' Jamie looked at ner watch. 'So, the three-point plan: TRUST, INFLUENCE, GOOD REASON. So, build trust first with people you know already, explain that other qualified people are leaving as well and then give them a reason to act. Dr Susan Durum has been working on a route out and we will share it here at four p.m., so come back here at four for an update. Now Gavin is going to make a note of which floors you are all visiting. No more than three floors per person. Good luck everyone.' Gavin looked surprised as paper was thrust in his hand.

'Susan,' Sam called over. 'I suggest our small group pick up any floors that have not been selected by volunteers.'

'Good idea.' She gave Sam a hug, and whispered in ner ear. 'I understand you have spoken to Paula.' She loosened the hug so that she could look into ner eyes. No words were needed but Susan's gentle smile filled Sam with warmth from ner very core. Sam pulled her tight and the hug became all encompassing, creating a single biological unit, their bodies touching in places where friends' bodies don't touch. They were sharing warmth, and it seemed to Sam that it was as if they were also sharing blood supply and heart beats. It could only have lasted a second or two, but it was the most powerful connection ne had ever had. Ne wondered for a second if this was the sort of hug ner mother would have provided. Ne didn't want to break it. But then Susan did. With a quick kiss on the cheek, she turned to check on Gavin. Sam stood, lost and dreamy.

'Thanks for that. Sam, this is Isabelle.' It was Jamie.

'No problem, lovely to meet you, Isabelle. Are you going to help us?'

'Yes, we've chosen the third floor, Isabelle's family are there.'

'Excellent.'

'So, what's going to happen to the people in the South Tower?'

Sam experienced a flashback to the bodies in the tunnel, and realised that shamefully, although gratefully, ne had not thought about them for a few days now. The smell, the horror, the calculated order, filled ner thoughts.

'Let's try and focus on the good things we can do in this block.' The young couple, probably no more than twenty-one or twenty-two, looked back wanting simultaneously, to ask more questions and not to ask more questions. In the end the desire to stay in the dark won and they turned to talk to other groups. Sam looked at the orderly queue lining up to give Gavin their floor number. It seemed their mission had started well. Sam was hopeful that it would work, now ne had to think about what would happen if their Russian invaders got wind of it. Group by group they set off, either to their apartments to collect things or directly to the stairwell. Soon it was just the group of them, and they made their way back to Sam's place.

Sam put the kettle on and started to prepare mugs of tea. Habit really, no one took up the offer. All the floors had been allocated so Sam and Susan could stay and be available.

'Have you heard from Simon at all? Impressive distraction last night.'

'No nothing yet. He was going to head back to the farm and create another distraction tonight. I tried to persuade him to join us this morning but he was adamant.' Susan looked resigned. 'What about Mary?'

'I think they reached the tower last night before us, so they should be safely in the building, maybe we should check on them this morning, those kids have been through so much.'

They sat and discussed options and potential problems for the evacuation and then set off to the thirty-fourth floor to talk to Mary.

The stairwell was quiet. Given they had twenty-six people moving around the building talking to people it was eerily quiet.

'We did tell people not to use the lifts, didn't we?' asked Sam

'Not exactly, hopefully they'll realise that the lifts can be monitored.' She smiled.

Mary answered the door immediately, came out into the corridor and shut the door behind her.

'Oh Sam, I need your help!'

'What is it?'

'It's the children, they want to see their parents and me repeating that we will investigate what happened to them when they themselves are safe is not working any more. I think they feel safe and Samantha is demanding to see them. Bastion cried all night. I think it is being back here.'

'I suppose this discussion was overdue. If delaying isn't working any more then we have two options, tell them the truth and then have two distraught children to keep safe, or we make something up.'

'I vote truth,' Susan said simply.

'I agree,' Mary added

'Then who?' asked Sam.

Neither said anything, it was understood. 'OK, let's do this.'

Sam took a deep breath and Mary opened the door. Joe looked up from the sofa, a child on either side. The children looked up in hope but it was immediately dashed when they saw Sam and Susan. The relationship they had built over the last few days was turning to resentment before their very eyes. There were only two people in the world that could take away the sadness in these two children's eyes and they were lying on a concrete floor, in a dark tunnel underground, that no longer went anywhere. There would be no light at the end of this tunnel.

Joe got up and Sam took his place. Ne breathed a heavy breath and then turned and sat on the coffee table holding a small hand in each of ners. Samantha edged towards her brother and took his hand with her spare one. The three of them locked together, almost seance-like but there was no false hope to be given here. Sam began.

'Mary tells me you didn't sleep last night, Bastion.'

'I want my mummy.' He looked at Sam and looked like he was about to cry, but he was empty.

'Has Mary been looking after you?'

'Yes, but…' started Samantha. Sam interrupted.

'That's good, she's a lovely kind person, who loves helping people, do you know she has helped me ever so much over the years. Don't tell her but I couldn't have done my job without her.'

Samantha smiled over towards the kitchen where Mary was standing with tears rolling down her cheeks. Joe took hold of Mary's hand and squeezed.

'Whatever happens, you two have four friends here who will help you, and we are all desperate to keep you safe. It was you, after all, Bastion that helped us find out all that information from outside, with your clever school internet suggestion. I think you are both clever and brave, we've been chased by wild boar, and slept under the stars.'

'I wish Daddy had picked us up from school, why didn't he pick us up? Why does Mummy have to work so much?' Bastion stared at Sam and Samantha looking for answers.

'We don't know all the answers yet, but we do know that many of the people who lived in the South Tower have died. I'm sorry but I think maybe your parents have died too.'

'You're wrong,' said Samantha. 'Daddy would come and find us, he'll be looking for us.'

'I know sometimes your parents feel like they will live forever, but my mummy died when I was a baby and as you may know my father died a few years ago. It is very sad, but they'd want you to be strong.'

'I want to find Daddy,' said Bastion. Thoughts went through Sam's mind of trying to identify all the bodies in the tunnel, surely that was impossible.

'We can't go into the South Tower now.'

'But he would have been going to the school, to pick us up. He wasn't at home when it all started.'

Sam couldn't fault the logic. 'I'm sorry, both of you, we need to keep you safe and at the moment this block is the only one that is safe.'

'I'll go.' Sam turned round, puzzled. Joe repeated it. 'I'll go and check the school, to see if your daddy made it there and if he left a message.'

'Can I come?' asked Samantha.

'Certainly not,' jumped in Mary. 'You stay here with me.' She gave Joe a look, a cross between pride and annoyance.

'I'm sorry Joe, how are you going to do that?'

'Same way we did before, from your apartment up to the roof and back down to the school. I can be in and out in an hour.' Sam looked at Susan, and she shrugged as if to say 'Fine by me'.

'If you're sure?' Sam aimed the question at Joe. Then at the children, ne said, 'Would that make you feel better?' Samantha nodded and Bastion looked at her. They held each other. Mary came over and sat next to the two children. She did a reverse nod with her head, ushering Joe to head off.

Joe headed off having been offered a gun. 'Be careful, there are only a few rounds left,' she whispered as she handed it over. Joe took the gun with care and his army training flooded back through his veins. His fingers found the trigger and it felt warm and familiar. He looked at the children.

'I'll be as quick as I can.' With that he left.

Joe met a few of Sam's neighbours in the stairwell, conversations with residents were going well. The plan seemed to be working. He had several offers of help, but Joe felt good doing this alone, not risking the lives of others. A solo mission into enemy territory on humanitarian grounds to hopefully rescue a stranded civilian, this was made for Joe. This was a major reason he joined the army in the first place. He never thought he would be doing this in the UK. Enemy territory in the United Kingdom. The very concept filled him with rage, which he allowed to rise within himself for the first time. He started taking the stairs two at a time and in no time, he was approaching Sam's level. He quietly pushed through the doors — all quiet. From Sam's apartment he took the private stairs to the roof. The sun was shining, and white clouds created a peaceful environment. No time to stop as Joe went through the back gate along the sky alleyway between the private gardens, over the bridge between the towers. It was more open on the middle tower with views into the distance. Joe took the opportunity to scan for activity. The land around the towers looked quiet, Joe got his bearings, and looked over to where the farm building must lie, but no activity or smoke from there. There was however, smoke in the distance, and clouds along the horizon to the south, no doubt out at sea. He heard sounds, no birds up this high, but it was rustling. It was coming from the South Tower. He made his way silently towards the southern skybridge. He crept along, the layout was like the North Tower, private gardens in the main for the apartments at the higher levels. He continued and then froze, as he heard clipping and muttering. Someone was gardening, as if nothing was going on. It was a woman. He followed the sound, to try and detect the language. English or Russian, come on English or Russian. Say something woman. Talk to yourself. Cut yourself. Swear. Anything. English or

Russian. Joe jumped as a loud male voice said something in Russian. The woman replied and he heard footsteps as she left the roof garden. Joe moved quietly back to the middle tower, and found the door they had used before. He started down the stairs, stopping and listening at each level. It was a long way down to the school. He took the stairs two at a time as he headed down, past the hotel floors, the restaurants on the sixth floor but then with a few levels to go he heard a door open below him. He drew the gun and listened, back against the wall. The door shut again. No noise, then very faint breathing, they must be just one floor below, between Joe and the school. Joe held his breath. What were they doing? Joe strained his ears to check if the breathing was getting louder. He couldn't tell. He inched towards the railing to risk a look down. When he heard a door open again, Joe held still, was it someone new or the person leaving? He waited. The door opened and then shut again. Silence. Joe was alone again in the stairwell. He stealthily made it past the door that had opened and made it to the second floor. He opened the door and soon was in the reception area. It seemed such a long time ago that he was here, everything was exactly as it was. The missing picture, which held the map they had been using, had left a mark on the wall, which he only just noticed. He decided to do a sweep of every classroom. He made his way calmly and steadily from room to room opening cupboards and checking offices. There was nothing. He wasn't really expecting anything, but his training was kicking in, he was on reconnaissance, and that meant checking everywhere. He finished up in the headteacher's office. He remembered the children hiding in here. What were they doing here? He went behind the desk where they'd been crouching, he sat on the floor. On the ground under the desk there was a pen, and written on the floor two messages, the first read:

'*Daddy, where are you? Bastion*'

Joe read the second message in a different handwriting, clearly written by an adult.

Bastion, Sammy, don't go home, I'll come and find you.

Joe, sighed, not the most helpful message. He added his own.

Bastion and Samantha are safe. Make sure you are safe too. See you soon. A friend.

There was no way they could find each other, if both were moving around. Joe copied the messages onto a piece of paper and put it in his pocket. While he was there, he logged into Schoolnet. The last message on the message board was all he needed to read:

This network has been compromised, may God be with you.

It was two days old.

What else could he do? He searched his mind for his training, how to leave a trail for the children's father to follow, but the challenge was, that he didn't know enough about him to be able to leave one. Joe sighed to himself and left the headteacher's office. If he was their father and he'd have gone back to the children's last known location, he couldn't go back to his own apartment. Where would he go. He then thought back to the door in the stairwell? Maybe just maybe, there was someone monitoring the stairs. Was it worth the risk?

Joe made his way to the stairs and quietly went up one floor. He stood beside the door to the third floor with his back to the wall, the doors opened into the corridor so when it opened, he thought he would have the advantage. Joe stamped on the spot making sure his footsteps could be heard. He heard movement on the other side of the thick fire door. He waited. The handle moved, the mechanism clicked as it retracted allowing the door to open. It opened slowly. Joe closed his eyes to focus his senses on his hearing, he judged that there was just one person there. He leapt into the opening doorway and used his full force to push the door away, making sure he didn't let go. He didn't want it to slam against the wall. It didn't. The man who had opened the door however, did. Stunned but still standing, a tall slim

224

man with a moustache and glasses, looked back at him and then launched himself at Joe. He kicked and fists made contact. Joe was still holding the door with one hand and trying to fend off this assailant with the other. He had no option, with his spare hand, his left, he punched the man in the face. He hit him square on the nose and the blood was instant. The man clutched his face and looked horrified, as if he been peaceably walking through a park on a Sunday afternoon and suddenly, he'd been punched by a stranger. He hadn't, he'd been hitting a man and the man had hit back. Russian or English? Joe wanted the answer, nationality this time not language, but he'd settle for language. Joe closed the door behind him and held the man by the throat up against the wall.

'Stop, stop, wait,' the stranger begged. 'Please!'

Joe smiled with relief, he loosened his grip. 'Sorry about your nose. I'm Joe, Head of Security.' And instantly felt as if he had failed in his job.

'Paul, Paul Stevens.'

Joe held out his hand. 'Pleased to meet you Paul, so tell me why are you listening to the stairwell?'

'My kids are missing, I got delayed picking them up from school, my wife is…' he trailed off, feeling his position helpless.

'I can guess about your wife, and I'm really hoping your kids' names are Samantha and Bastion?'

The man crumbled, and Joe had to hold him. He couldn't formulate words, hope flowed through him in an uncontrollable wave that almost drowned him in emotion. 'They're safe,' added Joe. 'Now let's get you safe too.'

'But...' Paul started but couldn't finish, he didn't need to finish, his babies were safe. He dragged his feet underneath him, they were leaden with relief, he should be skipping and running, but that's not life, the weight of emotion slowed him down as he tried to follow this messenger of good news. They were heading up, surely not to the roof. He had hardly eaten or slept for days, he tried to motivate himself, knowing they were safe was enough, but the relief led to dread. He had let them down, he wasn't there for them, they will be starving and tired. What will their eyes betray when they look at him? How can he possibly tell them about Mummy? She was always better at this than him, delivering sad or disappointing news. He'd always stood in the back supporting his wife as she announced the death of their grandparents, the guinea pig, the moving house away from their school. She was always the one to deal with scrapes and arguments.

'Come on Paul, keep going, your two are going to be so very happy.'

Paul looked up, positive and negative thoughts battling over control of his body and mind.

'Do they blame me for being late to school? When I got there, they were gone.'

'No of course not, we got to them that same day not long after school closed, you must have been just behind us. They've been very well behaved, and if it wasn't for Bastion we wouldn't have a plan, but I'll let them tell you all about it.'

'Where have they been all this time?'

'There's a group of us helping the mayor, and they helped us along, they've been in the woods.'

'The woods?'

'Yeah, we have a secret location in a farm! I think they have had an adventure. Although if it wasn't for Samantha, I wouldn't have come back looking for you.'

'You came back just for me?'

'Yes, I heard someone on the steps, and when I read your message on the floor of the headteacher's office, I thought it might have been you, so took my chance. They will both be so happy, if Samantha has a bone to pick with anyone, it's with us for having given up hope on you.'

They climbed more levels in silence. Paul wanted to hug this man, but thought better of it. In any case he'd have to catch him up first.

They opened the door at the top into the fresh air, and Paul breathed in, like he'd never breathed before. They crept across to the North Tower and back down.

'We're not going down as far as we had to come up,' Joe said with a smile.

'No worries, I'm OK, is there any food where we're going?'

'Of course, you must be starving, yes food, drink and a hot bath if you want one.' This man really needed a bath.

The steps down flew past and in no time, Joe was knocking on a door. Paul was nervous again but he needn't have been. The door opened.

'Is there enough tea left for one more?' he asked loudly so everyone in the apartment could hear. Within seconds, two young, very happy children came running to the door. Paul crouched down and scooped them both off the floor, something he'd no doubt done many times before. Joe had to steady him. No words were needed. Samantha was sobbing. Bastion broke the silence.

'Daddy, Daddy, I've been chased by a wild boar!'

Paul looked at the assembled group who were now all collected in the doorway and they all laughed, even Samantha laughed. The group calmed down and introductions were made. The children were competing for stories, and Bastion won each time, Samantha correcting and removing the exaggerations where necessary.

After a fashion Sam suggested they might like to go to ner flat for food and some family time. Paul nodded. Sam led them upstairs and briefed Paul on the plan for the rest of the day. Sam also explained that Bastion hadn't slept much so suggested that the three of them get some sleep, and be ready for ten p.m. All three of them thought that was a good idea.

'Here we go, help yourselves to food, and Paul feel free to take any clothes you need.' With that Sam let them into the apartment and left them to it.

Back at Mary's they sat down again. The kettle was put on again.

'This is like the calm before the storm!' said Joe.

'I feel as though it's more like the eye of a tornado, chaos behind us, in front of us and all around us. Here we are in the calm, drinking tea, and eating cake!' Mary remarked and they all smiled. It was an unreal situation. Hours passed in limbo. As the clock ticked, and conversations dried up, people tried to relax. The hour hand approached five p.m. and they were getting ready to leave to do their final house calls, when Sam's phone rang.

Ne put it on the table and clicked speaker.

'Sam, are you there?'

'Yes, I'm here with a group of us.'

'Bad news, I'm afraid. The Americans have just notified us that they are going to flatten the site. I have put them off as long as possible but you have one hour. Have you found a way out?'

Susan nodded, and Sam answered. 'We have a plan, but doing it in daylight is tricky. Are you sure you can't buy us any more time?'

'Sam, it is what it is. Good luck.'

Sam stood up put the phone in ner pocket, 'OK, action stations, floor by floor starting at the bottom so we don't overload the stairs, the last thing we need is a human pile-up. We can evacuate the building in sixteen minutes, so an hour is plenty!' No one looked like they thought it was plenty. 'You head off and signpost the route for people to take, and I'll go up and get the messengers lined up, I'll make sure they come down in thirty second intervals. We'll need to use all three stair routes, so Susan, make sure you get people in the car park showing the way.'

'Sam come straight back down when you've told people what to do, I'll need you at the sharp end.' They looked at each other.

'OK, will do.'

Gavin chirped up, 'I'll stay up on your floor, I have the list of names anyway.'

'Thanks,' said Sam. 'Mary, Ian, you go with Susan. Good luck everyone, see you on the other side.'

Sam and Gavin left first and headed up the stairs as fast as Sam could, it was clear that Gavin wasn't breaking into a sweat. It was now quarter to five. They kept going.

Just before five they opened the door into the lift lobby on Sam's floor, people had already collected ready for part two of their jobs. They had clearly been busy, there were discussions as to how many remainers they had encountered. The good news was that they seemed surprised at how many people they had persuaded. Sam clapped ner hands to get a bit of hush, it didn't really have much impact. Gavin thundered his hands together. Silence fell.

Sam cleared ner throat.

'Gavin has got the list here, when he calls your name, you should head to your floors and get people out, we're leaving now. Knock on the first door you find and get them to get everyone out, get them to use all three emergency exits, head to the car park. No discussion, answer no questions, give the instruction and move on. If you get push back just say, "If you stay, you die". We have forty-five minutes to clear the building, we know we can do it in sixteen minutes, keep it orderly. Gavin, first name please.'

Gavin read out the first name heading down to the bottom floor. Sam headed down the corridor. Gavin grabbed nim. 'Aren't you going the wrong way?'

'I need to get Paul and the children, I'm going to send them down now, they've been through enough.'

Gavin nodded. 'Be quick, we need you.'

Sam knocked on his door, and counted. No answer. He banged the door. Why did he have to leave the key with Paul? They were safe in the apartment. Oh, ne hoped they hadn't done their own thing, maybe just sleeping heavily. Ne banged again, looking at ner watch. Sam turned away, there was no time left. The door opened behind ner, Paul was at the door. Clearly just woken up.

'Get dressed all of you we're leaving. Make your way to the car park, people will direct you from there. Come on quick.' Paul didn't move. 'Go!' shouted Sam in his face. It shocked him into action. He ran back inside.

'Kids get dressed, we're going, Sam's here.'

The four of them headed for the stairs, taking a different set to the others, to avoid any collisions. Sam spoke aloud to ner father, 'Dad why did they have to be vertical villages, what were you thinking!' as, yet again, Sam found nerself going too fast down a set of stairs. Sam didn't really know the details of the plan that Susan had hatched, ne knew that they had plans A, B and C, and Susan had said that it was fine, but the plans must have relied on a distraction from Simon that wasn't arranged until ten p.m. This wasn't going to work, getting thousands of people out of a building without being noticed during the day, when everyone was awake, and perhaps patrolling. They carried on down the stairs. Sam started to worry, ne thought ne was good at delegating work but now ne wasn't so sure, ne should have gone through it with Susan, but she seemed to have it under control. She worked at Porton Down, did that mean she had had some military training? Maybe. They took it step by step. What else did Sam not know about Susan? Ne started to think about all the gaps. What films did she like, did she prefer music or comedy, what could she live without if she needed to? Did she prefer the cinema or live theatre? What was on her bucket list, did she want to get married, did she want children? As the questions got bigger, the thought of a relationship seemed to bring bigger and bigger questions. Somehow

Sam didn't think they would agree about these things and ne was looking forward to having the discussions, perhaps over a glass of wine, on the coast somewhere looking out to sea, but specifically not a beach. If this was a film, there'd be music playing balancing dreams and impending disaster. It wasn't a film. This was actually happening. They reached the third floor and were joining people already being evacuated. Sam scooped up Samantha, and Paul did the same with Bastion. There were a lot of people. Sam overheard a conversation below them.

'This is a waste of time, I don't believe any of it,' said the man

The woman replied, 'Well even if it is nothing at least we get out of the apartment for an evening, did you turn everything off?'

'I left everything as it is, we'll be back in no time, just you see.'

She made a noise which effectively seemed to say, 'I tolerate your opinions but you're wrong again.' In any event it seemed to signal the end of the conversation and they moved with the others down the stairs. It was orderly but restrictive, you couldn't deviate, and if you decided you'd forgotten something there was no turning back. The human flow carried on like ants with fresh leaves to collect. They carried on. Down step by step, the walk was steady so Sam let Samantha walk, ne went to grab her hand but she chose her father's hand instead, as it should be. Sam felt good, it had been a long time of just taking each step after another. All these people, the whole of the North Tower walking down step by step to safety, ne and the others had saved them all. Then ne almost fell, a thought had penetrated ner brain, blocked out until this moment. Ne grabbed the wall and steadied nerself. Tears started to flow. Sam was going to be sick, ne held it back swallowing hard.

'Are you OK?' It was Paul.

'Yeah, I think so.'

'What happened?'

'Just a memory.'

'A memory did that, it must have been a bad one. You sure you're OK?' They were causing a block, like a heavy stone in a river, they were all getting knocked by people trying to get past and it was getting dangerous for the children.

'We need to keep moving.'

They set off again, Sam swallowing hard and trying to clear ner mind. But here there were hundreds of people surrounded by concrete, the thing was that these people were living. Sam's thoughts went to Samantha and Bastion's mother who must certainly be one of the bodies lying on the concrete floor. Sam steadied nerself again and took it one step at a time. Sam tried to concentrate on anything, to try some mindfulness, thinking of happy places, concentrating on tiny details, calming the brain down, stopping it conjecturing, extrapolating, scenario building. But it was useless, all Sam could see was bodies and concrete, anonymous people, whose lives were on the line. Sam looked for anything to break ner mind away from death and despair, and saw a sign. They were at level 0. One more level twice the height of other levels so four flights of stairs instead of two, but still almost there.

They came through the exit door into the car park, like a crowd leaving a football game, funnelled through a door and immediately fanning out as if humans had a natural negative magnetic charge that forced them apart when the space allowed. Ian was ahead and directing the group across the car park.

'Paul, you follow the crowd, I'll see you all later, when this is all over, I'm going to find Susan.'

Paul nodded and was off, Sam noticed he speeded up, taking no chances. Sam glanced at ner watch — 5.13 p.m.

'Ian, where's Susan?' He pointed to Sam's left and Sam set off at a jog. It didn't take Sam long to find another flood of people exiting a door, which at maximum use looked wholly inadequate. Sam remembered visiting the O2 Arena, and there, whole walls of doors opened simultaneously. Sam wondered why that was not the same here. Crossing the current of people was not an easy exercise, Sam did away with any usual politeness and forged ner way through, out the other side and there was Susan. For a second or two Sam watched her, without her knowing. She was directing the crowd and cajoling them forward, keeping them moving at a steady pace, almost conducting them.

'Hi,' said Sam but it was lost in the noise of a thousand human footsteps on concrete. Sam approached and she caught sight of ner and smiled a huge happy smile, as if Sam had been the only thing on her wish list for that very moment, and indeed ne was.

'How's it going?' Sam said at a louder volume than before, but misjudged it as ne found nerself shouting in Susan's ear.

She jumped back and then deliberately shouted, 'FINE THANK YOU SAM,' and laughed. 'We have things under control we think, we've managed to open the doors to the Porton Down tunnel, and managed to block the access points into the car park, apart from the three exits that people are coming down, so we shouldn't be disturbed. One of the team is at the entrance that they are likely to use, below reception, and has a flare which he will set off if he needs help.' Susan pointed down into the distance of this cavern of a space. 'We have four people in cars near the vehicle entrance and if we have trouble at this end, I set off my flare and they drive through the barrier and create havoc outside.' She showed Sam her flare, which looked suspiciously like a firework.

'That sounds like a suicide mission.'

'Yeah, it may be, but there is a ventilation shaft which is accessible out in the woods so they can join us later. I will open it when we go though, I have told them where it is, hopefully they can head off, find Simon, who is waiting out there for ten p.m. and find their way

236

to the vent. At least it's daylight, they stand a better chance of finding it than if it was dark.'

'Well,' Sam checked ner watch again. 5.21 p.m. 'Soon the Russians will have other distractions to cope with. We all will. Let's just hope it takes them some time to realise that the Porton Down tunnel is their best chance.'

'Although James seems pretty on the ball to me, we have a plan for making sure they can't follow us through the tunnel. But you should go Sam, follow these people and get to Porton Down, they'll need someone to organise them when you get there. It's all quiet there, I guess James and his team had no use for the site, we went there last night and there was no one there, just empty rooms and burnt-out laboratories. It's such a huge site Sam, with thousands of people there normally, when we left, they were planning to stay. I don't know what happened, I just hope they were evacuated, I can't bear to think of what might have happened.'

Sam held her shoulders and looked into her eyes. 'Let's focus on these people we are saving, all of them are in our hands now.'

'Yes, you're right. I have people at the other end of the tunnel, it's a two-hour walk, although we're not telling them that. They should be safe as long as they are clear of the towers, so when it happens the last person needs to be at least fifteen minutes into the tunnel, otherwise the tunnel might collapse. It depends on so many things. Once at the other end, we are directing people to the auxiliary mess hall at level minus three, where security, cleaners, and catering have got their areas. It's a large space and there are fewer security doors to get to it from the tunnel entrance. I'll see you there in a few hours.'

'OK.' They kissed. Whatever happened, Sam felt she was the one. 'Excuse me.' Sam nudged a person in the flow of people. They looked at Sam but no answer. 'What floor are you from?'

'Twenty-six,' came the reply. Not even half of the people were down. Then someone who heard the question, said, 'Thirty-seven,' which was a whole lot better.

'Thank you.' Sam joined the throng and looked back at Susan, she glanced, smiled, and then continued her choreography. They weaved their way across the concrete car park, Sam allowed the flow to swallow ner and ne made ner way through so ne was now walking on the edge of the mass of people, but on the other side. Sam could see the other human line that Samantha and Bastion were in, hopefully near the front, they should be in the tunnel by now and heading for safety. 5.27 p.m. They have about fifteen minutes left, before the hour ran out, but no room for panic, just keep the flow going. Sam kept up with the speed of the line and was soon at the entrance to the Porton Down tunnel. There were three streams of people meeting and causing a bottleneck. Two of Susan's team were there, who hadn't been at the farm. She seemed to have recruited more people. They were getting people to speed up as they entered the tunnel, trying to avoid a crush at the doors.

'Hi, I'm Sam.'

'Yes, I know,' said one of the men on the door.

'Susan has asked me to follow the group and take them to the auxiliary mess hall.'

'Yeah, it's a good place and will be able to house everybody, as well as being underground.'

'Yeah, so I understand. Do you know where it is?'

'Yeah, of course, been there many times. Why?'

'I'd like to swap jobs with you.'

'No way, Susan has asked me to stay here until the flow of people stops and she joins us here. I'm not moving.'

'Look, I'm the mayor here, sort of, I can't leave until I've seen most of the people to safety. So, I either stay here watching you direct these people, or I send you to safety, and give you another job of making sure people don't get lost at the other end. Your choice.'

There was a pause, and then the guy reached behind his back and produced a gun and a flare. 'You might need these. Flare first if you need help, then gun if you really need it. Only enough bullets for a few rounds, so don't spray them about. OK?'

Sam nodded, and like a child given permission by a teacher to skip class, the man was gone.

'Come on all, speed up when you get into the tunnel, no running but just move faster. Come on move along. Speed up in the tunnel. Not long to safety now.

No stopping in the tunnel. Keep moving. Move quicker in the tunnel. No running. You can do this.' And so it went on, minute after minute. An old man came past with a bag he was struggling to carry.

'Sorry, you can't take that with you, it's a long tunnel, you'll drop it. Leave it here please, I'll bring it through.'

'That's OK, I know him I'll take it,' said another man. People working together. Sam couldn't help checking the time, and minutes were ticking past, the number of people was still as many as minutes ago.

'Come on everyone. Keep moving. Speed up in the tunnel. No stopping. There's food at the other end waiting for you.' Sam started to vary the statements. Sam braved a time check 5.38.

'Excuse me what floor are you from?'

'Forty-eight,' came one reply.

'Fifty-three,' came another.

A magic, 'Sixty-one,' came from a third. There were sixty-two floors in total, so they must be nearly there, but there was no visible end to the line.

Explosions

Boom! A massive explosion shook them to their core. It was deafening, the whole building shook and people stumbled, the screaming started and the panic. There was a massive surge of people towards the doors to safety. People were running, the line fragmented and people shot round the sides trying to jump the queue. Instead of a line approaching the tunnel entrance, Sam was faced with a wall of people, like an invading army, a swarm of humans, scared, shouting and running where they could. There were people falling over and trampling taking place, the scene had changed instantly from something that resembled a fire drill to some horror movie full of crazed zombie-like creatures desperate to put their needs first. Flare first. Gun second.

Sam risked it and fired the gun away from the crowd. There was a split second of hesitation from the screaming mob. Sam shouted as loud as ne could.'

'OK we knew that was going to happen, it's the road tunnel being cut off, now keep moving but SLOWLY.'

Sam hoped it would have an impact. Ne could hear on the other side of the throng. 'Keep moving you heard what the mayor said, no need to panic, we can do this, not long now. No stopping in the tunnel, keep moving.'

Gradually the calmer feeling spread like a virus through the group, the faces were scared, urgent, but no longer panicking. They were humans again, letting people go through the line was starting to take shape again. Sam could see the end of the line now, and then he heard them. Some cars were heading towards them, people turned and looked, maybe two of three, the noise of the engines echoing around.

'Keep moving you're doing well. No stopping in the tunnel, keep your speed up, stay strong, food waiting at the other end.'

The cars were coming closer, and fast, one of the cars swerved and headed for the end of the line. In the distance, there were people running from what looked like different directions. Another one of the cars swerved and headed towards a group of runners. The second car to swerve was heading straight for the stray people, and was getting close. It drove straight at them. Sam couldn't see exactly what happened but things flew in the air, bodies perhaps. The car stopped and then turned and headed towards them. All the cars were now heading towards Sam and the remaining people getting through the door. The line was reducing at last, when there was a second explosion. This one louder than the first. Then Sam saw it. Dust billowing towards them catching up with the cars, and then a noise, grinding metal and concrete, like the noise of a car dragging a loose exhaust but a thousand times louder. Then a piece of concrete flew across the car park and hit the wall just metres from where Sam was standing. The pillars were buckling, the pillars were collapsing. The cars were ahead of the cloud of dust but only just. The line was through the door, Sam was left with the other member of Susan's team.

'You go, I'll hold the fort.' Sam raised the gun and pointed towards the cars. Ne could see people running towards them in small groups. Snap decisions, Russian or British. Sam put ner faith in Susan. 'We managed to block the access points, so we shouldn't be disturbed.' Sam took ner finger off the trigger. The cars were being driven by Susan's team, they all got out. Susan was in one of the cars, she must have been the reason why the first car veered off course. Sam couldn't find the words, just looked at the other car that veered off and pointed in the direction of the mown-down bodies.

'Russians,' the driver said. The value of life was suddenly no longer equal, Sam wondered whether it ever was, or ever would be.

As the last of the residents made their way into the tunnel, they crashed the cars into the entrance to the tunnel, leaving a gap for them to climb through. 'At least it'll delay them a bit.' Shrugged Susan.

'Well, if the roof comes down, the entrance will be blocked anyway.'

Susan turned to one of her team. 'Have you heard from Simon?'

'Sorry, didn't get the chance to get out there, so we came straight here.'

She nodded sombrely and looked very serious. Sam would soon come to realise that this was her plotting face. They crawled through the gap and started down the tunnel, most people were far in the distance, but they caught a few slower residents and slowed down to stay at their pace. The tunnel was not like the other tunnels, this looked as if it had predated the building of New Horizons, this looked like a Second World War corridor seen in a film. Sam could almost imagine Winston Churchill walking along this path, maybe he had done. The floor was solid but not concrete, without bending down and exploring, it was difficult to tell, but Sam thought it was well-worn stone. The walls were brick and although the ceiling was curved, it didn't have the feel of a tunnel, it had the feel of a corridor in a stately home or a church, at least the functional corridors used only by servants or church wardens. There was a string of lights pinned to one side of the wall that stretched the length of the corridor. In fact, the only thing that was missing were doors, no doors for as far as the eye could see. It was damp down here too, and as the door behind them faded into the distance the feeling of claustrophobia increased. They had two hours of this walking and walking without a change in the view, it almost seemed that maybe they weren't moving at all. Your brain likes to play these tricks on you, like when you're sat in a train station and you're waiting for your train to leave, it's running late so you check your watch, you look out of the window with relief and your train is moving. A few seconds pass and you realise you haven't moved at all it was the train on the other platform moving in the opposite direction. Maybe they weren't making any headway, Sam began to feel like slowing down or even stopping, where were they even going? It was then that they heard the largest explosion yet. They were about five hundred metres into the tunnel, but the noise could have been just above them. It soon became clear that the blast had directly impacted the North Tower, and therefore, the car park they were in. It must have affected the end of the tunnel, because soon dust started to follow them down, chasing them like some huge ghost-like monster. They started to run again, Sam's muscles responded, and they easily made good progress. The cloud behind them seemed to be gaining, but they kept pace with the struggling residents. They could now smell, and more worryingly, taste the cloud of dust chasing them down.

'This way.' It was Susan's voice. She called them all to a barely visible door set into the bricks. It wasn't really a door, it was more of a gate made of metal. The sort of door used to keep a particularly dangerous animal behind it, but still wanted them to breathe. Susan got a key out and opened the gate. It opened into a small space no more than two metres by two metres, with a ladder attached to the wall. It was lighter in here, but

Sam couldn't see any lamps, ne looked up and saw sky above.

'Follow me.'

Susan started climbing. One by one they made their way up the ladder, there were ten of them now, seven of Susan's team, including Sam, and three slow residents. They climbed. The air vent was remarkably deep. Sam was last and it seemed to take ages, dust was filling the chamber beneath them and starting its own journey up. It billowed beneath Sam. Sam headbutted the person in front, and ner hands banged with their feet. Sam stopped. The dust was rising, and it was leaving no space for air. Sam heard a click and a rattle. Something was wrong. There was shouting above and banging, then lots of banging, then a loud crash, then, silence.

Sam tried to climb, to breathe, ne was almost on the back of the person above ner, arms still holding the ladder but the legs of the person ahead between Sam and the ladder. Then there was movement. The person in front started to climb, and in doing so lifted their leg away from the ladder to move up a rung, they kicked Sam in the face pushing Sam away from the ladder. One hand broke free, and with the twisting, Sam lost a foot on the ladder. Time slowed, dust continued to rise, the light faded and breathing was impossible. Sam's head hit something. Eyes now closed, ne had swung round and was now holding on with one hand and one foot except that the foot was completely twisted in the ladder, with ner back to the chamber. Sam tried to pull

246

ner body weight round, but it was made so much more difficult as the rising dust had filled ner nostrils. Opening ner mouth seemed dangerous, Sam tried not to breathe, and to concentrate on keeping the air pressure constant in ner nose, like learning to go under water in a pool without holding your nose. Sam pulled nerself towards the ladder and made contact. It hurt, but at least Sam could use both hands now. Hands pulling up, feet following suit, Sam was heading up. It was getting difficult but Sam carried on, eyes closed, mouth closed, foot hurting, lungs burning.

'Sam, I've got you.' A hand had grabbed Sam's left hand and was pulling, it threw ner off balance and ner good foot slipped. Sam let out a scream, as ner full weight seemed to be on ner twisted foot. But the helping hand above was strong and soon, the weight was taken and Sam was dangling free of the ladder. A massive drop below, thick with dust, but although it looked light and soft, Sam knew it would not protect from the hard surface below. Sam could feel beads of sweat on ner palms of ner hands. The hand above held ner hand so tight it was now painful. Ne hoped that the feeling of being lifted was not a trick of the brain, the urge to breathe was now overwhelming, pain from different sources fighting for control of the body's muscles was scary. The mouth wanted to open and breathe in. The hand wanted to be released from being crushed, the foot wanted to bang itself against the wall. Seconds passed, they felt like minutes.

Sam was now horizontal and still being dragged by one arm.

'Sam, Sam, can you hear me?' It was Susan. She was scratching Sam's face, it was hurting.

Sam groaned. 'Don't open your eyes.' Then cold water was thrown at Sam's face.

'Aargh!'

'Sorry, you're covered in dust, and your nose looks hurt. Can you sit up?'

Sam was being helped into a sitting position, face dripping and a mouth full of dust.

'Here, drink some of this and spit it out, also you'll need to clear your nose, get as much dust out as you can. It's horrible if it gets into your lungs.'

Sam, did as instructed. After a few minutes of care, and wiping, more gently this time, Sam was able to breathe and open ner eyes. They were outside, in the fresh air. Surrounded by trees.

'Are you OK?'

Sam looked at Susan as if to say, 'You're kidding, right?' and smiled.

'I'll take that as a yes. This is the rendezvous point for Simon. In the original plan I was going to meet him in…' Susan looked at her watch, 'about five hours' time, but hopefully he'll come here earlier if he has been watching what's going on. So, Sam you stay here with the residents, I'm taking my team and we're going to see what's what. We can't use the tunnel for another half an hour at least and that assumes there isn't another blast. OK?' She didn't wait for an answer. 'Come on guys, fan out and report back here in twenty minutes.' And with that she was gone.

Sam sat with the three residents and felt useless. Ner's foot was throbbing. With the help of one of the residents they removed ner shoe and sock, what they saw did not look like Sam's foot, and certainly would not have matched the other one! It was immediately obvious that they should not have taken the shoe off, because it was clear it was not going back on any time soon. Sam touched the skin and winced, replaced the sock and looked at ner helper, Matt.

'Any suggestions?'

Matt took off his shirt to reveal a T-shirt. That too came off. He put his shirt back on and proceeded to rip up the T-shirt. With significant skill, he created strips of material. He delved inside the now redundant shoe and pulled out the insole. Sam watched in silence. Matt expertly used the strips of material to wind round the ankle and Sam's foot, making sure the insole was protecting the sole. By the end Sam had quite an attractive, almost Roman centurion-like, sandal. That was firm and comfortable.

'Does that work?' replied Matt after looking at his handiwork.

'That was very impressive.'

'I'm a paramedic by trade, long retired, but still got it!' Matt went to high five Sam, something not done for thirty years, and they laughed as Sam hesitated and then high fived back. There were so many rituals that were lost post covid. The French habit of cheek kisses when meeting someone, the Latin hugs, the shaking of hands, all casualties to a disease control culture.

'Help me up, would you?'

'Sure?'

'Yup,' said Sam, nis brain already preparing to send pain signals up ner leg, wincing ahead of the agony to come. Sam got onto one foot and then gingerly put the other foot, with human and rubber sole, onto the ground. So far so good, the wincing stopped as the pain was not as expected, and then Sam carefully put some weight on it. The wincing returned as the pain shot up ner leg. It was as if Matt had carefully attached a drawing pin between the two soles, and the sharp point was digging its way through the bone.

'Ah, ah, ah, OK, that hurts,' gasped Sam. 'Could you help me find a stick or something, strong enough to walk with.'

Matt helped Sam sit back down and took the other two off to find something. With no tools it was going to be a challenge but they seemed glad to have something to occupy their minds. Sam sat alone, trying to take ner mind off the throbbing foot, running through what had happened to see if any plans needed amending or accelerating. There was the first explosion, that made a noise and seemed not to cause any damage to the columns in the car park, then the second that damaged the columns and was louder, then the third, louder still.

Sam tried to organise ner thoughts. What conclusion could be drawn? Perhaps that third one was closest, if so the first might have hit the South Tower, the second the main tower and the third the North Tower. If that logic held, thought Sam, then was there enough time between the first and the second to escape? Somehow, the Russians knew, because they were seen in the car park. Any others in the car park would have been killed by the third blast, if Sam's theory held. But anyone in or near reception in the main tower would have been able to get out, they just needed to be careful.

'Who are you talking to?' Matt was back.

'Oh, no one, just thinking, was it out loud? First sign of insanity you know!' They smiled.

'I think you might be right, three blasts, three towers, makes sense.'

'Question for you Matt, how would you feel about going back and looking at the damage?'

'Fine by me if I don't have to go in that tunnel again, it gave me the heebie jeebies.' Sam smiled at Matt's use of twenty-ninth century expression.

'In fairness, I'm not sure I'll make it down the ladder! Let's see what Susan has discovered and then we can decide.'

'Oh, almost forgot, will this do?' Matt took a long log from one of the others, grabbed it about halfway up and used it to drag himself into an upright position, and it worked.

'More Gandalf than Yoda, but it works,' said Matt. The references meant nothing to Sam but it seemed to be meant as a compliment.

'Yes, thank you all.'

'Oh yeah,' Matt looked towards the other residents. 'Becky and Stuart, this is Sam.'

Smiles all round.

'So I guess we now wait for Susan to get back.'

'Anyone for a tot of rum?'

They all looked surprised, as Becky produced a hip flask and handed it round. All of them looked very nervous, as their lips touched the same surface one after another. Each one hesitating before taking a sip. But the taste of the alcohol was massively improved by the thrill of doing something that for twenty years has been frowned upon, and given the latest outbreak was possibly fatally dangerous.

'Don't worry, I'm not Russian!' Becky said with a laugh. The three of them laughed, but looked at each other, as if to ask, do you know her?

'Don't mind my wife, her idea of a joke,' said Stuart and they all relaxed a bit. The flask went round a second time, and if nothing else, it helped Sam's brain manage the pain.

'Well, I've been sharing bottles with people for a week now,' said Sam which only made them all more nervous.

They sat for ages, discussing life in New Horizons, they all felt Sam was doing a good job, but what else would they say at this point? The conversation was getting gradually more forced, and slower, so they were all relieved when Susan returned.

'How are you all doing?' she said with a smile as Becky put away her hip flask like a naughty schoolgirl.

'Well, you know things have never been more peaceful and relaxing,' replied Sam.

Their eyes locked, and the communication flowed easier than ever, it was like when creating a communication device using yoghurt pots and string, it worked best when the string was taut. Well, the way they were looking at each other now created a similar link, every message understood, every mood acknowledged. 'Any news?' Sam smiled.

'You're not going to like this, but I think we should go back.' The laughter broke out among the group and for a split second all seemed good with the world. Susan looked perplexed.

'It's just that we were thinking the same thing, and I'm never going to get down that ladder like this!' Sam got up using the log and lifted the bandaged foot.

'Well, that's very impressive, to be honest Sam, didn't know you had that skill in you!'

'I don't, he does.' Pointing at Matt. 'Matt, Becky, Stuart. This is Susan.'

'Excellent.' Susan introduced the other group members.

'No Simon?'

'No, but I'd like to leave a message for him here. Any ideas?'

Becky produced a small notepad and pencil, from the bag she had round her waist and they fixed a note to the air vent entrance.

Matt grabbed Sam round the waist and they set off back to the towers, or what was left of them.

It wasn't long before Sam could taste the dust, the walk was slower than in the tunnel, particularly for Sam, but the air got thicker and thicker. They needed some wind, but the trees were preventing any air flow.

'Don't worry it gets better up here, there's a clearing,' Sam heard Susan call back, they kept moving, Sam bit by bit, step then wince then step then wince. As promised, they came across a clearing, where the air was noticeably clearer. They stopped.

'Sam, we're only a few hundred yards from the edge of the woods at this point, so be prepared all of you, but particularly Sam, this is shocking.'

Sam's mind kept racing ahead, so ne nudged Matt forward and they took the lead. Faster now, Step. Wince. Step. Wince. Sam broke free from Matt. And continued under ner own steam. Although Sam was still wincing with each step, the brain was no longer processing the pain. The thoughts of seeing the towers in tatters, towers that for so long had been part of ner father's legacy and time. Ner only link to ner father. Something that made ner so proud to be nis child. Sam came out of the woods. The open grassland that they had

254

crossed several times over the past few days. In the distance Sam could see the trees. Sam should not be able to see the trees. Between Sam and the trees was cloud. Just cloud. Swirling. Sam stood and stared, the towers, the tallest towers outside of London, reduced to nothing. As the air swirled, Sam saw glimpses of rubble, but it was as if the towers were never there. Sam looked to the air, to where ner garden would have been, and couldn't even fathom how high in the air it had been. All that concrete and those apartments, all those people. Oh my god. All those people. The reality of the extermination that had just happened. Was this genocide? Had they been complicit in a war crime? Were they now a secret that no one would ever find out about? The group gradually came through the trees and lined up looking towards where the towers had been. The dust was already settling, or dispersing, whichever it was more glimpses of rubble were visible, and then almost as if choreographed the rain started. Slow at first and then soon torrential. They were being sheltered by the trees, and they stood as if watching a film, as the rain cleared away the dust and cleaned the air. The view became clearer, such that human activity would now be visible, but there wasn't any. Sam's thoughts went back through the steps taken and the information shared with Amardeep. Were they too open? Did the information they gave lead directly to this? Were they responsible for this? Were they to blame? Sam felt an arm around ner waist. It was Susan. Sam returned the gesture and they stood, perhaps supporting each other. They stood there for some time, and then one by one they made their way towards the pile of rubble. In hindsight doing this in daylight was a blessing as they could see what was what. The precision targeting of missiles now meant that buildings could be destroyed without destroying neighbouring buildings. In Afghanistan this was always reported how the Western nations, who were still in the country and had been for the last forty years, were able to use drones to take out specific buildings, sometimes even specific floors in specific blocks were targeted. Some drones were equipped with facial recognition and were given a specific target, they would spend days, sometimes weeks, patrolling the skies looking for targets. The destruction in front of them had all the hallmarks of an ECM. An Engineered Cluster Missile, a missile equipped with a dozen or so explosive charges. Feeding the design of the building into the computer, based on an engineer's report, the missiles target the structural parts of the building so that it drops vertically wherever possible. Demolition militarised, Sam was gearing up to seeing three piles of rubble that don't cover much more ground than the footprint of the original building itself.

In fact, as they drew near, the pile of rubble was tiny, it looked like they'd demolished a family home.

'Where have the buildings gone?' It was Matt.

Sam thought for a while and then realised. 'It's all underground. The building was designed with a massive double height car park, so that in the event of a flood, it would fill up and minimise the amount of water above, but it looks like the basement was big enough to swallow the towers whole.' And as they got closer and started moving to their left, the rubble they could see, was just elements that hadn't broken up — part of a lift shaft, a three-storey length of stairs jutting precariously up, a stairway to hell. In the rain, which had reduced to a drizzle, it was becoming clear that no one would survive this, and now that it was open to the elements, anyone trapped below, would surely drown if the rain from a few weeks ago came back. As they walked steadily in their clockwise direction, they approached what would have been the front of the building. Sam stopped and held up a hand, they all stopped and then followed Sam as ne crouched down. There was a small group of people just ahead, they were observing the damage as well, too far away to pick out faces. Sam looked towards Susan and waved her alongside.

'Could it be Simon? How many were with him?'

'It could be, there were four of them in total.'

They looked at the group they could see to count them, there were four maybe five. Sam tried to crouch as ne walked and ended up walking like an impersonation of an old witch, but it seemed to work. The others crouched with more ease and followed. Sam tried to remember Joe's effective hand gestures, but realised ne was making this up. The rubble was taking all the attention of the group ahead, but even so, Sam drew the gun out from ner belt and took off the safety catch once more. They were getting close enough to hear that the group was talking, but not close enough to discern a language. They inched closer, trying to keep unobserved, the group seemed to be looking at something or someone on the ground. The next thing they saw and heard, was one of the group shoot whatever was on the ground, then they moved off in the opposite direction. Sam and the others were soon able to stand.

'OK what now?' Sam asked, part rhetorically, part in desperation for ideas.

'Back to the tunnel?' suggested Matt without much enthusiasm.

'What about the farm?' asked Susan. 'Do you still have the phone on you, Sam?'

'Yes, and there is still some charge on it.'

'We could try and phone Amardeep from the farm, see if he has suggestions or needs information from us, plus Simon might be there.'

'All in favour, hands up.' Sam addressed them all, Susan and her team immediately put their hands up, then Matt and finally Becky and Stuart raised theirs too. Only after, did Becky ask, 'What's the farm and how far is it?'

'It's like a safe house we've been using and it's about an hour's walk if we don't get lost, we can spend the night there if needed.'

So that's what they did. Maybe it was the fact that Simon was somewhere here, or maybe the main threat had been neutralised, or just the thought of going in the doorless tunnel for two hours, that made them think this was a good idea. Susan drew a mental map in her head where the towers had been less than an hour before, where the ventilation shaft was. She determined that they needed to head to the left and then straight for the trees. She planned to follow the tracks that Simon would have taken in the truck. They set off, Susan at the lead and Sam at the rear, step then wince, then step then wince. Matt saw the pain across Sam's face and took hold of the stick and hoisted Sam up, Stuart went the other side and before long they were making their way across the open grassland in a relatively pain-free manner. Both men must have been in their seventies at least, but their pace was good, and although they had been walking slowly in the tunnel, they now were keeping up with the rest of the group. It was approaching seven p.m., and dusk was closing in. Soon they were in the protection of the trees, Sam took one last look back at an empty park, a resting place for so many. As Sam looked, he called to the others. 'Look over there.' They all looked over, there was now a larger group of people and several vehicles. They stood and watched feeling safe, protected by the shadows from the trees above and behind them. At a guess it looked about twenty people.

'Let's keep moving, we're not safe here in the open.'

They worked their way through the undergrowth, trying to find signs or tracks, but found none, nevertheless Susan did an excellent job of making them all feel in safe hands. Matt and Stuart also worked wonders in helping Sam along.

They met no wild animals on this journey, maybe the explosions had sent them all into hiding. Soon, they would have the whole site to themselves.

'This way,' Susan declared enthusiastically, and as Sam approached, ne saw there were tyre tracks crossing their path diagonally. It meant another slight left which made Sam think they would end up back where they started, but said nothing and followed. The temperature was falling sharply now and none of them had brought clothes for this eventuality, and the clothes they were wearing were wet. When Sam grew up April showers was a thing, but now rain showers were rain, the UK almost had its own rainy season starting in April and lasting 'til the end of May. Although the world had woken up to climate change very late, there was a time lag, scientists reckoned there were still many years of unpredictable weather ahead of them. Sam would normally have been depressed by these thoughts, but suddenly realised ne was thinking about a future, a future of years, not months or days. Each year, rainfall levels exceeded the year before. They were lucky the rain wasn't heavier, although thoughts of hypothermia drifting into Sam's mind. The group trudged on in silence. Step by step Sam hoped with all ner mind that they were closer to the farm. But none of these trees, were familiar, they were following a path that Sam did not recognise. Was it possible they were going completely the wrong way, or that these tracks led somewhere, completely different? Sam shouldn't have worried. The tracks curved to the right and there was the truck that Simon had been driving. They were round the back of the farm buildings. They crept round a small plant room, and then the area opened up to a familiar sight of the farm with lights on. Susan held up her hand and they all stopped. She pointed two fingers to her left and two to her right and her team obediently took up positions. She crouched and inched her way until she reached a window, and slowly peered in. Simon was sat at a chair, but he wasn't moving. She looked again and it seemed he was strapped to the chair. Susan crept back to Sam, and was about to explain when they heard the engine noise.

Within seconds two vehicles approached, full of people, mostly Russians, but some faces that Sam thought ne recognised. But what there were most of were guns, each of the Russians seemed to have at least one. Yakov was not one of them, but there was certainly a senior person in charge. They were surrounded and had guns pointing at them.

'Go move,' said one of them and jerked his pistol towards the door of the farm. The six of them moved towards the farm door. Sam caught sight of the four of Susan's team who had been sent left and right, they were melting into the background. Sam wondered if they were armed.

They were pushed and shoved into the dining area that had until recently been a laboratory but they had turned back into its former use. Sam wondered how the Russians had known about it and also whether they had opened the cupboards where the equipment was held. The answers to both followed quickly.

'They followed me yesterday, so…' blurted out Simon

'Silence,' yelled one of the captors.

In the corner were three slumped bodies. Next to them the contents of the cupboards. It seemed they had been rumbled.

Susan was strapped to a chair opposite Simon, and from there could see that he had been severely beaten. The rest of them were frisked and sat in a row along the floor. Sam was disarmed.

'So you in charge yes?' the man asked Susan.

She didn't answer, the slap across the face startled everyone, and the noise reverberated around the room.

'Answer.'

She didn't and he slapped her again, this time so hard that her head spun round to the side, she held firm.

The man pointed his gun at Becky, who screeched in terror and surprise.

'Yes, I'm in charge,' said Susan.

'What are you doing here?'

'Our homes were destroyed. I came here for shelter.'

'How you know this place?'

'I used to walk here when I first moved in.'

'Where you work?'

Susan paused. 'In the school, I'm a teacher.'

The man looked at her, he looked over to the older man who Sam had thought was in charge. The older man shook his head. They grabbed Susan and sat her down with the rest of us.

'You, wait.' They all sat.

They all seemed to be waiting for orders, but none would be coming. They grabbed Becky and said, 'You. Food.' She was dragged to the kitchen and the next thing they heard was general food preparation noises. Becky had never been to the farm so they could hear her opening cupboards and closing them again looking for things to cook, which luckily confirmed the story that they'd not been to the farm before.

Sam looked around, there were five Russians, or at least presumed Russians in their room, two had left with Becky, so seven. There must have been some already there before they arrived and it was difficult to say but Sam guessed about a dozen arrived while they were outside, so where were the others? Sam looked towards the window to see if ne could see anything and saw a shadow moving slowly. Sam decided to act.

'Aargh, my leg, I need treatment for my leg.' Sam made a point of trying to move.

'Sit! Silence!'

'But it hurts, I'm in pain. Aargh.'

Matt joined in. 'I need to change the dressing; he's hurt his leg. I'm sure there is something here I can use. Have you got anything that would help?'

'Shut up all of you.' Three of them were now looking directly at Sam and Matt trying to decide what to do. At that moment there was a noise outside, Sam heard it. One of the Russians twitched and jerked his head to listen.

Susan must have heard it too. 'Becky!' she shouted. 'Do you need any help?'

'No, it's OK,' she called back.

'What do you want from us?' Asked the one person of Susan's team who was held captive.

'Yes, what exactly are you going to do to us?'

The Russian closest to Sam lost patience and shot his gun in the air. That shut them all up. They sat, and Sam wondered whether a rescue was being planned. There were four Porton Down staff members out there, with hopefully at least one gun between them and some military training perhaps, and some prisoners in here. What would their next move be? Sam tried to formulate a plan that would help, but beyond being a nuisance and acting as a distraction, ne found it difficult to come up with anything. Becky came through with bread and what looked like soup and placed it on the table. It looked like she had also made mugs of tea. The man in charge said something in Russian and one of their group left, and brought back more of them. They were now outnumbered as more of them piled in. It looked and felt hopeless. Was this indeed where Sam's story was going to end?

Sam watched helplessly as the Russians spoke and ate. It was clear from their body language that they were making up their plans as they went. The person 'in charge' seemed to be senior rather than in charge. Was he the ambassador? Sam didn't think so.

'Hungry?' one of the Russians asked. Matt nodded and all the Russians laughed. It was going to be a long night.

It was getting darker outside, but Sam kept seeing shadows pass the window. Apart from the four members of Susan's team, the rest of the group were now in the dining room. Simon was still strapped to his chair and Susan was now with Becky, sat on the floor next to Sam.

There was a strange noise through the kitchen and one of their captors went to investigate. He didn't come back. That left five of them in their room, three sat eating at the table and two watching them.

They looked towards the door waiting for their man to return. A few seconds passed and the boss said something in Russian and one of heavyset men watching them disappeared through the door, this time his gun was raised and he was alert. The next few minutes went crazy and with horrible consequences for everyone.

It went quiet for a few minutes then a scuffle, everyone in the dining room stood still, until one of the captors shouted.

'Sit. Floor.' And they sat, although Sam noticed that Susan crouched rather than sat, and therefore, ne did the same.

Then there was the gun shot, it was close and loud. The shouting was confused and panicky, the man in charge stood up and rather than take the lead he moved to the corner of the room and stood behind one of the armed compatriots. It seemed he was more of a VIP than a commander. Sam thought, if they had a gun, he would make a good hostage. Sam watched and crouched slightly higher, to be ready for action. Susan did the same. They looked around for something that could be used as a weapon, but the only thing Sam could see was a chair and they looked quite heavy and cumbersome. Up until this moment all the fighting and death had happened elsewhere or at least before Sam had arrived on site. Sam realised ne had not seen someone die right before ner. That was about to change. Anyone entering the room would be staring down the barrels of four loaded guns, two handguns and two machine guns. They would need lightning reactions to survive.

Susan saw the movement first, maybe a shadow of someone coming into the room, she'd clearly decided to create a distraction, and Sam followed her lead.

Together they launched forward and she grabbed a leg of the table. Sam guessed she was trying to create a barrier, so grabbed the other leg, it lifted and turned, pivoting with only one leg now in contact with the floor. Simon got knocked to the floor, and yelped. The captors who had all been watching the doorway, turned and a shot was fired. Sam was not clear where the bullet had ended up, but it had not hit nerself. Matt had jumped up and had clearly reached the same conclusion as Sam and now had his arm round the neck of the VIP, who was not a small man and they started to struggle. Their captors knew they were losing their grip, and the entrance of one of Susan's team from outside made matters worse. The captor nearest the door, opened fire with the machine gun. It was mayhem. The table was still precarious, but taking a lot of bullets. Simon spasmed on the floor, Becky was screaming and trying to hide behind the table but it was heavy and between them Susan and Sam were struggling to keep it upright. A shot fired from the doorway and the shooter then crumbled to the floor, another shooter arrived, that was no doubt from Susan's team and they too were gunned down, then another and the same fate greeted them, then a shot came through the window, and the guy with the machine gun dropped to the floor. There were now more guns on the floor than in use. The fight in the corner was heating up and Stuart tried to rugby tackle one of the gunmen. They fell to the floor. The melee of bodies made guns redundant without the risk of reducing their own numbers.

The gunman started shouting in Russian.

Susan looked at Sam and simply said, 'Now,' She lurched forward still holding a table leg. Sam took the long way round so the table spun round while heading forward. Becky took a second to realise what was going on and then followed round still hiding behind the table. Simon was now on their side of the table and still alive. Becky started untying him. They carried on moving round until a gun was now on their side of the table.

'OK,' shouted Sam to Susan and they dropped the table and crouched. Sam passed the gun to Susan. And in a flash, she stood, fired and dropped to the floor. There was another flurry of bullets. The wall behind them was being plastered with bullets as was the old farm kitchen table. The volley of bullets stopped and Susan went again. Up, aim, fire, down. This time the down was not voluntary.

She hit the floor, bounced, and then her head snapped back and hit the stone floor. Sam and Becky screamed. Sam raised the leg of the table and rammed it forward, not realising the obvious that ne was the only person holding a leg of the table. It pivoted and twisted, catching Sam unawares. It knocked Sam sideways, it also caught the gunman holding the machine gun and he lost balance. Unlike the handguns, his gun was on a strap, and it went down with him. Matt got the better of his VIP in the confusion that followed and managed to get him to the floor and free himself. He grabbed the last remaining captor and got his handgun off him, two, gun shots later, and the only surviving Russian in the room was the VIP groaning on the floor. Sam lay sprawled on the underside of the upturned table, which was lying across Susan's leg. Simon was still half attached to his chair. Becky was holding Susan and sobbing. Matt came over and helped Sam, Stuart tried to console Becky. The gunman who shot through the window, whose name they later found out was Richard, appeared through the door, and looked around. The VIP moved and groaned and before Sam could stop Richard, a shot was fired. Sam could only mutter one word. 'Susan.'

Richard joined Becky crouching over Susan. Matt helped Sam to sit and then went over to look at Susan. He took a pulse and started what looked like a resuscitation procedure. They waited, and hoped. But it was not to be. She had gone.

***

Simon spluttered and Matt turned his attention to him, checking for broken bones and then sitting him up. Sam watched in silence, unable to move, while Matt and Stuart righted the table. Becky and Stuart then righted the chairs and Sam and Simon were helped onto the chairs. Sam let nerself be moved, as if ne was a shell of a person, or a mannequin, empty and without resistance. Meanwhile the bodies were dragged outside. All except

Susan, she lay there. Matt laid her straight and closed her eyes. He even tidied her hair. Sam sat in silence as tears once again flowed down ner cheeks. There was nothing to be said. Simon put his hand across and took hold of Sam's. Matt quietly pulled up a chair and sat the other side of Sam. The three of them sat there. The table in front of them had taken so many bullets, some of them still embedded in the wood, but not the most important one. Sam glanced down and saw that Susan was now in a pool of her own blood. Sam knew that ne should be down there holding Susan. But it was too difficult. Sam's body would not let the muscles work. Becky and Stuart appeared at the door, and they quietly moved away. Sam tried moving ner hand, and was able to release the hold with Simon, muscle by muscle Sam was able to move and made ner way next to Susan.

'Leave us please,' was all Sam could manage. Sam lifted Susan up so she was leaning in ner lap, and ne stroked her hair. Sam kissed her forehead. Sam sat there only half aware of what was going on around, as Simon and Matt collected guns of all shapes and sizes, and brought them in and laid them on the table. There were car keys and ammunition cartridges also brought in. Becky appeared with what looked like mugs of tea.

'I've put lots of sugar in, it's supposed to help with shock.'

She put them on the table. Sam stayed on the floor as an unattended mug of tea waited on the table.

'What next?' whispered Becky to the others.

They shrugged and took a sip of their tea.

'I think we stay here tonight,' Simon answered eventually. Becky, Stuart and Matt looked round the sparse room, and looked questioningly at Simon.

'I'll show you,' Simon said in a half whisper. They got up and took their mugs with them for a tour of the farm, no doubt. Sam was left in a bullet-strewn, derelict room with a broken window and a mug of steaming tea out of reach on the table. Ner legs were straight out on the floor, and ner trousers were soaking up blood. Susan lay peacefully with her head still on ner lap. Sam moved her gently to one side leant forward and leaned up towards the table. Any onlooker would have thought Sam was reaching for the mug of tea waiting, instead Sam picked up the handgun. Ne settled back down stroking Susan's hair. Ne held the pistol so its barrel was touching ner ear. Sam pulled the trigger.

What Next

Simon took the small group round to where he had been sleeping only a few days earlier, the beds were still laid out as before. The barn still dry. The group agreed that they would sleep there tonight. Becky insisted they move the bodies, so one by one they put the bodies in one of the trucks and made a note to move it away, once they had given Sam enough time and could retrieve the keys. That left one truck which they could use to get back to the ventilation shaft and join the others at Porton Down. They were all tired and although none of them wanted to admit it, they were hungry. It turned out that at times of stress what people do most is eat, that's why so many people had put on weight during the first pandemic. People eat for comfort, they eat to solve boredom, they eat to feel useful. Becky led them back to the main farm building. The sitting room at the front was quiet and there were no noises coming from the room at the back. It had been a science laboratory, then a dining room, and then minutes ago, was the scene of a carnage. Becky went straight to the kitchen area to prepare something. Stuart joined her leaving Simon and Matt to check on Sam.

As they approached the doorway there was no sound. The centre of the room was dominated by the table, and they could see Susan's and Sam's legs under it. Simon walked round the table, and saw Sam slumped, with a gun in ner hand, eyes fixed. How had he not thought of this as a likely outcome, why did they leave Sam alone? The two of them sat there motionless. The air seemed thick with tragedy, like a Shakespearean play, two lovers lying on the floor in a pool of blood, in solemn silence.

'Oh, Sam!' cried out Simon.

Sam looked up, making Simon jump out of his skin.

'No bullets.' Sam shrugged, as if this was a final bit of failure, robbing ner of the chance to join Susan.

'Thank God for that Sam, come here.' Simon gingerly leant down and tried to help Sam up, but their combined bruises and injuries made that impossible. Matt took over and helped Sam into the front room, where a more comfortable chair awaited. Simon followed with Sam's mug of tea, still not drunk. Handing it to Sam, he said, 'I'm so sorry Sam.' That was all that could be said.

Becky came in with some bowls with food, pasta maybe and the other three ate.

'What next?'

'I've no idea love,' Stuart replied. 'Let's just rest a while and make decisions tomorrow.'

'But are we safe here?'

Sam looked over and they all looked for a reply in ner expression, but there was nothing. Sam's face could be described as having lost its soul, the eyes had turned off. But it was the loss of hope or reason to continue that had gone. Sam felt emptier than ne had ever felt before.

'Well?' Becky asked Stuart.

'We're safe here.' For a second no one knew who had spoken, the voice was not familiar to any of them. But it was Sam who had replied. A hollow voice much deeper than Sam's usual tone.

So they sat and waited, not a word was said while the four of them finished eating, going through the motions, eating on autopilot. Matt cleared away the dishes. They heard noises in the kitchen and then Matt reappeared with glasses and an almost empty bottle of brandy. It caught the light of the one lamp that was on in the room. Sam looked over, it was the one ne had taken from the kitchen larder all those days ago, when they had purpose and friends, children to care for, responsibilities. Now what did Sam have, sat here, aching from head to foot, hungry although not caring enough to eat anything, alone with three people that ne only met a few hours ago, and Simon who ne'd known for many years now, but never really had become a friend. Matt seemed to sense the mood.

'OK, I think we all need a drink, and tomorrow we'll take the truck and join all the others that were saved tonight, head back into the tunnel, and see what help we can provide in Porton Down. But for tonight, let's rest.'

Becky seemed comforted that a plan was in the air. Matt put a shot of brandy in front of Sam and Sam drank it in one go, no cough or splutter, no sign of swallowing even, it was as if Sam had simply poured the liquid down a hollow tube. Becky and Stuart had a sip of theirs, Becky no problem, Stuart coughed and spluttered like a sixteen-year-old trying alcohol for the first time. In any other circumstances, Becky would have laughed one of her loud, cackling, hiccups of a laugh, but here she just smiled, as did Matt. Stuart smiled too, as they looked at Sam. No change. Simon too was impassive, maybe his injuries were worse than they thought, maybe he had suffered more than being slapped around the face.

An hour or so elapsed, and then Matt helped Simon up and together they went to the barn. Simon's movements were more laboured now. Becky and Stuart helped Sam and they walked across the yard to the barn, Sam's foot still bandaged, giving Sam a limp but the pain had subsided, or maybe just overtaken by other pains.

They were in the middle of the yard when there was a noise, a quiet noise, but quiet noises in the dark always seem louder. Stuart grabbed Sam closer and started to move faster. Sam yelped in paid as dormant bruises were pressed into action. The three of them got to the barn, looking for the noise.

'What was that?' asked Becky.

'Don't know sounded like a phone or a walkie talkie,' Stuart said, trying hard to hide his alarm.

'Are we being watched?' Becky again.

'What's up?' asked Simon.

'We heard a noise out there, someone's watching us.'

'What sort of noise.'

'It was a phone, definitely a phone, but it can't be, there hasn't been a signal for days.' Becky was thinking fast trying to put thoughts together that made sense, but nothing made sense any more.

'Sam has a signal on his phone,' announced Simon

They all looked at Sam. It took ner a few minutes to realise what was going on, and that they were now using ner name. 'What?'

'Sam your phone just went off.'

Sam looked at Simon, puzzled at first and then recollection came back, and as the others watched, so did some colour to ner complexion. Sam got the phone out and looked at the screen. There was a message:

Is it safe to call?

'Can you call them?' asked Simon. Sam looked at Simon, but instead just texted back.

Yes

276

They waited in silence, stood up, at least two of them aching, but ignorant of the fact. They waited. It seemed like a strange amount of time given the texts. Sam and ner dad used to communicate like this. Ner dad hated speaking to Sam if ne was doing something, on a train, cooking, on a walk. So this first message was, "Are you free to talk?" which actually meant, "Are you doing literally nothing, or at least doing something you could stop doing while I talk to you?". Sam would get the message and then pause the TV or find a bench or otherwise pretend ne wasn't doing anything. The texts came through so rarely that it was not an opportunity to be missed. Sam had tried to call ner father a few times, but it was never answered. Messages were left, that were never responded to, sometimes Sam would get a message "Can't talk now", and that would be that for days. But this message from Amardeep, supposedly, should prompt an immediate call.

'Should we call them?' It was Becky.

'No, we wait, it might no longer be safe for them.'

So they waited.

It could only have been about five minutes, but it felt longer, they were all now sat on the ends of beds, both actual and makeshift. The phone rang.

'Hello!' Sam answered.

'Sam is that you?'

'Yes Amardeep, it's me. With a very small group of people.'

'Are you safe?'

277

'We believe so, back at the farm.'

'You haven't left?'

'We came back, a lot of the residents made it to Porton Down.'

'I know, I'm there now, I've been looking for you. We thought… well never mind what we thought. We're sending drones over to survey the damage and check for survivors, but perhaps you could tell us what you know.'

Sam talked them through the three piles of rubble they saw and the group that had them captive.

'OK, we'll need images of the VIP you mentioned, so we'll send a drone, if you could meet it and show the operator the body, that would be good.'

'Why don't I just take a photo and send it to you?'

'The network we have is an emergency network set up before MMS so it can't cope with a photo, just voice and text, like the old days.'

'OK, we'll look out for the drone, is there anything else we can do?'

'If you have food and shelter, then we'd like you to stay put, inside the wall.' It went quiet on the call as if Amardeep was checking with someone else. 'Yeah, as I said it's really helpful if you could stay in the grounds, can you keep the phone charged?'

Simon nodded at Sam.

'Yes, we think so.'

'OK, the drone will follow the signal of the phone so keep it switched on, that should happen within the next hour, then tomorrow morning we'd like you to carefully check out the towers. Are you on foot?'

'Yes, we are.' Sam stopped as Becky put her hand in Sam's field of vision. 'Yes, Becky?'

Becky spoke, clearing her throat first. 'We have two trucks available, one of them has a full battery, and seats six people.'

'Thank you, Becky,' said Amardeep. 'Very useful. One last thing, Sam we're going to seal you in.'

'What? Why?' Sam on full alert now.

'We need to protect all the civilians here and the area of most risk is the tunnel, they are sealing it this end. I'm sorry, we'll be in touch.' The call ended.

Sam sent a text.

we have civilians here too

No answer.

what news from outside the walls?

No answer

are we at war?

No answer. There was a long pause and then a simple message:

Stay safe

They looked at each other, and sat for a while. Matt was the first to speak.

'I suppose, we get our VIP ready for his photo?'

Matt and Stuart got the huge man off the truck and sat him up against the rear wheel. Becky manoeuvred the other truck so the headlights lit up the body. His head kept slumping down so when they eventually heard the buzz of the drone approach, Matt had the job of lifting the head of the corpse. The drone arrived and surveyed the scene, as if it was alive. Drones were commonplace in deliveries, when they replaced postal workers in 2031, and despite the resulting strikes, it was a real turning point for drone use. Now they were everywhere, most of them controlled by AI so there was a pattern to their movement, straight lines and jerky movements. This one, however, clearly had someone doing the controls. Its movements were more animal-like as it took in the information it was recording and then adapted its position. Soon it was hovering a few feet off the ground directly in front of the dead body. It then turned to Matt, pointing directly at him and effectively nodded, and flew away. Sam watched from the doorway of the barn and thought how like the encounter was, to the encounter with the deer, a few days ago with Samantha.

Their job done, they decided the truck was more useful to them than the bodies so they drove the truck away from the farm and laid the bodies in a pile. All the care taken with them just a few hours earlier forgotten as Matt, Becky and Stuart had grown into their new roles, with new standards of behaviour, they were now effectively in the army albeit completely untrained. They were employed in the defence of the United Kingdom.

The five of them sat, back in the barn, and all looked at each other, realising that sleep was not something that was going to come easily, so minutes later they were back in the farmhouse drinking. Becky and Sam did an inventory of the food, and determined that they could last a week, if they ate normally, maybe two weeks if they were careful. Matt and Stuart were despatched to do a perimeter check and came back all clear. In silent communication it was agreed that they would take Susan's body and bury her outside, which they did. Sam stood and watched and then sat with her while the others went inside. They tidied up the dining room and tried to remove the bloodstain as well as they could. They hid all the weapons at various points just in case there was an attack, and then they sat down round the table. The pack of cards had been found and they were playing Chinese patience. Sam eventually came in, it was now past midnight and the temperature had dropped, Matt set about starting a fire in the hearth and it looked peaceful, warm and comforting, but that was lost on all of them.

The five of them sat and drank, the brandy bottle was finished off and the plates were cleared away. It was gone two a.m. when they gave in to the need for sleep. They collected a gun each and made their way to the barn.

Simon looked at Sam holding a handgun. 'Are you sure you're going to be OK?'

'Yes, I'm sure.' Ne wasn't.

In the event, tiredness both physical and emotional, dragged Sam into a deep sleep, so deep that dreams filled the night, those dreams that hover between dream and nightmare, fitting into neither binary category very well. Dreams involving Susan and ner father. Dreams randomly including Gavin. Dark dreams involving Yakov and images of the dead VIP. All muddled up with images of deer and wild boar. Even though Sam's mind had been busy all night, ne awoke fresh and alert. Sam sat up and realised that as well as being alert, ne was also alone. A quick look at the time, eleven fifteen a.m. Sam got up, still dressed, aware that they were living in a world where clothes washing was a luxury. Ne crossed the yard and into the main house. Simon was sat on the sofa, dozing. The sound of the door roused him.

'Morning Sam, sleep well?'

'Ah, yes, where is everyone?'

'Well, the others have headed off to do the recce that we agreed to do. They've been gone about an hour, so should be back soon. Hope you don't mind, they took the phone.'

Sam checked pockets and all empty.

282

'No problem, us war wounded can take a back seat for once,' Sam replied while looking towards the dining room.

Simon smiled. 'I suppose that's what we are! How's the foot?'

Sam looked down and it was still bandaged with ner shoe sole still attached. 'Let's see.'

Sam undid the bandage and freed ner foot, it felt good, fresh air eased it and Sam was able to rotate it with only minor aches. 'Well looks like nothing's broken, and walkable with only minor discomfort, shame I didn't keep hold of my other shoe.'

'I think Becky put it in her bag, we'll check when she gets back.' With that they heard the sounds of tyres crunching across the yard. Simon grabbed his gun and listened for voices. It was their group returning.

'Morning, both, how are you?' It was Matt who came through the door first. It was a genuine question, rather than an upbeat question of habit that is heard so often.

'Much, thank you.' Sam lifted and rotated ner foot with a surprising amount of ease.

'That's good,' Matt came across to get a closer look.

'What have you found out?'

Stuart took over the update, with regular prompts and additions from the other two. They seemed to be fully invested in their new roles, and in fairness Sam and

Simon were glad of other people taking the lead. During the update, mugs of tea were served.

The upshot of their exploration was in fact, nothing they didn't know already, the area seemed deserted, no one else about. The towers had dropped almost vertically and the pile of rubble was not extending far beyond the footprint of the original buildings. There were elements of the gardens from the roof which were amazingly still intact. Trees almost upright and planters still holding their plants. All the external infrastructure was intact, the makeshift zoo, the swimming pool, the vegetable garden, all as it was a week before. The only other area that was untouched was the lift block at the tower end of the train access tunnel, in fact amazingly the lifts were still operational.

'Did you go into the tunnel?' asked Sam. They hadn't. Becky had just gone down and back up in the lift. For a second the sight of the dead lying there, flashed through Sam's mind and ne wondered whether it would have been kinder if that tunnel had been buried too. If normality ever came back then there would need to be proper burials and ceremonies. A church was never part of the original design, but now it seemed one was needed.

'Did you go over and check the access ventilation shaft we came through yesterday?'

'We thought about that, Sam, but we weren't sure which direction it was in and the truck is on fifty per cent battery so not sure how long it will last.'

'They have a one-hundred-mile range, so we have a bit of time yet, although I don't think this terrain is what they use in the calculation. Talking of power, there's a solar array stored in the plant room, we should get it set up, I'll show you where we set it up before.' Sam stood up unevenly because of ner shoeless foot. 'Apparently, Becky you might have my other shoe?'

She did and once socks, insole and shoe were on, Sam helped them set up the panels. They then moved all the beds back into the farmhouse reinstating it as a family home, with separate bedrooms. Simon worked well to make them watertight, Becky and Stuart got a room to themselves and Sam and Simon shared. The water levels were checked. They set about cleaning, chopping wood, and creating a more relaxed place, not knowing how long they would be there for. The broken windows were boarded up, and they generally kept busy. The day passed with no messages on the phone, but at least they had everything working. When Simon and Stuart came up with the idea of going hunting, it seemed the natural thing to do. All the twenty-first century trappings of New Horizons had gone, they were now in a nineteenth century building sealed off from the outside world, with nothing but the resources they could harness from their environment to sustain them. Sam remembered an article which compared communities in Africa, South America and Indonesia which had remained unchanged for centuries. These remote communities hadn't industrialised at all, but they had all adopted technologies like solar and wind. Their farming patterns were sustainable and they were now exporters of power to towns and cities, providing a revenue stream. An example, it was said of how the past could light a direction for the future. A simpler lifestyle, and the article concluded, a happier way of living. Maybe the five of them could live that life for a few days, maybe even a few weeks. They were sat later that evening in the front room, having eaten a rabbit stew made with the spoils of the hunting expedition, that Matt had prepared. The pack of cards was brought out again, bored of patience Matt taught them to play whist and they played until after dark. Sam had spent the day checking the phone but nothing had come through, and in fact they had all been quite busy during the day, that it wasn't until late that the others really noticed that no contact had been made.

'Shouldn't we have heard something by now?' Becky said as she watched Sam check the phone.

'It is a bit odd,' Sam acknowledged and sent a message on the phone.

update available, call when you can

Sam put the phone down and they dealt another round of cards. After about twenty minutes a message came back.

Busy day here, call tomorrow

Sam showed the message to the others, and they carried on playing. At about midnight Becky and Stuart retired to their room, and Matt followed a few moments later. Sam grabbed a couple of dining chairs and took them out to the front of the farm. They sat, the two of them, mugs in hand, in silence. Simon and Sam just listening to the world, listening to the environment, the natural environment.

'What do you think will happen to this place?' Simon pondered

'No idea, what do you think is going on outside the walls?'

'No idea.' They looked at each other. Both had jobs which involved decisions affecting others, both had worked hard to create safe environments but here they were without information, unable to make any decisions beyond their immediate surroundings. They had to settle for the situation they found themselves in, which was both frustrating but also incredibly liberating.

'If this was a film, we'd be trying to get out of here you know,' Simon observed.

'I suppose so. Is that what you think we should do?'

'To be honest, I've got absolutely no idea. We've got food, water, energy. We could survive here possibly indefinitely.'

'Yes, I suppose we could.'

'I'll be honest, Sam, when we speak to Amardeep tomorrow, there's a bit of me that is worried we're going to have to give all this up. Jess would be happy here.'

'I'm sure she would, you'll be back with her soon.'

'I hope so.'

Sam nodded looking over towards where Susan lay. Sam was not sure ne could ever leave this place. They put the chairs back and retired to bed.

The following morning, Sam was woken at eight a.m. by the phone beside the bed. Simon also woke and they sat up and read the message.

Hi Sam, Mary here, how are you?

Sam leapt up, and ran downstairs and replied.

can I call?

She replied instantly, Sam went back and suggested ne called in five minutes, woke everybody up and they all congregated round the dining table. Sam checked the number and called Mary.

'Mary?' Sam said with hope returning. 'Are you OK?'

'Yes, we're fine, they moved us to a refugee centre near Salisbury yesterday. It's like a small city here of tents and prefabs. How are you and Susan?' She said with a smile in her voice, almost mischievous. Simon took over.

'Hi Mary, Simon here, it's been difficult. We've had issues.'

'Simon, what are you saying?'

'I'm sorry, Mary, there was a gun fight of sorts here at the farm, people died. Susan was shot.'

'Oh my God, is she OK?'

'She didn't make it.'

There was a silence at the end, after a while Mary asked, 'Is Sam OK?'

'Yes, I feel so bad, she wouldn't have come here had it not been for me.'

Sam had not told Simon, but it was nevertheless true, that Simon was the reason they were here, the reason Susan was dead. Sam looked at Simon. 'I'm sorry, Sam, I know you wouldn't be here if I had been able to find my way to you, but I was sat here waiting for ten p.m. like we said, when the explosions happened. I didn't know what to do. I sent up a flare to let you know where I was and to create a diversion. That's why they came back. I thought you were all dead in the explosions. I'm sorry.'

'It's OK.' Sam put a hand on his shoulder.

'Mary, are the children OK?'

'Yes, they're with their father at the other end of the camp. There's an informal school been started taking the children and helping them come to terms with what has happened.'

'What about Jessica?'

'Jessica?'

'Simon's girlfriend, is she with Steve still?'

'Oh yes, they're all here too.'

'Why Salisbury?'

'Well, the site was already set up taking evacuees from the south coast, from the tsunami.' Sam suddenly was struck by the other things going on outside.

'What else is happening?' Sam asked

'Well, they are sending up drones today, so that all the areas with no mobile or TV signal, will be able to get information and broadcasts. Apparently, there are parts of Britain that have been unaffected by what's been going on. Northern Ireland, like Ireland, are virtually virus free. So there is a lot of help coming down from there. I spoke to Amardeep, and he said he is arranging for a drone to act as a relay over to you, so you'll be able to access the Internet. You'll get it by lunchtime today.'

'That's great, but we only have one phone between us.'

'Oh, maybe not, Ian said there is some computer equipment stored at the farm, Simon should be able to get it working.' Simon nodded.

'Thanks Mary, so you and Joe are OK?'

'Yes, Sam, thank you on behalf of all the residents here, thank you for saving so many people.' There was a massive cheer in the background and Sam welled up inside. Becky, Matt and Stuart applauded too and for a minute Sam felt that everything had been worthwhile.

'Amardeep has let me keep this phone, so you can call

me whenever. If it's OK, he's asked me to be your point of contact outside. He wants you and your team to stay there for at least another three days, making daily inspections of the sites. If you find anything or anyone, then please contact me immediately, but they can't spare any rescue services at the moment unless there are known survivors, by which I think he means residents. They haven't decided what to do with the site, but I guess they'd want you to help decide.'

'OK, thanks Mary, anything else?'

'Oh yeah, once the drone is in place, you'll get an encryption key to get access to the news sites, there's a lot to catch up on.'

'OK, stay safe, hope to see you soon.'

'Me too.'

Sam ended the call, as Simon, who was already digging out lab equipment left behind by the scientists, appeared with three laptops and set them up one by one. They watched in anticipation. Becky brought them all back to the present.

'Breakfast anyone?'

Nods all round.

'I'll make up some more milk and we can have cereals.' She disappeared with Stuart to mix the powdered milk and prepare breakfast. Sam went out and sat with Susan for a while, giving her the updated news, something that ne would do every day from now on. As Sam sat with Susan, a deer approached and watched, and as they looked at each other Sam began to believe it was the same deer from those years ago, when Sam first found the farm. Sam decided on the spot to call the deer Susan.

'Hello Susan, you are beautiful you know, will you help me get through this, as I'm all alone now, everything my father built is in ruins. Everything I was working towards has been taken away. I really don't know what the future holds for any of us, and I'm scared, Susan. I'm scared that I'm not enough, that I won't recover. Will you help me?'

To an onlooker, the deer did not move, but in Sam's head it bowed its head. They both stayed for a short while longer and then Sam went back and joined the others. Sam stopped as ne approached the front door, the sounds of people inside and activity, voices and laughter, brought the farmhouse to life for the first time. Ner brain had categorised this place as a safe haven, and now despite the casualties Sam's heart felt that it was indeed a safe haven. Sam decided ne would never leave.

They sat and talked and waited for the drone or the encryption key whichever came first, in fact the drone won. They could hear it faintly above, they didn't know if it was equipped with a camera. The cost of the camera probably meant it wasn't, although Stuart was more of a conspiracy theorist than the others, and decided that all drones had cameras, especially the ones they tell you don't. In truth, Sam didn't care, it connected them to the outside world, and if there was a camera, it just made them safer. As they came back in from trying to spot it in the air, the phone pinged with the encryption key. Simon input the key into the laptops and suddenly they were reconnected, they hadn't realised how much they had missed. Becky and Stuart, Sam noticed, went straight to their social media accounts to check if they were active. They were, they posted updates. Matt went straight into the NHS portal to see if he was needed and how he would connect. Simon was emailing. Sam had no one to engage with, so he opened up the BBC News website.

It resembled a BBC website from the noughties. The rotating story cube which held fifty-four instant stories, constantly updated each with a video icon which you could select, had gone, instead it was a simple 2D list of news items.

Under world news, Sam clicked the story, 'Europe Divided Again'. The story went on.

After late night talks last night, Germany has agreed a ceasefire with Russia, on condition that the European Commission will not seek to enforce the membership commitments for countries who have signed agreements with the Russian Federation. A line has been drawn down the map of Europe, from Slovenia in the south, through Hungary, Poland, the Baltic states, and controversially, Finland, which are now part of a new economic and health block which extends east to Russia called 'Russian Supported States' or RSS. Italy and Greece have remained part of the European Union.

Turkey have renewed with urgency their request to join the EU which is being considered imminently.

The article finished with the chilling statement.

Peace in Europe has returned, but at what cost!

Under medical news, Sam found an article on the state of vaccines headed:

Hoarding is the new sharing.

The article went on:

Despite the experience of sharing of vaccines in Pandemic number one, this time countries have been more generous, but only just. China has reached agreements with all its neighbours and reassuringly, included Japan, which has severed its previous links with Russia, to supply details of its treatment programme. France was the first European country to roll out a treatment programme and is sharing this treatment with the now smaller European block. America has joined forces with Brazil to vaccinate both American continents in a move which has brought all the countries of the Americas together, including, with much relief, the USA and Cuba. The UK vaccine developed at Porton Down, scene of a worrying Russian spy mission reminiscent of the Salisbury Novichok mission in 2018, (see story on the heroes who saved Britain) has now been rolled out across the UK and Commonwealth countries and, along with the French vaccine, is being sent to countries across to Africa.

Sam read on as death tolls were announced. Russia was proudly stating that their death toll was less than five per cent in any country that had signed agreements. But no one seemed to believe these reports. Across Europe the death rate seemed to be around thirty-five per cent which seemed to be the average. At the time of going to press, no rates were available from Edinburgh, the new temporary seat of government for the United Kingdom.

Sam scrolled back up, and clicked the link: The heroes who saved Britain.

The tears rolled again as the headline was followed by photos. Small photos that had been sourced from an archive, of everyone except Ian who seemed to be the source.

'Hey, Simon you might want to see this.'

Simon came over as did the others, looking over Sam's shoulder.

The article began:

Details are still unclear, but there are witness reports coming out of Porton Down, of a heroic series of acts, in the face of atrocious circumstances. The two key people involved are Susan Durum, a senior scientist at Porton Down and the mayor of nearby New Horizons

Vertical Village, Sam Brown. The child of Sir Andrew Brown whose work on protecting the UK in exactly the circumstance we have found ourselves in has no doubt saved countless lives. Both Susan Durum and Sam Brown are currently location unknown.

The article went on to name other members of the group including Simon, whose location was also listed as 'currently unknown.' Sam read on:

While under attack from an elite Russian underground network, designed to take control of the whole of the United Kingdom once the virus had taken its toll, these brave citizens managed to get a viable vaccine out of the laboratory, into a safe house. While under constant threat, they managed to finish the testing and were even able to send copies of the vaccine with instructions to medical centres locally. One package was sent to the local MP, who released this statement:

"We had this drone appear in our back garden, the dog got hold of it, but luckily, we were able to get hold of the contents. At first, we weren't sure what to think, but then I drove it to our local treatment centre and they knew exactly what to do. I can't believe the bravery of my constituents who managed to make this happen, we owe them an enormous debt of gratitude. It should be noted that Russia have denied any link to this underground network, claiming that it was the actions of a small group, based in the UK.

Sam sat back in the chair, as they all read on. Becky patted Sam and Simon on the shoulder. 'Well done both of you, I see honours coming!' They all smiled. Once everyone had returned to their own screens Sam clicked on the next story that was suggested: 'Cumbre Vieja,. Where are we now?'

The article described how most of the waters had subsided now and people were returning to tsunami hit areas. Norway and Denmark, largely unhit by the virus having closed their borders immediately after the first pandemic cases were announced, had offered support and hospital ships. Brighton and Southampton survived, and services were resuming as residents returned. Portsmouth was the largest casualty, with the whole of Portsea Island still under water. The decision looked to have been made to rebuild a city on the hill, with Lisbon/San Francisco style trams, rising up above the ruins of the old city which would be flattened and allowed to rewild naturally, providing a level of protection as sea levels continued to rise. A number of historically important sites would be rescued, including the Mary Rose, making her the first ship to be rescued from being submerged twice in her lifetime.

The five of them carried on reading, taking it in turns to make drinks as if they were in some IT workplace. Becky and Stuart got in touch with family members, and as video calls filled the room, Sam made a coffee round and quietly left them to it.

A few days went past, with trips to the bomb site and reports back through Mary, the group had formed a routine. On the third day the message came through that the tunnel was back open and they could now leave and would be picked up at Porton Down. Simon got them all ready, and was not surprised to hear that Sam had decided to stay. 'OK we'll arrange a food drop for you, to keep you going.' Tears were shed, but Sam smiled as ne waved one of the trucks, goodbye. Sam wasn't sure but a nearby bush seemed to twitch. Susan was watching.

2045

The chickens in their coop often woke Sam up, and ne lay there listening to the morning chorus of birds. Sam stroked the cat still sleeping on the bed, and padded downstairs. The sun was trying to make its way through the trees. It was six a.m. Sam did ner favourite thing when woken this early, made a cup of tea, dressing gown on, and then climbed the spiral steps to the tower that Simon had engineered on the site of one of the outbuildings. The stairs led up to a platform that touched the sky, sitting as it did at the level of the treetops. This took Sam straight back to boarding school. Ner best friend, Jeremy, had a huge house and many school holidays the two of them would spend most of their time making dens and camps. Sam's father was always too busy, and staying with Jeremy was better than moving in with the childless headmaster and his wife.

One year, Jeremy's parents had had a tree house built during the summer term. Jeremy and Sam both agreed that was their best summer ever. Sam looked around at ner grown up version and smiled to nerself. From here Sam could sit and see the sun rise and set over New Horizons. It was being rebuilt, not as skyscrapers but as twenty individual manor houses, each providing their own communities. They circled a memorial garden where once the towers stood. Now it was a wild meadow, where butterflies and bees thrived and in the summer months it was dominated by poppies. The miniature zoo had survived and was now famous over the world. It was hoped that the rebuilt complex would become a place to visit for reasons other than the tragedy that took place. The wall was still intact and all the tunnels were now open. The trains had started stopping again, in fact, with the building work in full flow and one of the mansions already ready for occupation, it seemed that a normal life was returning. Sam hadn't left the farm, not even to collect the George Cross ne was awarded in ner absence. It was sent by special envoy. Sam felt safe here. Sam drank the tea and watched the sun rise, then the daily mail-drone arrived, and deposited its contents in the post crate designed to receive the mail.

Sam made ner way back down, wondering whether ne should ask the mail to be delivered to the tower now that it was possible to pick any square metre you required at any height, even a balcony, if you wanted. Maybe not.

Sam picked up the mail, which today, included a personal letter. Sam made some breakfast, fed the cat and sat in the front room to read the letter.

Dear Sam,

We hope you are well. As you know there is a reunion next week for the survivors, I do hope you will come along. This year they are holding it in the grounds of the mansion that is completed, together with marquees and a band. It should be an excellent time to catch up, and you could walk there. Please come.

In other news Joe and I are getting married, Samantha has agreed to be my bridesmaid and Bastion is going to be, I bet you can't guess, he's going to be Joe's best young man. I have included an invitation for you, but more in hope than expectation.

We've been offered an apartment in the new block, with the insurance pay out from the apartment. I think we will be happy there. Joe is hoping to resume as head of security, although he has had to face some questions, back in London, about how it came about, but it seems that most of the responsibility is being laid at James' door. I really misjudged James, but I guess we all did. Thinking about London, there was a garden party at Buckingham Palace that a group of us went to, people asked after you. The cakes were lovely, but I didn't much like many of the savoury bites, you know me, a ham sandwich and I'm happy. We stayed in a lovely hotel, on Park Lane. London is getting back on its feet, the death toll there was over fifty per cent so they are trying to get people to move to London. They have an advertising campaign with posters everywhere using

Dick Whittington, which as you can imagine have been defaced a bit.

Also, and I promise this was not the reason for the letter, the Natural History Museum want your permission to build a statue of your father in the foyer. I told them that you would be receiving your post and you will reply if you want to, but they are very keen, and I think your father would have liked that.

Anyway, that's enough of me prattling on. My email and phone numbers have been reinstated, so please get in touch, and we'd love to see you at the reunion.

Your friend always
Mary

Sam folded the letter, put it back in the envelope and slid it behind a number of other letters, that one day might be responded to. Ne looked at a letter, also personal, with a US stamp, the envelope still sealed. Sam took the envelope and sat on the front step looking out into the trees, a calming place to read this letter that had arrived six months before. Sam felt that today maybe the day to open it.

To my dearest Sam,

I know I have not written since your father died, and I'm sorry for that. We have seen what you have been through and what you have lost. We wanted to make sure you knew our door was still open. Your mother, my sister Abigail, would have probably wanted us to be there for you more than we have, but my father would not let us, he still has not forgiven your father for taking you to England. He died last month. That is not the reason why I am writing, but it is the reason why I can. I have wanted to reach out to you for so many years, you have cousins here who are so proud of what you have done. We have many Vertical Villages here now, some of them based on your father's designs, In California there is even one that is based on New Horizons. I was horrified when I heard what our government sanctioned with regard to your home, so many people lost their lives. We hear you lost people close to you.

Your grandmother is still alive and would love to meet you, she still lives in the area of New York where your parents lived all those years ago.

As I say, we would love to see you, and I have therefore, taken the liberty to include below details of a flexible flight that I have pre-paid for you to come to New York. I do hope you will consider using the voucher, we would all love to meet you.

With love,

Your aunt Christina and all your American family.

Sam looked at the voucher, it had expired two weeks previously. Sam folded the letter, put it neatly back in the envelope, and placed it back on the mantelpiece. Would ne ever travel there? At the moment it was difficult to imagine leaving the farm, let alone getting on a plane and travelling across the Atlantic. There was a bit of Sam that still wondered about ner mother, what was she like? What traits did Sam have that came from her? What advice would ner mother give Sam now?

For now though, Sam was content, settled. After the death of ner father Sam had felt less anchored, without focus. New Horizons and then Susan had provided a purpose, an anchor. Now alone, Sam let life drift past, the farm was now completely self-sufficient, two happy goats, some chickens and vegetable patch. A perfect sustainable, even carbon positive, lifestyle, which ne had achieved five years ahead of the global target for carbon neutrality. Sam took a daily walk through the woods, sometimes joined by Susan, who would follow silently behind, and Sam would talk to her. There was a log on the edge of the wood that Sam would sit on, perhaps for hours, watching activity in the distance, as the building works progressed. Sam's personal hygiene had dropped quite significantly, without the supplements that Sam used to take, ner facial hair had grown again. Sam looked quite different now, and wasn't sure if people would recognise ner.

Sam finished breakfast and went for the usual walk, maybe ne would go to the reunion. Then again, probably not.

Sam sat and watched the cranes in the distance, equipped now with binoculars it was easy to pick out the different buildings and the stage of work on each. The plans online showed a tree-lined avenue creating a circle around which each building would be built.

Unlike the towers, all the accommodation in these new blocks would have their own identities, from garden flats, attic spaces with hidden roof terraces to duplexes and studio apartments. Priority was given to existing residents, many of whom had decided not to return. There were vacancies in jobs as well as properties, and with a much lower UK population, estimated at around forty million, automation and robots had increased — robots making robots. Sam had read a story about a robot in Maidenhead, one of the latest generation of home-help robots, which had gone to the shops on behalf of its owner, bought some spare parts for itself, was served by a robot, and even the part bought, had been manufactured in one of the few fully automated factories in Japan. The article went back through the supply chain and could not find any evidence of human interaction throughout the whole process. Just human company owners making profits. In fairness, without self-driving lorries, cargo ships, diggers and busses, there would not be enough humans to build what was happening in front of Sam's eyes. Sam knew that to live in one of the mansions would be turning ner life over to automation, no digging in dirt to find the best carrots, or sitting with a chicken on ner lap or even dealing with goat droppings in the kitchen.

Days passed, no drone deliveries, peace. Sam logged on to ner laptop, wondering if a new one would be required soon. Ner bank account had been reactivated, and the insurance pay out was due soon, but with no expenditure Sam wondered what ne was going to do with the money, maybe give it away. The laptop could last a few months longer. It was the day of the reunion, calendar reminders popped up, from an invitation no doubt sent by Mary. An email from Mary which simply said 'Please come' in the subject, and no text in the message itself.

Sam, went up to get dressed for the day, something ne tried to do most days. Ne looked in the mirror, naked, slim bordering on thin. Hairs had sprouted in places ne had forgotten grew hairs. It was ten a.m.

***

The party was due to start at seven p.m. but Mary and Joseph had arrived early, but everyone called them Mary and Joe for obvious reasons. She had dressed to kill, and was glowing, Joe was clearly proud to have her on his arm. It was important how she looked, as Mary had said when getting ready, they were the VIPs really. Mary busied herself, offering help to the team in charge, and keeping out of the way of the army of dumb waiters, who were patrolling with drinks and canapés ready for the arrival of guests. Trays were being held by child-sized mannequins that balanced on a single wheel and lights hidden on the painted-on hair. In fact, they were anything but dumb waiters, they were controlled by a sophisticated AI system, which had facial recognition. It monitored who was drinking what, how fast they were drinking, automatically sending updates for more drinks to be despatched. All the robots worked as a team and voice recognition allowed people to set their preferences for the evening or change them at any time. Mary went to a control centre.

'One champagne followed by alternating tonic water and gin and tonic. After three gin and tonics, just tonic water. Latte at ten p.m.'

'Thank you, your orders have been placed please look at the screen for facial capture,' said the automated voice, which was based on an old woman's voice. Mary did as she was told.

'Thank you, enjoy your evening, and watch out for my colleagues.'

Mary wasn't really a fan of the amount of technology that now existed, but recognised the need for it, what with full employment having been hit within months of the pandemic, and the staff shortages had led to a massive increase in automation. She particularly liked the recent move to use older softer voices, rather than children or electronic voices, both of which had been used in the past. It had started in care homes where now almost all the routine tasks were completed by AI, leaving humans to provide entertainment, storytelling and management.

The red carpet was one of the last things to be laid down, as it was effectively still a building site. A drone display was greeting the guests and providing a light path for them to follow from the train station exit. Mary saw Ian coming along and went over and they hugged and then behind, Gavin hovered, still not putting himself forward, even though he had become a bit of a poster boy for the site. 'Hi Gavin, I love the long hair, how have you been?'

'So, so, haven't decided whether to move back yet, are you moving back?'

'Yes, we are,' she said with a smile that belonged on the face of a child. She looked round but Joe was not in sight.

'Is Sam coming?' asked Gavin, with, Mary thought, more interest than most.

She was expecting to be asked the question about a thousand times and she had prepared a stock answer, "I sure hope so" but this was a more personal question and it required a more personal answer.

'I don't know, probably not Gavin, do you want me to call you if I see ner?'

'Yes please.' Gavin looked sad, and almost as if he was about to turn around and leave. Nerves maybe. Mary put her arm though his and said cheerfully:

'Come on handsome, let's get your drinks ordered.' She dragged him off.

They walked quickly but still people stopped them, to say hi and take selfies. Mostly with Gavin. He was definitely a hit. He took everything in good grace and smiled for everyone there.

The band were good and were playing in one-hour sessions. They had just completed their second set, so it must have been about nine p.m. The marquee was full and the dumb waiters were now delivering food and plates, with precision accuracy as it was rare now for someone not to have a special dietary requirement. It would have been impossible for humans to orchestrate this level of personalisation, as everyone in the room was delivered their own personalised buffet selection. Although Mary's tray was exactly what she would have picked up from a buffet, she did miss the wandering up and down trying to find things she both could eat, and fancied eating, that particular night. She looked down at her plate of smoked salmon, calamari and six mini Scotch eggs and smiled. There was a hush in the room, as people ate, or so Mary thought. But gradually Mary noticed there was a parting of the group, people's phones pinged in their ears, and voice updates were shared. Someone close to Mary stepped back, and soon an empty path was being created from Mary leading towards the entrance of the marquee, as people nudged each other. People were now looking at their phones, and Mary's phone pinged, she looked at the photo. She hesitated, could it be? She hoped so. Joe appeared out of nowhere and grabbed Mary, he looked down the gap in the crown, and couldn't believe his eyes. It was Sam, but a different Sam, ne seemed taller, more focussed, more serious, more staged.

Ne walked slowly towards Mary, tears flowed down Mary's cheeks. Seeing Sam at last, bought all the memories back, they flooded through Mary like a tidal wave. Sam, alone, single, solitary. Mary wept for the loss, for Susan, for everybody. As the wave of emotion receded, it mercifully left happiness behind. They hugged. This was Sam.

'Hello Mary, oh, and congratulations.' Sam looked at Joe and winked, full of composure and authority. Sam's back was straight and proud. Joe couldn't work out whether it was confidence oozing from Sam or pure terror keeping ner in position, but in any event, it was an impressive performance.

'Oh, Sam, Sam, Sam, I've, I mean, we've missed you sooo very much.'

'It's been a long time. How are you all?'

'Much better now.

'Can I get you a drink?' She took Sam by the arm and directed ner to a voice control panel, as a round of applause rippled through the room, gradually evolving into cheers and whistles. 'I'll take you on a tour, but first there's someone here who wants to see you.'

'Just the one!' smiled Sam with mock affront as people all around started to raise their glasses in salute.

'Well, one in particular.' She then whispered, 'I think they are only here in the hope of seeing you again, I really hope they are.' A dumb waiter approached. Mary spoke to it. 'Find Gavin White.'

Sam lost composure for a second and then regained it, ne wasn't sure if this was what ne wanted, ne looked at Mary and ner eyes were gleaming with mischief.

'Gavin, as in Gavin?' Sam asked

'The very same, tall handsome Gavin.'

Over in the distance where tables were available, a dumb waiter weaved its way through the crowd looking at faces, and scanning. It stopped as there was a partial match on a face that was facing the other way.

'Please stop and turn around,' the robot asked gently.

Gavin kept walking, speeding up, he'd guessed what had happened, and now couldn't face the public meet up. What if Sam didn't remember him? What if Sam didn't feel the same? Sam seemed happy in ner farm, Simon had explained how well set up ne was, how Sam was enjoying the self-sufficiency, the solitude, being close to Susan. How could Gavin think he could compete with that?

'Please turn around, someone has asked for you.'

Gavin kept walking. He was outside the tent now, and turned to the right, following the lines of the guide ropes. The dumb waiter had slowed, their wheels hadn't been designed for such an uneven surface. As Gavin turned, enough of his face, was within the scanning field of vision.

'Please, Gavin White, Mary Johnson wants to see you.'

Gavin turned. 'Yes, but who are they with?'

'Unknown, facial recognition not completed.'

'Ask the stranger to meet me here, can you do that?'

'I have sent the message.' The dumb waiter scanned the floor and chose a route back that was flatter.

Mary had placed the order for drinks, orange juice followed by water, a nearby waiter lit up.

'Mary Johnson, we have a message from Gavin White. Would you like to receive it?'

'Play message,' said Mary

'Ask the stranger to meet me here, can you do that?' Gavin's voice came through the speaker on the device. Sam's stomach lurched.

'Lead the way,' Sam said to the machine, and followed it across the marquee, people smiling, silent clapping and a few taking photos as Sam followed in silence.

Sam stopped. 'Excuse me droid what do I call you?'

'I am DW56, you can call me that.'

'OK, DW56, I need a drink, can I order that from you?'

'It's not the protocol that has been agreed.'

'I understand but can I do it nevertheless?'

'Please wait.' The robot shone purple and then a green light appeared on its head.

'Citizen Brown, glad to meet you, I'm Tom, I'm in the office, looking after the waiters tonight, what can I do for you?'

'Thank you, Tom, I'd like a triple whisky on the rocks, can you deliver it to me here?'

'Sure, we can, it's being poured now. Just wait while I key in your position. OK, it's on its way.

Eighteen seconds and you'll have it. Anything else I can do for you?'

'No that's perfect.'

'Well thank you, we are all so glad you came and thank you for everything you have done for the community.'

'OK, Tom. Oh, I see the drink has arrived, wish me luck.'

'Good luck?' Tom said, not knowing what he was wishing it for, and the call ended. The AI took over control of the robot waiter and waited for Sam to take the drink from the recently arrived robot server. The two machines, motionless beside each other, unlike humans they made no reference to each other's existence. Just robots. Sam finished her drink and followed DW56 out of the tent.

The droid turned right and bumped its way along, for a second Sam wondered if it was a trap, but then ne saw Gavin.

He looked over and raised an eyebrow. He looked at the robot as if to say, 'You can leave us now.'

After a fashion of it standing waiting, Sam said, 'DW56 you can go back to the party.'

'Thank you, have a good night,' it responded and having surveyed the ground it took the exact same route as the earlier droid.

'Hello, Sam, you look,' he paused, 'fantastic.'

'Thank you, Gavin. I nearly didn't come, but I'm glad I did now, I think.'

'Well, I'm glad you came, I nearly didn't come myself, but I just felt it was time to come back on site and see how it felt. They've offered me a place to live here if I want. How's the farm?'

'Just how I want it.'

The conversation had stopped, they looked at each other, they both knew that the next words would either close this chapter as friends and get back to the party, or more likely their separate homes, or the conversation would begin a relationship, a connection, even maybe chemistry. The silence went on, neither person wanting to open their hearts for it to be stamped on. Sam stepped up.

'I've thought a lot about you over the past few years, do you think there is something worth investigating between us?'

'Oh, Sam, I do, if nothing else Mary will be pleased if we are talking. It will avoid her having to answer calls from me which simply ask if she's heard from you.' They smiled.

'Shall we go for a walk?' Sam took Gavin's hand and together they walked along the road, past the first mansion and the marquee towards increasingly unfinished buildings, until the road was covered in mud and the buildings were mere footprints of concrete. It was dark but their eyes adjusted and the moonlight crept around clouds, providing a backdrop of silver linings. They walked the complete circle and it took them almost an hour. They talked about the farm, the deer called Susan, they talked about trips to London and Buckingham Palace. They approached the marquee once more, and Gavin pulled Sam to a stop. He turned ner so they were looking at each other.

'Sam, I think you're amazing, and I have thought about you every day. Will you let me be a part of your life, in whatever form you want?'

Sam looked at Gavin and the journey she had taken.

'Gavin, I think I'm ready, let's open this chapter and walk the journey together.'

They didn't kiss then, that would come later, but they walked hand in hand back into the marquee. This felt right, maybe Sam was ready to acknowledge that ne had been trapped in this place, by the experiences and the losses, maybe Gavin was the person to set ner free.